BOOKSHOPS & BONEDUST

BOOKSHOPS
&
BONEDUST

TRAVIS BALDREE

TOR
Tor Publishing Group
NEW YORK

BOOKSHOPS & BONEDUST

Copyright © 2023 by Travis Baldree

All rights reserved.

A Tor Book
Published by Tom Doherty Associates / Tor Publishing Group
120 Broadway
New York, NY 10271

www.tor-forge.com

Tor® is a registered trademark of Macmillan Publishing Group, LLC.

Library of Congress Cataloging-in-Publication Data

Names: Baldree, Travis, 1977– author.
Title: Bookshops & bonedust / Travis Baldree.
Other titles: Bookshops and bonedust
Description: First U.S. edition. | New York, NY : Tor, 2023.
Identifiers: LCCN 2023024232 (print) | LCCN 2023024233 (ebook) |
ISBN 9781250886101 (trade paperback) | ISBN 9781250323224 (trade paperback) |
    ISBN 9781250886118 (ebook)
Subjects: LCGFT: Fantasy fiction. | Novels.
Classification: LCC PS3602.A59529 B66 2023 (print) | LCC PS3602.A59529 (ebook) |
    DDC 813/.6—dc23/eng/20230601
LC record available at https://lccn.loc.gov/2023024232
LC ebook record available at https://lccn.loc.gov/2023024233

Our books may be purchased in bulk for promotional, educational, or
business use. Please contact your local bookseller or the Macmillan Corporate and
Premium Sales Department at 1-800-221-7945, extension 5442, or by email
at MacmillanSpecialMarkets@macmillan.com.

First published in Great Britain by Tor, an imprint of Pan Macmillan

First U.S. Edition: 2023

Printed in the United States of America

0 9 8 7 6 5 4 3

Because right things happen at the wrong time.

BOOKSHOPS & BONEDUST

PROLOGUE

"Eighteen!" bellowed Viv, bringing her saber around in a flat curve that battered the wight's skull off its spine. She laughed and rammed her shoulder through its body before it could begin to fall, shattering bones in all directions. In two more steps, she'd already brought the blade back in an upswing, catching another in the ribcage. Splinters sprayed like wood-chips from a felling-axe.

"Nineteen!" She grinned savagely, baring her fangs and forging ahead with massive strides.

Every breath sang pure and clean in her lungs, her muscles bunched and released in perfect rhythm, her blood roared in her veins. She was youth and strength and power, and she meant to push all three as far as they would go.

Varine the Pale's army of gaunt, skeletal soldiers crowded amidst the bastion oaks, nimble despite their desiccation. They battled in deathless silence, short-swords and pikes snapping toward Viv, and she dodged or hacked them aside, relentless as the tide.

She was far ahead of the rest of Rackam's Ravens, leading the charge. Old warhorses, the lot of them. Old and *slow*.

They'd tried to keep the new blood in the back, but that wasn't what she was built for.

Somewhere ahead, the necromancer lay in wait, and Viv meant to reach her first. When the stragglers finally caught up, they'd find her with her blade at ease and their quarry in a heap at her feet.

Her count increased with every stroke as she laid about her with her saber. Still not fast enough. She yanked her maul from its loop and went to work with both hands, crushing and shearing through the skeletal ranks with hammer and sword. Their shields were bashed aside. Their ring mail tore like paper. Their skulls collapsed like winter melons.

Harsh cries echoed behind her as Rackam's crew dealt with the chaff she left in her wake or the wights that tried to flank them. Someone shouted for her to slow down. She huffed a scornful laugh.

And then her leg lit up with a cold fire that turned hot in half a second. She staggered and pivoted on the other foot just as a pike's rusty head withdrew from a long wound in her thigh. It darted forward again, and she stared disbelieving as it disappeared through her trousers and into the meat of her leg in a perfect parallel slice. Then the blood came. A lot of it.

She roared, knocking the pike aside with her maul and following with an upward slash of her saber that ripped the wight in half. Its horned helm spun skyward in an absurd twirl. Viv would have laughed if agony hadn't overtaken her when her weight shifted from the swing. Her wounded leg collapsed under her like a cornstalk.

Suddenly, she was on her side in the moss and muck, bleeding everywhere.

Another skeletal revenant loomed above her, curls of blue

light flickering in its empty sockets. On its forehead Varine's symbol burned bright—a diamond with branches like horns. It hauled a rusty tower shield into the air, preparing to bring the edge down in a crushing blow. The only sounds were the creaking of its sinew and Viv's own ragged breaths.

She just caught the edge of the shield with her maul, knocking it to the side, but she lost her grip on her weapon. Tears of pain blurred her vision. Viv hadn't managed to disarm the thing, though. Implacable, the revenant raised the slab of metal once more. This time, the angle was all wrong to shift the saber between her and the falling edge. In shocked disbelief, she could only watch as the steel dropped toward her neck.

A ragged cry, but not her own.

Rackam barreled into the creature with his shoulder. As the wight staggered back, the dwarf obliterated the thing with a single swing of his flanged mace.

He glanced down at her, and the disappointed grimace on his lips made her nausea double. "Hells-damned fool. Clap a hand to that. Stay put, and try not to die, if you can."

Then he was gone, and Viv was breathless with shock as Rackam's Ravens charged past in a line of blades and bows and arcane fire that leveled the foe before them.

They disappeared into the mist, and she was alone, staring in disbelief as her life pumped out of her leg.

～⌇

"Still with us, hey?"

Viv groggily regained consciousness. She felt like she was going to be sick. Maybe she already had been.

The first things she saw were Rackam's flinty eyes, glittering above the braids of his muddy salt-and-pepper beard. Viv shook her head and looked around; the edges of her vision seemed smeared with grease. Somehow, she'd braced her back against one of the oaks. She'd apparently also had the presence of mind to tear off the bottom of her shirt and bind her wound around a handful of moss. The cloth was soaked through, and the earth underneath was a churn of mud and blood.

At the sight of it, she began to drift, and Rackam brought her back with a surprisingly gentle slap to the cheek.

He sighed and shook his head.

The battle was done. If his presence hadn't been enough to tell her, then the unhurried movement of the warriors behind him would have.

"I figured it when you signed on. Hoped I'd be wrong, but nah, I knew this was the way it would go. Younger is always dumber, and wising up takes blood and time." He looked away, as though into some other possible future, then back at her. "Every new prospect, I give them even odds. I look at the hands, the arms. No scars? Then it's even odds that the first one they get kills them."

With one gloved hand, he patted her massive forearm. Corded with muscle, but the skin unblemished. Viv stared past it to the wreck of her leg.

Rackam stood, and she still didn't have to look up far to meet his eyes. "Is this the one that kills you, then?"

Viv swallowed down her nausea and narrowed her eyes, feeling stupid. Feeling stupid made her feel resentful. And resentment was only a half step from angry. "No," she said through clenched teeth.

He chuckled. "Don't guess it will, at that. But you're done for now."

She blinked. "Did we get her?"

"We didn't. Wasn't even here, near as we can tell. Only a little trouble she stirred up just for us. We're heading north. We'll find her."

Viv struggled to push herself to standing against the trunk with her left leg. The other felt too big by half, and every pump of her heart was a dark drumbeat all through it. "When do we leave?"

"We? Like I said, you're done for now. They tell me it's only a few miles to some sea town. I'll send you that way. You'll heal up, and we'll pass through when we're done. If you're still around and able when we roll through, we'll take you back on. Probably a few weeks. If you're gone when we show . . . ?" He shrugged. "No shame in calling this the end of it."

"But—"

"It's done, kid. You survived a stupid mistake today. If you want to make another so soon after, well . . ." His gaze was hard. "Want me to tell you the odds I give on that?"

But Viv wasn't a stupid orc, so she shut the hells up.

1

Viv lay on the floor of the tiny room. Well, almost on the floor. The place hadn't been built with orcs in mind, and the bed was too short by at least two feet. Someone had wrestled the straw-tick mattress onto the floor, and though her legs still went off the end, they'd positioned her pack so her foot was propped, keeping the wounded leg elevated.

It hurt like all eight hells.

She'd caught a fever while bouncing along in the litter behind a pack mule, coughing through all the dust it could raise. Which was a *lot*.

Viv might've been bedbound for two days, in and out of consciousness, a muddle of circular dreams and throbbing agony. The surgeon had come and gone multiple times. Or maybe he hadn't, and she'd just been hallucinating it over and over. She half remembered the man's face, tangled up in a shame she couldn't identify.

Now, her head was clear. Which mostly meant she could also *feel* everything with complete clarity. It was a debatable improvement.

What's more, she was absolutely ravenous.

Staring around the room, the place was mostly barren. A crude bedframe and a tiny table with a lantern and a basin on it. Gray, raw wood for walls. A small, slatted window. She smelled the sea, and dry beach grass, and fish. An old sea chest sat opposite. Her saber leaned against it, alongside a crude wooden crutch. Her maul was missing. There wasn't much else worth considering.

The building was absolutely quiet. The only sounds came from outside—the hissing of grass, the remote grumble of waves, and the occasional call of a seabird.

Viv had been lucid for less than a single hour, and she thought the view might drive her insane if she had to endure another.

Her leg was cleanly wrapped at least, splinted so the knee wouldn't bend. Her trouser leg had been cut away. The bandages showed some discoloration where she'd oozed through, but it was a big step up from moss and a dirty wool shirt.

"Well," she said. "Shit."

She made it up by degrees, hauling her butt onto the bedframe and sucking air through her teeth as she swung her damaged leg around. Her left boot fit, but the right foot was so swollen, it would have to stay bare. Tottering to her feet, she made it to the basin of tepid water, where she scrubbed herself as best she could with the rag she found there. Feeling less foul, she limped toward the door, but each thud of her heel against the floor pulsed black at the edges of her vision. Gritting her teeth, she changed direction and grudgingly seized the crutch.

It galled her to admit how much better that was.

While she was there, she belted on her saber out of habit.

Unfortunately, she discovered that the room was at the top of a flight of narrow stairs. She fumbled down them, catching herself every other step with the crutch. The saber did nothing to make things easier. With every impact, she found a new, more colorful epithet for Rackam. Not that it was his fault, of course. Still, it was a lot more satisfying to curse someone by name, even if that name should've been her own.

She could smell the ghost of bacon as she descended, which was plenty of incentive to carry on.

The stairs opened into a long, rough-timbered dining area in an inn or tavern or whatever they called it around here. A big, stone hearth crouched cold along one wall, yawning like a disappointed mouth. An iron chandelier hung askew, entombed in candlewax. Glass floats and storm lanterns were strung or nailed up in the rafters, alongside netting and weathered oars with names carved into them. The handful of scarred tables were unoccupied.

A long bar ran along the back wall, and the tavernkeep leaned against it, idly cleaning a copper mug. He looked as bored as the place warranted. The tall sea-fey's chin was grizzled gray. His nose was a hatchet, his hair hung kelp-thick past sharp ears, and his forearms writhed with tattoos.

"Mornin', miss," he rumbled. "Breakfast?"

Viv couldn't remember anyone *ever* calling her *miss*.

His gaze sketched over her, brows rising as he spied the saber, then returned to the mug he was polishing.

"Bacon?" asked Viv.

He nodded. "Eggs, too? Potatoes?"

Her stomach grumbled aggressively. "Yeah."

"Five bits ought to do it."

She patted at her belt for her wallet, looked toward the stairs, and swore.

"I'll get it next time. Worst case I climb those stairs myself."

The man smiled wryly. "Don't think you could outrun me, could you? You'd better fall onto one of these stools while you still can."

Viv was so used to her very existence being an obvious threat that it was honestly startling to hear a casual joke at her expense, even such a mild one. She supposed clunking around on one leg tended to dull one's fearsomeness.

As she accomplished the suggested maneuver, he disappeared into the back. Viv dragged another stool close enough to prop her bare foot on one of its low supports.

Drumming her fingers on the counter, she tried to distract herself by studying the interior further, but there *really* wasn't much else worth marking. The sounds and smells from the back were all her mind could dwell on.

When the tavernkeep brought out a skillet and set it on the counter along with a fork and a napkin, she almost seized the hot handle with her bare hand in her hurry to drag it closer. The hash of potatoes, crispy, fatty pork, and two runny eggs was still sizzling and popping. She almost burst into joyful tears.

Viv caught him watching her devour the food from the other end of the bar and tried to slow down, but the potatoes were salty and rich with the egg, and it was hard not to shovel it in without pausing. The noises she made as she ate were not polite, but they were definitely sincere.

"Feel better?" the sea-fey asked as he slid the empty pan off the bar-top.

"Gods, yes. And thanks. Uh, I'm Viv."

That wry grin again. "Heard when you came in. We've met, actually, but I'm not surprised you don't remember. Not with all the commotion."

She didn't *remember* the commotion, but his amused tone made her wonder. "So, did the Ravens pay up my stay?"

"Hoped I'd see Rackam himself," said the barkeep. "Still, the fellow he sent to put you up was practically a gentleman. Paid four days. Said you'd be able to foot it past that. I'm Brand."

He held out a hand, and she shook it. They both had hard grips.

"Back to your ease then?" he asked.

"Hells, no. I'd go crazy. Um. Where exactly *am* I?"

His wry grin went all the way to amused. "Let me be the first to welcome you to Murk, jewel of the western coast! A very *small* part of the western coast. And this here is The Perch, my place."

"Seems awfully quiet around here." She'd almost said *depressingly* quiet.

"We have our loud moments when the boats are in. But if you're looking to rest and recover, most days you're not going to be bothered by the noise."

She nodded and hopped onto her good foot, easing the crutch back under her. "Well, thanks again. Guess I'll be seeing a lot of you."

With hot food in her belly, Viv felt more herself. The thought of hobbling her way around a little of the town was a lot more attractive than it had been a few minutes ago. She rapped a knuckle on the counter. "Think I'll take in the sights."

"See you in ten minutes then," said Brand.

Viv laughed, but she had to force it.

2

As Viv lurched off the porch, grabbing one of the newel posts for balance, she glanced back. A battered sign hung under the shingled awning, bearing an indifferently carved fish, with THE PERCH chiseled above it and stained dark.

A light sea breeze teased her curls into her face, and she gazed out over what she could see of Murk.

The ocean was visible for three-quarters of the horizon, until it was obscured by a tall, chalky bluff to the north. She could discern the barest sketch of some small structures and fences, but not enough to identify their purpose. Dunes swelled back from the shore in flattening waves, crested by shaggy fringes of beach grass.

An old stone fortress wall surrounded most of Murk proper, marching uphill, with the town tucked inside. The Perch wasn't within its protective encirclement but on a sandy upslope beside the southern road, affording a view over the ramparts.

Outside the walls and nearer to The Perch, long ranks of narrow buildings curved in dwindling arcs toward the beach. Their clapboard sides were bleached pearly gray by sun and salt mist, burnished silver in the late morning light. Uneven boardwalks stitched them together, and old, sparsely cobbled roads wound between, sifted over with sand in places.

Four long piers extended out into the sea, jumbled with crates and rigging. Fishing boats nibbled against the pilings like minnows after bread, while bigger ships plied the waters beyond. A few tiny figures moved on the piers, and their faint calls rebounded across the water.

The whole city seemed half asleep. She doubted it ever woke up.

A sudden, powerful sense of being left behind swamped Viv. Rackam had dumped her in these misbegotten borderlands, and a wild certainty crawled up from her gut that he never planned to come back this way. It was all a convenient excuse to be rid of a troublesome kid.

She gritted her teeth and wrestled that feeling back down into the dark.

As Viv limped out of the shade, the full weight of the sun fell upon her. Not noon yet, but getting close. She closed her eyes and soaked it in for a moment, trying to enjoy the heat on her skin.

Drawing in a huge breath of the sea air, she let it out slow. "Well," she said to herself. "Let's get this over with."

Navigating the cobbles with the crutch was tricky, but she was glad they were there, because sand alone would've been far worse. Her progress was glacial, but methodical, and her underarm was already chafing at the unfamiliar crutch. She'd have to wrap it in something until she could get rid of the damned thing entirely.

The slope was downward, but slight, which was a blessing. Gulls startled from the dunes that climbed on either side of the road.

For a wonder, the first person Viv saw was another orc. He tromped stolidly toward her, dragging a wagon behind him with the traces tucked under his arms. His chest and head were bare, and his shoulders crisscrossed with old scars. Bundles of driftwood and split kindling were stacked in the wagon.

"Morning," she said, offering a joking salute with her unoccupied hand.

He nodded as he passed, his eyes flicking to her sword, and she stopped to watch him go. He didn't look back, which vexed her for some reason.

The first buildings she reached were a series of shops that led down to the beach, where a network of wooden causeways made the sand more navigable.

Viv maneuvered up onto the boardwalk connecting the shopfronts. Every impact of her crutch on the salt-blasted wood was like a hoofbeat.

Most of the shops were tall and narrow and seemed to be leaning away from the breeze off the ocean. Up close, the clapboard and shingles were shaggy with splinters.

The first few businesses were closed. Permanently, judging by the cracked glass with tarps or paper pinned inside. Then a bookshop of some sort. Through a pair of narrow front windows, she spied chaotic piles of books, charts, and miscellaneous junk. She could almost *see* the smell of mildew. The door had once been red but was now streaked with nothing but the memory of a color.

A little sign to the left read THISTLEBURR BOOKSELLERS.

Viv shook her head and hobbled on.

A sail-mender's. Then a junk shop crammed with shells, sand dollars, glass floats, and nautical flotsam and jetsam. Viv couldn't imagine why anyone would want any of it.

She caught a whiff of baking on the breeze, cutting through the pungent odors of brine and seaweed. Not surprisingly, she was already hungry again. The effort of getting around and the demands of a healing body notwithstanding, Viv burned hot, and her late breakfast was nearly consumed in the furnace of her belly.

At the very end of this strip of shops was the first real sign of life she'd seen, unless you counted the stone-faced orc hauling firewood. Which she didn't.

This place was at least double the width of the others, with two chimneys puffing away and folks actually coming and going. SEA-SONG BAKERY was stenciled on the glass, and the letters looked tidy and freshly painted. Not that you needed anything more than your nose to figure out what the shop was about.

Woven baskets crammed with big round loaves, buns, and biscuits showed through the window. A bell over the door tinkled as a dwarf with a sailor's swagger emerged, cramming the last of something into his mouth.

Viv peered inside for a minute, cursing herself again for leaving her wallet in her room. The gigantic, flaky biscuits promised to exceed the lofty expectations the scents had already set. She wiped her lips with the back of her forearm and turned reluctantly away.

Pa had always told her that hunger could be cured with sweat, one way or the other. She began lurching her way determinedly across the sand-washed road. Most of the buildings on the other side seemed to be residences, or maybe lodgings for vacationers. Nobody seemed to be about though.

A long hitching post ran along the road, and that would do well enough for what she wanted.

She'd spent several days on her back, and her body made sure she felt it. Not that she'd be running footraces any time soon, but you could hardly expect to stay alive slinging steel if you didn't keep your own edges sharp.

Leaning her crutch and saber against one end, she gingerly swung herself under the main beam, gripping it overhand. She stretched her legs out into the street, wincing as pain spiked along her right thigh.

She lowered herself until her elbows nearly locked. Then she pulled herself up, over and over, warmth building in her back, chest, and upper arms. The pain in her leg drifted to the aft of her mind.

When her biceps quivered with the strain and sweat traced her temples, she lowered herself onto her rear, tucking in the heel of her left leg and letting herself breathe heavy and even.

The orc with the wagon of firewood was staring at her, stopped on his way back downhill. His cart was a lot emptier now. A variety of worn tools dangled from hooks along its slatted sides—a maul, a sledge, an axe, a saw.

Viv narrowed her eyes at him. "What're you looking at?"

He shrugged, and when he responded, his voice was deep but surprisingly mellow. "Back at it awful soon."

"Did I already meet you when I got here, too?"

He shrugged again. "Not a lot goin' on most days. Hard not to notice when somethin' excitin' happens. It was pretty excitin'." The shadow of a grin. "You almost strangled Highlark."

"Highlark?"

"The surgeon."

"Oh," she replied with a wince. Well, that wasn't ideal.

"Pitts," he said, indicating himself. Then he ducked his head, hitched the traces higher, and tugged the wagon into motion. He didn't wait for her to offer her own name.

She found that vaguely annoying. "Viv!" she hollered after him. He just nodded without looking back.

"Eight hells," said Viv. "Great town. I can see why everybody stays."

She struggled to her feet. Gathering her crutch and saber, she went to the end of the boardwalk, retreating out of sight into a valley between two dunes.

She couldn't see the water, the wind was cut off completely, and the stillness itched at her so much that she tossed the crutch to the sand and limped to the crest of the beachward dune, hissing in pain the whole way.

The breeze up there was sweeter, and she gave her breath a minute to even out before unsheathing the saber. Viv tried to execute a couple of sword forms, keeping her weight mostly to her undamaged leg. She'd hoped to at least manage a few sets of transitions from high to low to feint, focusing on precision and upper body work, but it was a lost cause. Her leading leg shifted suddenly, and when she rocked back, the weight of the blade forced her onto the weak heel, and then she was tumbling over in a plume of sand and profanity.

Five minutes after her embarrassing flail down the dune, she stumbled back onto the main thoroughfare. Angry, thwarted, and keenly aware of the mix of sand and sweat up inside her shirt, she started the grueling trek up the hill toward The Perch. The gentle slope was more of a trial than it had any right to be, and all she had to look forward to at the end was an empty inn, an empty room, and a set of very narrow stairs.

She should've been shoulder to shoulder with the Ravens. She should've been hacking her way closer to Varine.

She should've been anywhere but here.

With most of her attention fixed on the sand-covered cobbles and where she'd next place the crutch, she was startled when a shadow stepped into view.

Glancing up, she found herself staring into the slitted serpent's eyes of a tapenti. The woman wasn't as tall as Viv—few people were—but situated upslope, Viv had to look up at her.

Or maybe it just felt that way.

She was powerfully built, the delicate patterns of her hide sculpted over muscular shoulders and legs. Her scaly hood flared along her temples and neck, salmon where the light glowed through it, and the long, rattle-like braids of her hair slithered dryly in the breeze.

The lantern of a Gatewarden gleamed where it hung at her waist opposite a longsword, and she wore a badge on her blue tunic.

The woman cocked her head in a way Viv couldn't interpret as anything but disdainful. "A stunning display of martial prowess." Her eyes darted beyond Viv to the crest of the dune and the site of her aborted blade practice.

Viv's skin crawled in a hot flush, the kind that could tip from embarrassment into rage with no more than a feather's weight. She wasn't fool enough to let it happen, not with the local law, but she didn't have to be polite either. "Guess there's not much else to look at, huh?"

The tapenti smiled thinly, and her eyes narrowed. "It's a sight I'd rather not see around my city. I like it quiet, and little girls hauling swords around promise to be noisy. I suggest you keep your steel sheathed, or better yet, back in your room. No reason you shouldn't stay there too, in my estimation."

Viv sputtered, "Little *girl* . . . ?"

The Gatewarden rode over her roughshod, her voice a relentless hiss. "When they dragged you in, I took one look at you and knew I'd need to watch you. *Highlark* certainly won't forget your arrival anytime soon. If you cause the slightest trouble here, I won't hesitate to toss you in a cell to ride out your convalescence until your . . . *friends* show up to take you off my hands."

Viv could only stare in mute fury. Her hand twitched toward her saber's hilt, but she mastered the impulse even as she saw the tapenti's eyes follow the motion with grim amusement.

"Good day." The woman tilted her head mockingly toward the inn. "And be careful on your way up the hill. A bad fall might extend your stay, and neither of us would want that, would we?"

Then she was gone, and Viv could only stare up the street toward The Perch and fervently long for something to stab.

If Rackam didn't come back soon, she'd have to leave and find him herself, before she did something she might *really* regret.

3

Still seething from her encounter with the Gatewarden, Viv considered The Perch with a renewed lack of enthusiasm. Unable to face a tedious, lonely walk to a tedious, empty room for the rest of a tedious, pointless day, she angled for the boardwalk and the nearest occupied shop.

As she brought her crutch down in front of Thistleburr Booksellers, there was a tortured crack. She swore as the rotten wood buckled beneath the weight. Viv almost went tail over tusks for the second time in a quarter of an hour but managed to hike the crutch up before it went all the way through.

She stared at the half-disintegrated plank. "Shit."

With adrenaline still sizzling up her arms from the near miss, she pushed open the door and staggered into the dim light of the bookshop.

The interior smelled almost exactly as she'd imagined—of old paper, mildew, and disappointment—but with the additional odors of dog and . . . *henhouse*. She wrinkled her nose.

Books crowded a long, narrow shop—squeezed into leaning shelves, scattered on top of them, teetering in stacks on the floor. Some volumes seemed new, but most were old, with errant threads poking from leather or cloth-covered wooden bindings.

Sea charts and maps lay in a disorganized heap on a low shelf below the front windows. A hurricane lamp with a cracked chimney flickered weakly where it was mounted on the wall.

The inside was constructed of the same planks as the exterior facing. Once painted white, they now looked tea-stained and peeling.

Charting an unfortunate path through the room was a shabby carpet crusted with salty sand and . . . stray feathers?

A tiny countertop crouched at the back, with another wall of books stacked behind. It seemed in danger of disappearing under a landslide of old words. A crooked hall ran into the rear, and she thought she heard rustling around the corner. A battered old woodstove—*also* piled with books—squatted to the left of the hall. Nobody appeared to be manning the shop.

"By the Eight, what a pit," said Viv, curling her lip. This had been a terrible idea.

As she awkwardly turned to go, her saber slapped three piles of books, which scattered in a tumble of pages and dust. Viv winced, took a breath . . . and then two adjoining piles slumped over to skitter atop the rest.

A strange, barking *hoot* echoed from the rear of the shop. Suddenly, a thunder of paws preceded the appearance of a squat little animal that barreled directly toward her in a cloud of feathers and shed hair. Its claws caught in the ragged carpet and bunched it together in dusty humps beneath its belly until it shot forward again, sounding for all the world like a dog barking underwater.

She didn't flinch as it came to a skidding stop before her,

bouncing on four stubby legs, its short golden hair abristle along its spine. Its head was owlish and oversized, with great luminous eyes and a small black beak. Sprigs of fur and pinions hinted at vestigial wings. Triangular, canine ears were folded back over the feathers of its head in the righteous fury of a guard dog.

Viv put a hand on the hilt of her saber, but despite the creature's aggressive squawking, she couldn't imagine she was in much danger. Her surprise was already turning into a dis- believing chuckle.

"Oh, *fuck!*" cried a small, high voice. "Potroast, *no!*"

Viv glanced up, surprised at the profanity. The really *sincere* profanity. But she was even more surprised by the owner of the voice.

A tiny rattkin wearing a short red cloak hurried into the light, shaking a severe finger at the animal.

"It's okay," said Viv, wrestling her laugh into a lopsided grin. The absurdity of the situation had scrubbed away the last traces of her raw fury over her encounter with the Gatewarden.

"I'm *so* sorry!" exclaimed the rattkin as she bent to wrap her arms around her vibrating savior. Then she caught sight of the tumbled volumes and slumped. "Oh, gods-dammit."

"Yeah, *I'm* sorry about that one. My fault." Viv gestured to her leg and crutch, even though they hadn't been the culprits. She was almost embarrassed to be carrying the sword now, which was weird.

"Potroast! Get in the back! Go on, get!" the rattkin hissed. To Viv's surprise, the creature obeyed, its stubby tail drooping as it slunk behind the counter. It popped its head out the side and regarded Viv with distrustful eyes the size of grapefruits, but it stayed put.

Viv began the laborious process of squatting to help gather the confusion of books.

The rattkin stopped her. "Forget it." She heaved an enormous sigh. "Let's not tempt fate, hm?"

It didn't take her long to create new, more precarious piles, but at least they weren't scattered across the floor. While she did, Viv surreptitiously straightened the carpet by dragging one end with her crutch, which triggered a ridiculous, bubbling growl from Potroast.

"All right. Shit. I'm flustered," said the rattkin, fanning herself with one paw. She shook out her whiskers and inquired, "Can I help you with something?"

The words were delivered in a polite tone so at odds with her very foul mouth, Viv couldn't help it anymore, and a laugh finally escaped.

"Oh, gods, I'm sorry," she said, trying to choke it off. "It's just . . . every rattkin I've ever met was such a soft, shy little thing, and I thought—"

The rattkin's eyes narrowed. "And *I* thought all orcs only *ate* books, but here we are."

And then Viv lost her grip on her laughter entirely.

After a second, the rattkin managed a chuckle or two as well, wiping her forehead and staring around as though wondering how on earth she'd gotten there.

"Fern, by the way." She held out a paw to shake.

Viv obliged, swallowing it in her own massive grip. She tried to be gentle about it, though. "Viv. Again, real sorry for the mess."

Fern waved it off. Sort of. "You buy a book, all's forgiven."

"Uh, so . . . I left my wallet back at The Perch . . ." She

gestured at her empty belt. A convenient excuse, since she hadn't really intended to buy anything anyway.

Another big sigh from Fern. "From the look of that leg, I don't imagine you'll be galloping over the hills with an ill-gotten novel, so take it on credit and come back tomorrow. Does that work for you?"

Cornered.

"I guess. But"—she glanced around—"gonna be honest, I don't read a whole lot, and I don't have any idea what I'd be looking for anyway."

Fern looked her up and down, as though measuring out her weight in words. She tapped her lower lip with a claw as she considered Viv's sword and the overall . . . Viv-ness of her.

"*Ten Links in the Chain*," she said, running a finger along the spines of some of the books. "It's a classic."

Viv made a dubious face. "Sounds . . . stuffy."

"It's about a jailbreak," Fern called over her shoulder. "Swordfights. A nighttime ship battle. Curses. There's a dwarf with one eye and a murderous streak." She looked back, and her black eyes gleamed with certainty. "Trust me, hm? Ah, here it is!"

She withdrew a slim volume bound in red leather and brought it over. Viv reluctantly took it. The title was embossed into the cover and painted in flaking gold, and the author was R. Geneviss. Flipping it open, Viv stared doubtfully at the small words.

"Any pictures?" Then she thought guiltily of the mess she'd made and the rotten wood out front. "Not that that's important, I guess?"

Fern laughed, a soft, musical sound. "A *few* woodcuts. But none of the gory bits."

Viv mustered a smile that she hoped looked appreciative. "Uh, yeah. Of course. Anyway, thanks for this. How much do I owe you? For tomorrow?"

"It's not off one of the newer printers, but with that leather binding—thirty bits." She saw Viv's expression and sighed. "Shit. Okay, for you, twenty."

"So, I hate to bring this up, but . . ." Viv told her about the destroyed plank out front.

The rattkin covered both eyes with her paws and uttered several surprisingly creative profanities, as well as some words that Viv was *pretty* sure were profane, before visibly gathering herself. "I'm just glad you weren't further injured," she said carefully, like she was walking a tightrope after a tumbler of brandy. "Tomorrow."

As Viv stepped out the door, Potroast delivered a triumphant hoot at her retreat.

~

A fog rolled in off the sea and the beach grass seethed in long gusts as Viv staggered back toward The Perch. The weather was changing fast. The prospect of soaking through her bandages and orc-handling her crutch through wet sand was unappealing in the extreme, so she quickened her pace. The chafing in her armpit was getting pretty fiery, though.

The first few drops scattered dark coins across the sand as she mounted the three stairs to The Perch and reached the safety of its awning. Only seconds later, thunder growled like potatoes down a washboard and licks of lightning flashed through the mist. Sinuous curtains of rain slid in from over the dunes, and the odor of hot sand gone wet overrode every other scent.

When Viv ducked inside, the inn was a lot more populated than earlier.

Sea-fey and humans with ropy arms and salt-scaled clothes clustered around the tables or lingered at the bar, and a muddle of convivial conversation filled the room. Brand glided effortlessly back and forth behind the counter, attending to this and that. A narrow-shouldered half-elf kid wove between the tables, dropping off copper mugs or bowls of stew. Somebody was lighting a fire in the hearth, and raindrops hissed in the kindling.

Viv was starving again. One lonely table in the back was unoccupied, and she figured she'd be able to park herself comfortably. She thumped over to a chair under the mounted skull of some toothy sea predator. Sighing in relief as she transferred her weight from her uninjured leg to her backside, Viv fumbled with the sword-belt and dropped it underneath her chair, keeping her crutch in reach against the wall.

Laying the red book on the table, she stared at it while she waited for the kid to make his way over. She wondered where Rackam and the rest of them were—Lannis, Tuck, Sinna, and Malefico. Pitching camp by now, no doubt, drawing lots for the watch. Or had they already caught up to Varine? Was everyone still in one piece? Viv had barely been with the Ravens two months, and already she was falling by the wayside. She worried at her bandages and chewed her lip, staring off into a growing distance.

"Get you something?" A nervous voice brought her back to herself. The tavern kid, a bunch of empty mugs dangling from his fingers.

"A couple of those," she said, pointing to the mugs. "And whatever everybody else is eating? Three of that." She caught

Brand's attention, raising her brows at him. He gestured back. "Let Brand know, and I'll pay up tomorrow." She patted her bum leg.

"Uh, sure."

While he was gone, she centered *Ten Links in the Chain* before her and sighed deeply. It felt like giving in to even consider reading it. A tacit admission that she was now a different sort of person. Weak. Soft. Sleepy.

Someone who idled and studied, rather than fought and won.

She flipped to the first page. The chapter was titled "In Which I Dismember a Man." Viv thought of Fern's knowing gaze and huffed a laugh. With reluctant interest, she began to read.

> *When I first tell you that I was wrongfully imprisoned, you may have some sympathy. But when I also relay even a few of the dire things I've done, your sympathy will, perhaps, become strained beyond its limit. I can only ask that you hear me out, dear reader. Indeed, because I cut the man's head off and then his legs and his arms and stuffed them into three barrels of brine to survive the voyage, I may seem a monster. But by the end of my tale, I think you may again consider me worthy of your regard.*
> *Besides.*
> *He was a bastard.*

Viv continued reading after her drinks and food arrived. She chewed and sipped absently, turning page after page, and was surprised when she noticed all three bowls were empty, her mugs drained. She didn't even look up when the kid took them away.

The glow in The Perch dimmed, her corner untouched by the blast of light and heat from the hearth across the room, so she asked for a lantern to read by. The kid obliged, and despite the uncomfortable chair and the ache in her leg and the backwater in which she'd been abandoned, she was absorbed.

She was transported.

She was elsewhere.

4

That night, Viv dropped the wooden shutter in her room against the rising wind and sheeting rain. Striking a sulfur match, she lit the lamp, then shuffled the mattress around so she could sit on it while leaning against the bedframe. Not terribly comfortable, but the low boom of blood in her leg made that small by comparison.

Viv read until the wee hours, until she couldn't keep her eyes open and her jaw creaked in an enormous yawn. Then she lay with the book facedown and open across her chest as the sounds of the storm crossed over the boundaries of sleep and colonized her dreams. Swords flashed on the foredeck of a frigate lashed with rain under a bruised sky. The keening of the wind twinned in her slumber, and Viv voyaged through seas unknown.

When Viv navigated to the ground floor of The Perch the following morning, the storm had blown itself out into a miserable drizzle. Raindrops murmured on the shingled awning, and through the open door, runoff pitted the sand below the eaves.

She'd bound the butt of her crutch in the remains of the wool shirt she'd ruined to bandage her wound in the woods. It was considerably more comfortable now, though it would take a day or two for the raw flesh under her arm to forgive her.

Thinking of the looks she'd gotten, she'd left the saber behind, though it chafed her to do so.

A scattering of folks breakfasted at a few of the tables, and Brand must have been in the back. Viv mounted one of the stools and realigned its neighbor under her foot again. She slid her book onto the counter and found her place on page 196.

Madger had just infiltrated the island fortress of General Dammerlight with her crew of down-and-outers, and if Viv could've read through the prior night, she would've. Her subsequent dreams had been vivid fragments of past scenes and imagined futures, and she'd never experienced anything quite like them. It might've been the wound prodding her sleeping mind, but she awoke itching to recapture the light and fury of it all.

"Been to Thistleburr then?"

She startled, already absorbed after only a couple of pages. Brand passed her with a few empty plates.

"Oh. Yeah." She glanced out the door at the rain. "Something to do indoors, I guess."

"Looks like you should've gotten two." He indicated the slim number of pages remaining. "Always dishes to do when you get bored, though." A half-grin.

"That reminds me." She fished a handful of copper bits from her wallet. "For yesterday, and some breakfast again, if I can get it."

Brand nodded and disappeared into the kitchen once more. When he returned with a plateful of fried sausages, buttered grits, and peppered eggs, Viv marked her page and closed the book. As he scooped her coins off the bar, she pulled the plate closer and asked, "So, that tapenti Gatewarden . . . ?"

Brand laughed. "Met Iridia, did you? Eight hells, I would've paid to see *that* stare-off."

Viv blinked at him.

"Sometimes you spy a couple of dogs on either side of a road before they see each other, and you know the teeth are going to come out. I would've said the same about you two. Iridia's a hard lady and wants to make sure you know it. In her mind, it saves trouble later." He shrugged. "Can't say it doesn't work. And I guess she barked loudest, since you're sitting here this morning."

She frowned and put down her fork, bite uneaten.

"It's a compliment. She's the head Gatewarden around here. If you'd been fool enough to press her, you would've spent a lot harder night. In a cell, I figure. Means you've got some sense, that's all." He patted her considerable forearm. "Besides, in a dogfight? I'd put my copper on the one who hasn't been stabbed in the leg yet." He chuckled and strode off, wiping his hands on his apron.

Viv tried to let that roll off her, with limited success, but the hot food helped. The really *excellent* hot food. If there was a bright side to forced convalescence, it was eating something besides cold, dry trail rations.

Even thinking that put her in mind of Rackam and all the rest, forging northward without her. The fried sausages were more than fine, but she would've traded them for a blanket on the cold ground where she really belonged.

Brand was right. She *should've* gotten two books. Viv moved to the table she'd claimed the night before and settled in to finish *Ten Links in the Chain.* Madger's long-delayed revenge, the heartbreaking betrayal of Four Fingers Legann, Dammerlight's poignant end, even *after* the hells he put her through. Viv kept wishing she had a bowl of nuts to chew through.

When she closed the book at last, running her fingers over the red cover, the drizzle still hadn't abated.

"Well, Fern, don't suppose I'm going to show today. I'll just have to make it up to you," she said. She imagined the rattkin charging through the door, fur soaked flat and cursing her out in that high, sweet voice of hers. That dredged up a grin.

Viv was turning back to read the first chapter over, just to keep the taste alive, when someone *did* charge through the door.

Rain slicked off his oiled cloak as he flapped it with one arm and withdrew a big, black leather bag. The elf tossed back his hood and flicked errant drops from his valise in exasperation. A pair of spectacles dangled on a cord around his neck, which was odd, since elves rarely needed them. Even Viv knew that.

Something about his face tickled a memory.

He glanced around the room, and when he saw her, his expression didn't exactly light up, but it did . . . *resettle* into one she couldn't immediately identify.

Then she noticed the purple bruising on his neck.

"Oh, shit," she groaned.

He marched over and dropped his bag on her table with a bang and a rattle. He could've been one century old, or five. It was hard to tell with elves. He kept his silver hair cropped short, and his face was smooth and severe.

". . . Highlark?" asked Viv. Her apologetic smile felt awkward and huge on her face, her tusks too large in her mouth.

"You didn't remember our appointment, did you?" he said. There was something surpassingly strange about hearing such a beautiful voice express annoyance. "I don't suppose I'm surprised. You were barely lucid."

"I'm *real* sorry about . . . about *that*," mumbled Viv, pointing a limp finger at his throat.

His mouth thinned. "Well, I'm not going to do this down here in front of half of Murk. Up." He hiked a thumb toward the stairs. "Let's get this over with."

"Get what—?"

"Child, if you want to roll the bones on gangrene, then I'll be on my way. Out into the weather. Again. Otherwise, I'll kindly ask you to limp your way up those stairs. Yes?"

Viv grabbed her crutch.

And her book.

～

She kept up a running stream of apologies all the way up the stairs, into the room, and until the moment after he'd unwrapped her leg. When he began prodding the tender areas around her wounds, she wanted to knock him through the wall.

Viv sat on the bedframe, leg extended, with her heel propped on her pack again. The long tears in her thighs oozed afresh as he wiped old salve from the angry flesh. Viv dug her teeth into her lower lip hard enough to draw blood but forced herself to stare at what he was doing.

"You've been hobbling around too much, I see," he observed. He adjusted his spectacles on his nose.

"Mmm," she grunted. "Keeping limber."

"Yes, I see that's working out well for you."

"Spectacles?" She hissed through her teeth. "Never met an elf that needed 'em."

"Magnifiers," he said. "Helps detect creeping foulness. Which, luckily, doesn't appear to be present. The more you rest, the more likely it is that this happy situation will persist."

"In here? I'd go crazy. I can barely turn around without hitting something. Besides, if I lie around for a couple of weeks, I won't be fighting fit when it's time to go. And then . . ."

He gazed at her over the top of his glasses, and while his annoyed expression didn't quite make it to sympathy, it inched in that direction. "Look, child, I know you're young and you've got the constitution of a prairie ox. But you can afford to lose a little of *this*"—he patted one enormous bicep—"to keep *this*." He tapped her thigh.

"So, let's say I take your advice . . ."

Highlark snorted.

". . . when *can* I move around?"

He studied her with narrowed, lavender eyes.

"I hesitate to make the suggestion," he said, "because it will be very annoying if you misbehave and I have to saw your leg off."

Viv swallowed.

"But." He rummaged in his bag. "Callis oil. I normally wouldn't use this. You've heard of it?"

She shook her head and watched as he removed the lid from a small earthenware pot containing a yellow cream. It smelled like pond scum by way of raw lye.

"It was once used on battlefields where the side effects were worth enduring, given the dire circumstances. The sensation it produces is . . . well. It's been compared to hornet stings."

Viv almost laughed. "That's not so bad."

"Continuous hornet stings at every point of application, for hours and hours and hours," Highlark elaborated.

"Oh."

"However, its healing properties are unrivaled, especially when it comes to stitching together rent flesh on the quick. Were we to apply it today, then by tomorrow morning, I might approve of *limited* mobility. As long as the bindings are left undisturbed, and you make use of that crutch."

"I *have* been."

"Then I take it you'd like to give it a go?"

Viv glanced around the tiny room, at her leg, and at the crutch. She nodded. "Do it."

When he first slathered the callis oil on with a small wooden spade, the sensation was cold, and she thought he'd been blowing smoke. Or that orcs might be immune to the effect.

Then the burn began to set in.

Then it was a forest fire of needles.

Then she would've traded it for being stabbed all over again.

She decided it was a good thing she could still see the bruises on Highlark's neck while he rewound her bandages, because it kept her from throttling him a second time.

～

She skipped lunch and dinner. Indeed, she didn't rise from the straw-tick mattress again that day. Food was as far from her mind as Rackam and his Ravens were from this gods-forsaken place. The pain was incandescent, all-consuming, and Viv lay on her back, breathing long, shuddering breaths while sweat slicked every inch of her.

Pain tolerance was a point of personal pride, and for the first thirty minutes, she'd been positive that she'd be able to master the flayed feeling in her thigh. That it would dull into a throb. But the edge stayed sharp, unblunted by passing minutes or by careful breathing. Perversely, it honed itself ever sharper.

In the face of that, she clutched for the story she'd just read. It was slippery, like muck-slick rope running through her fingers. She caught a good grip on it only intermittently, but flashes of Madger and Legann, of rooftop swordfights and nighttime flights astride huge black horses, kept her eyes on an interior vista.

In the darker hours, she didn't even manage a doze. Not really. Not well. There were simply snatches of time where her thoughts were on the insides of her eyelids.

Before the pink of predawn, the storm blew itself out at the same time as the fire in her leg, and the straining muscles of her body collapsed into a tremorous unconsciousness.

She slept hard. She slept late. And when she woke, she wanted to eat the whole world.

5

Viv paused before crutching her way down the front steps of The Perch. In the wake of the storm, the sky burned hot and blue, and the beach grass seemed to have flushed from yellow to green overnight. The sand was pitted and dimpled, as though a million tiny creatures had traversed it in the dark.

Her leg wasn't miraculously mobile, but the flesh *did* feel less tender, more solid. When she tested it through the bandages with her fingers, it seemed to take more pressure to set off a nauseous ache. The feverish memory of the callis oil's burn wasn't one she'd soon forget, though.

In stark contrast to her first, solitary trip down the slope, Viv spied others strolling along the boardwalks. A passenger frigate wallowed at the pier, gangplank down. The bay must've been pretty deep. Gulls wheeled in fluttering loops, their cries rebounding off the gentle swells. The activity below trickled up the causeways and through Murk's gates, but plenty of figures headed her way as well.

She passed Thistleburr Booksellers, which didn't seem to be benefiting from the increased traffic in any appreciable way. Viv stayed in the sandy street, distrustful of the decrepit boardwalk. And maybe she didn't want Fern to spy her through the windows just yet. Viv glanced at the door as she thudded past, but she had another errand in mind.

Sea-Song Bakery had apparently soaked up all the custom before it could reach the bookshop. A line stretched out the door, with a mix of dockworkers, tradesfolk, and passengers from the frigate. Viv joined the queue, earning a few wary looks from the gnome in front of her. *Thank the Eight I didn't belt on the saber today.* She tried for a smile, but that got her nothing but a raised eyebrow.

The scents were even more appetizing in the fresh, post-storm breeze. When Viv finally clomped her way indoors, those savory and sweet smells redoubled.

Hot and humid, the bakery was open all the way to the back. Moisture beaded on the glass of the front window. Two brick ovens and two enormous cast-iron stoves faced each other beyond a counter, with long marble workspaces flanking them. Down the center ran a pair of open shelves, stacked with an impressive variety of breads.

More baskets lined the front, sorted by type. There were long loaves with slitted crusts, salted rounds, the massive, flaky biscuits Viv had spied two days ago, and buns studded with huge crystals of sugar.

When she reached the front of the line, the dwarf behind the counter looked her up and down, then gave her a pink-cheeked grin. Her sleeves were rolled past the elbow, her forearms evidence of hard work wrestling dough. She fairly glistened with sweat, and she wore her hair bound in a thick blond braid. A startling quantity of flour dusted her apron.

"Well, ain't you a big piece of somethin' sweet?" she said, winking. "What can I getcha?"

Viv was baffled by the wink and stared back wide-eyed for a second before recovering herself. "Uh, can I get three of those biscuits and . . . I guess the same of whatever the dark ones are?"

"Ginger lassy buns. You got it, hon. Fresh off the boat?"

"No . . . no, I, um—"

"Oh, hang on!" The dwarf snapped her fingers and pointed at Viv's leg. "*Highlark!* Hells, you're the one that—" She clutched at her neck and poked her tongue out. Then she laughed and slapped the counter, an explosive sound in the open bakery. The sea-fey behind Viv actually flinched.

Viv flushed, although she thought she ought to be immune at this point. "So, I wasn't exactly in my right mind when I—"

"Ha! Nah, don't fret over it, sweet thing. He's a sour apple. You probably squeezed a little sugar into him." She snapped her fingers again, this time at a willowy human girl with her hair up in a bun. The kid dutifully flapped open a paper sack and filled it from the shelves.

"For you, six bits," proclaimed the dwarf as she folded the top of the sack and handed it over. "Gonna be in Murk for a while?"

"A few weeks," replied Viv as she fished around in her wallet. "I guess."

"Suppose I'll be seeing you again then."

"These are *that* good, huh?" Viv tried for a teasing smile. To her astonishment, it seemed to work.

"I *know* you'll be back tomorrow. Hells, you try my biscuits, I bet you decide to stay *longer*. I'm Maylee. Welcome to Murk."

"Um. Viv." She took the bag.

"Try not to eat 'em before you get home, Viv," Maylee called sweetly as the line shuffled aside to let Viv maneuver out into the air.

~

When Viv cracked open the door to the bookshop, the scent of pastry almost managed to beat back the musty funk of the place. Fern looked up from her stool behind the counter where she'd been writing notes in a ledger.

Potroast darted into view from around some shelves, his yapping hoots strident and self-important. He scrambled to a stop at Viv's feet, and she was careful to maneuver her crutch between him and the precarious piles she'd overturned last time.

His barks dwindled when he caught sight of the sack in her hand, at which point he began darting glances between it and her face. His eyes goggled in furious consternation and a pink tongue like a tiny spade lolled out of his black beak.

"Back the next day, hm?" said Fern, closing the ledger and leaning an arm on the counter.

"Bandages aren't so good in the rain," replied Viv. "Brought an apology, though."

"Hm. Hope you brought enough for three. Potroast, at least, is very susceptible to bribes."

"That's what I was counting on. So . . ." She dug into the sack and withdrew a biscuit, pinching it between two fingers above the creature. His tail blurred, and he uttered a long, plaintive hoot. "What exactly *is* he?"

"A gryphet." Fern climbed down from her stool and approached. "If you don't break it into pieces, he'll try to swallow it whole, and then we'll have to fish it out of him. He's incredibly greedy."

Viv couldn't manage a crouch, so she handed the biscuit over to Fern, who tore a little off and dropped it. The gryphet snatched the morsel out of the air before it reached the ground.

"I've got more," said Viv.

Fern tossed another piece to Potroast and then waved Viv over to the counter, where she unpacked the sack, laying out her bounty.

"Maylee's, hmm? You *did* want to apologize."

"Yeah, she seems . . . nice. Friendly."

"She does, does she?" The rattkin selected one of the lassy buns and took a surprisingly enormous bite. "Oh fuck," she said around her mouthful. "Forgot how *good* these are."

Viv laughed. Her leg really was less sore today, and her mood was up. She slid twenty bits onto the counter beside the baked goods and picked up one of the biscuits. "Been wanting one of these since the first day." She inhaled deeply and took a bite. The bread was still warm—moist and crumbly, with a hint of sourdough tang. "Eight hells, it's *made* of butter. You could have this every day, and you don't?"

Fern frowned. "Well, *some* expenses are more pressing."

Viv stared around at the state of the shop uncomfortably, especially since she'd only just squared with Brand for another few weeks of lodging, with coin to spare. Mercenary work was deadly work, but it paid to match.

Potroast whined, and the rattkin eyed him, then polished off her bun before heaving a pleased sigh. "Anyway, never mind that. Any thoughts on *Ten Links in the Chain*? How are you faring?"

"I'm fared. It got me through a rough day and then some. I've never really read like that . . . just to *read*."

"You finished it?" Fern's brows shot up in surprise. "Well, I'll be damned."

"Thanks for the suggestion."

"You really want to thank me, you could subsidize this place by buying another."

Viv propped her crutch against the wall and put an elbow on the counter, easing the weight onto her leg. "Business that bad?"

"I sell a lot of maps and sea charts, but . . ." Fern picked up one of the biscuits and examined it. "These days, that's just bailing water. The ship will go down eventually." She took a bite, closed her eyes, and mumbled another crumb-filled profanity.

An awkward silence followed, during which they both chewed and looked anywhere but at one another. Sadly, the shop itself remained not much to look at. At last, Viv swallowed and said, "Well, a sea chart isn't going to keep me from going stir-crazy, and I'm stuck with this crutch for a while, so . . . any other suggestions?"

The rattkin studied her for a moment, and Viv thought she looked more weary than someone so young ought to ever be. Fern shook herself, though, and brightened. "First, tell me about *Ten Links*. I want to know your thoughts."

Viv frowned. She'd enjoyed the hells out of it, honestly, but . . . she wasn't sure how to put that into words.

"Well. I *liked* it," she tried lamely.

Fern snorted. "Yes, very illuminating."

"The swordfights were great. Not realistic, but, you know, fun."

"I'll have to take your word for that, I guess. How about the characters, though?"

"Uh. Well . . . Madger was—She was . . . complicated."

"Mmmhmm. How so? What stood out to you?" She stroked her whiskers, seeming honestly interested.

Viv thought about it. "She was hard. And I guess you like her for it. At least, I did. But sometimes . . . *too* hard. And then . . . Legann, he kind of pushes back, I guess? Sort of like they're each only half a person. But if they press hard enough toward each other, then—"

Something ignited in Fern's eyes. "Legann was *always* my favorite, despite how everything ended for him. When Madger lost Legann—"

"She lost everything," finished Viv. "Even though he betrayed her."

"Did he though? *Really?* Or was he trying to keep her from betraying herself? And then the more important question . . . did he *succeed?*"

Viv frowned. "Huh."

"Well, while you wrestle with that, I think I have something you might want to try."

As Fern rounded a shelf to rummage in a pile, Viv looked down at the gryphet, who was watching her with narrowed eyes.

"Still enemies?" whispered Viv.

Potroast burbled deep in his throat in what she thought was a growl. The feathers of his ruff fluffed.

"Your loss, then. This one's for me," she said, popping the last piece of lassy bun in her mouth.

His burble intensified.

"Here go you," said Fern, sliding a green volume onto the counter. It was thicker than the last and entitled *Heart's Blade.*

"By Russa Tensiger. A little more modern, but I have a feeling you just might like it."

"Well, it's got 'blade' in the title, so that's a good start."

Viv thought Fern's smile was secretive, but the rattkin nodded.

"How much do I owe you?"

"Actually, I have a little deal in mind. Take it for now. Another twenty bits if you like it. If you don't, you keep your money."

"Uh, I'm not qualified to give business advice or anything, but that might be why you're only selling sea charts."

"You have to read the whole thing though. *All* of it. And if you don't finish, you *also* have to pay up."

Viv frowned at her. "I'm getting the feeling this book doesn't have as many swords as I was expecting."

"It's an *important* sword. So, agreed?" She stuck out her paw.

Viv thought about it but shrugged. "Agreed."

Fern's eyes twinkled with amusement. "I'm so interested to hear what you think."

6

Viv almost planted her good foot through the wrecked plank in the boardwalk, catching herself just in time. "Eight hells," she said in exasperation. "Two busted legs really would put a crown on it."

As she carefully made her way into the street, she saw the scarred orc and his wagon, tools rattling against the slatted sides. Folks streaming up the hill toward The Perch parted around him like trout skirting a gar.

"Hey!" she called out. She finally dredged up his name. "Pitts!"

He slowed to a stop, watching her limp nearer.

Close up, Pitts was younger than she'd expected, his scalp shaved clean. He studied the book in her hand with interest.

"Look, if I wanted to get a couple of planks around here, where would I do that? I figure you'd know," she asked.

He frowned, then gestured over her shoulder. "Mill's 'round the other side of the walls, on the stream."

For some reason she expected him to follow that up with a question, but he dropped his hand and waited on her again.

"Uh, so . . . how do I ask this . . . Do you ever get over that way? If I wanted to maybe pay you to pick up a few boards for me, and also for a little time with some of your tools, would that be something you'd do?"

"Suppose that depends."

"On?"

He shrugged, still holding the traces, so that the wagon tilted as he did. "On what you're plannin'."

She waved at the shop with the book. "The wood's rotten up there. Almost put my foot through it. Figured I'd replace it."

Pitts's brow wrinkled doubtfully at her bum leg. "Why?"

Viv frowned in return. "Because it's dangerous?"

He shook his head. "I mean, why you? Somebody ask? Know what you're doin'?"

"I guess *no* to both, but how hard could it be to knock in a board? Pretty sure I can hit a nail hard enough to get the job done. I don't know, I think Fern's got enough to worry with, so I figured . . ." She trailed off.

Pitts thought about that for a second, then nodded once, very slowly. "Tomorrow at noon."

"At noon . . . what?"

"Meet me here."

"Oh. Uh, what do I owe you?"

"We'll see."

And then he was off and rolling again.

Viv blinked at his departure. "Well . . . thanks!" she called after him, but he didn't turn back.

"See you at noon," she said to herself, shaking her head.

Viv stepped into The Perch anticipating a leisurely lunch at the table she was coming to think of as *hers*. She'd been looking forward to dipping into *Heart's Blade* and figuring out if Fern was teasing her or not. Instead, she found the bottom floor absolutely packed.

Apparently, Brand's inn was well known to the passengers and crew of the docked frigate, because they *all* seemed to be there. It was louder than she'd ever heard it, thick with chatter and the occasional bellow of laughter. Her table had even been commandeered—although there *were* two open chairs there.

Any time before this week, the atmosphere would've been welcome. A beer and some food and conversation might've been just the thing. But with a book in hand, and a surprising interest in cracking it, she felt properly thwarted. She supposed she could go upstairs to her room, but . . .

Sidling through a crowd with a crutch caused more than a few bumped shoulders, and she mumbled apologies that were lost in the hubbub. But her natural size helped some as she approached her preferred table.

Her favorite chair—the one that faced the rest of the room—was occupied by a gnome with a look about her that Viv had seen plenty of times before.

She had to be younger than Viv by at least a few years. A pair of goggles held back her spiky orange hair, and a set of bare-bladed knives gleamed on her bandolier. Hardly bigger than a human child, her head didn't clear the table-top by much. Clad in fingerless gloves, her hands toyed with the copper mug in front of her, and she didn't seem to be eating.

"Hey," said Viv with a forced smile. "Any chance I could convince you to swap so I could sit in that chair? Easier to be out of the way with the leg." She patted her thigh lightly.

The gnome eyed her up and down. Viv recognized the look

of a new recruit with something to prove. Unfortunately. "After I'm gone, you're welcome to it," she said with exaggerated indifference. The girl ran a finger around the rim of her mug, very slowly.

Viv's eyes narrowed, and she breathed in hard through her nose. Then with great deliberation she laid her book on the table and dragged out the empty chair, raking it across the floorboards with a squeal. She didn't break eye contact with the gnome as she eased into the seat and swung her stiff leg around to the side.

A smile teased the gnome's lips, and Viv had to deliberately unclench her fists and lay them flat on the table.

Doing her best to shake off her irritation, she figured she'd dive into *Heart's Blade* while waiting for the tavern kid to make his way over. It'd probably take a while, given the crowd. Also, it seemed like an excellent way to ignore someone while they were sitting right in front of you.

CHAPTER ONE
❧

The steel that brought them together was the steel that kept them apart. Or possibly, it was the other way around. Like the blade in question, their story has two edges.

It was a simple longsword—nothing elaborate about it. Even so, it was the work of a master bladesmith, perfect in its utility, a burnished blue that made one think of evening fog on the river.

Tamora wielded it in the spirit that it had been forged. Never flashy, never ostentatious. She drew it, swung it, and sheathed it as part of work done well and right.

She stood on the backboard of the coach as it rumbled through the night, and her broad features were cast in harsh shadows by the lantern light. Tamora kept her eyes fixed on the lane behind them, ever watchful.

Mirrim Stanhood gazed out the small window in the coach door at the dark stripes of trees as they flickered by. She wielded weapons of her own, but they were of another sort, from the finely sculpted ringlets of her hair to the sharp words she slid between the ribs of the unsuspecting.

Lately, she'd been sliding a lot of them into Tamora, who also wouldn't have minded returning the favor in a much more physical way. Only necessity saw them occupying the same coach.

But when Tamora saw the red glow, and smelled the smoke, she still—

"Whatcha readin'?"

When Viv glanced up, she found the gnome tapping her lips, eyes half-lidded with amusement.

"You don't care," Viv said flatly.

"Must be interestin'. I mean, *you're* readin' it."

"What's that supposed to mean?"

The gnome shrugged. "Oh, nothin', really. Lookin' atcha though . . ." She gestured to Viv with a hand, as though the answer was obvious. "Guess I just figured you're more of a steel-swingin' sorta gal? Probably gotta be pretty good to catch *your* attention. Or, I dunno. Short."

Viv simply stared at her. Usually that was pretty effective.

The gnome didn't seem to mind. "C'mon, what's it called?"

"Piss off."

"Okay, that *does* sound like a book you'd read."

"Can I get you anything?" the tavern kid asked breathlessly as he squeezed through the crowd, dirty mugs looped around his knuckles.

Viv worked the frown off her face and pointed at his hands. "Same as last time. A couple of those, and a couple of whatever lunch is."

"For both of you?" The kid gestured between them with the mugs.

"If she's buyin', I could always eat," piped the gnome.

"No," replied Viv firmly.

When he disappeared back into the crowd, Viv sighed and set the book on end so that the girl could read the title. "There."

"*Heart's Blade*, huh? Well, that *is* a better title."

Viv snorted and shook her head, very pointedly returning her attention to the pages.

"How'd ya get the wound?"

Viv glared at her. "In a battle."

"Oh, hey, now *that's* the kind of story I wanna hear."

"Not interested in telling it."

"Aw, come on. Tell you what, you spill, and I'll swap chairs after. We both get what we want. Deal?"

"Everybody wants to make a deal today," muttered Viv. "Fine. But we switch first."

A pause. "All right. You welch on me though . . ."

"And what, you're gonna stab me with one of those?" Viv scoffed.

The girl drew one of the knives from her bandolier, flipped it a couple feet into the air, and caught it point down on one fingertip. She shrugged as she balanced it there.

"Very flashy." Viv rose, which took a few seconds as she heaved herself up and onto the crutch.

True to her word, the gnome swapped places, and Viv settled with real satisfaction into her accustomed chair. "Thanks for warming it up for me."

"Yeah, yeah, get to the tellin'."

The kid reappeared with Viv's food and drink, and she waited until he was gone, then took a long pull of the beer.

"Okay, fine. I run with Rackam's Ravens. We're on contract with three north Territory cities to hunt a nasty woman with a bigger army than anybody is comfortable with. We were rolling through a forest near here, and one of her soldiers got me through the thigh with a lucky strike." She gulped another swallow and set it down forcefully. "And that's it."

The gnome's eyes were wide. "*Rackam?* You run with Rackam?"

Viv shrugged. She tried to be nonchalant about it. She probably wasn't very successful. "Sure."

"Well, where are they now?" demanded the gnome.

"Back in a few weeks. I'm just . . . resting up until they show. All right, I kept up my end, so I'm gonna read now, yeah?"

The girl sat back in her chair and folded her arms with a speculative look.

Viv was about to resume her story, but then sighed and said, "What?"

"Introduce me to him."

"*What?*" Viv repeated incredulously.

"You heard me. I figured I was gonna have to take a coach all the way to Thune to find somebody to take me on, but this is perfect! Look, I'm *real* good. What'd you have to do to sign up?"

"I was recommended," said Viv. "By someone who knew me. And *liked* me," she emphasized.

"See, that's the way it works! You gotta know somebody. But you know me, you intro me, bam!" She pounded a fist into a palm. "I'm in!"

"I don't even know your *name*."

"Gallina." The gnome shoved her hand across the table. It didn't come close to reaching halfway.

Viv ignored it. "How am I going to recommend you? I don't know the first thing about you."

"You need a demonstration?"

"I need to read my *book*."

Gallina grimaced at her. "Y'know, people like us gotta look out for each other."

"People like us? What the hells does that mean?" Viv massaged her forehead in exasperation.

"New blood. Everybody's gotta start *somewhere*. What's *your* name?"

"Viv." She wondered if she'd regret answering that. "And now that we both know each other, I'm going to read this and eat my lunch. If you want an introduction to Rackam, I guess you can wait around here until he rides in and do it yourself. What in the hells could I possibly tell him? 'I ran into this kid in a bar, and she was a relentless pain in my ass? Please, sir, I just thought she could be a pain in the ass for the Ravens?'"

Gallina's expression could've curdled cream. She slid down from her chair. "Well, fuck you, too," she said, and disappeared into the crowd.

"Good gods," muttered Viv, wondering if she hadn't jammed her foot into a hole after all.

7

Viv had the feeling she was going to be paying Fern twenty bits, and not because she liked the book.

She headed early to the boardwalk, moving slowly toward her noon appointment. Her leg felt remarkably stable, and every few steps she let her weight settle onto her right heel a bit, just to test her tolerance. Still, she stuck to a reserved pace, mostly thinking about the chapters of *Heart's Blade* she'd read.

There had been a lot less swinging of the titular blade than anticipated. As in, nearly zero, which she should've figured out from Fern's grin. In fact, the first third of the book mostly seemed to be about Mirrim's political misadventures with a bunch of upstart arcanists, Tamora the bodyguard's intimidation of said arcanists, and increasingly loud arguments between the two of them. There was a lot of clever wordplay that Viv was pretty sure was mostly sarcasm. Tamora was a stone-fey and had a few centuries on Mirrim, who was human. They hated each other. *Sort* of. It was increasingly hard to tell. Viv kept wanting them to either punch one another or hop in the sack, just so they'd sort it out. If things didn't change soon, she wasn't sure she could make it to the end.

She figured she'd be waiting for Pitts to show, but he was already at Fern's shop. His wagon was parked to the side of the thoroughfare, and he sat on the boardwalk with his hands dangling between his knees. Four planks lay beside him, along with a saw, a mallet, and a couple of other tools.

He hoisted himself to his feet as she approached.

"Hey, thanks," she called as she set her crutch against the boardwalk rail and held her balance against the post.

"Ought to be what you need. Got things to do, so I'll come by in a few hours to get my tools." He leaned toward her and earnestly added, "Don't leave 'em out, mind."

"Of course not."

He looked from her to the stack of supplies and back. "Brought extra. Just in case."

"I'm pretty sure I can manage."

Pitts shrugged. "Guess the worst that happens is there's a new hole." Then he stepped into the traces and trundled off.

"It's just a gods-damned board or two," muttered Viv. She thought about poking her head in to greet Fern, but then figured she might as well get on with it.

Pitts had also provided a wooden box of long iron nails, a steel pry bar, and a charcoal pencil.

Viv eased down to her butt on the boardwalk and hefted the top plank, then slid it alongside the rotten board. Too long.

"Not *that* complicated," scoffed Viv, marking the plank with the pencil.

Taking the saw in hand, she arranged herself awkwardly with her bandaged leg kicked out and her torso twisted to try to get the right angle. With one hand on the board, she set to cutting. Unfortunately, the other end slithered around with every backstroke, and the saw's teeth hitched and hung.

Swearing under her breath, she muscled the sawblade back and forth, ripping down through the board until the end canted away. She snapped it off with her fingers, leaving a ragged spine of wood projecting.

Staring at the lopsided cut and the fringe of splinters around the edge, Viv sighed and looked at the remaining planks, which suddenly seemed too few.

"Well, shit."

~~

It took another two boards to get a properly clean cut, which involved a very uncomfortable and awkward arrangement of her legs to keep things steady. By then she'd figured out how to make sure, smooth strokes. She decided that the end result wasn't *too* embarrassing.

Ripping out the old board was simple, at least. She popped it off easily with a little muscle applied to the metal pry bar.

Hammering in the nails was trivial too. Too much so. She delivered sharp, accurate strokes, with nary a bruised thumb, smiling as she did so. This was a language in which every muscle of her arm was fluent.

On the final stroke, she brought the mallet down so hard, a crack shot from the nail almost to the center of the entire plank. She swore so loudly that the door flew open behind her.

"What in the faithless *fuck*?" cried Fern. Potroast yapped anxiously behind her.

Viv glanced up guiltily. "Uh, just . . . doing some repairs?"

Fern stared at her open-mouthed, taking in the powdering of sawdust, the boards tossed into the street, and the ruined, half-installed plank.

"I . . . why . . . ?" The rattkin seemed at a loss for words.

"The rotten plank I told you about. You remember? I almost put my foot through it. Well . . . I *did* put my crutch through it first, and . . ." Viv looked at the hammer, then squinted back at her. "I've almost got it?"

Fern closed her mouth, seized the clasp of her cloak like she wanted to crush it, then shut the door on Potroast and walked in the direction of the beach without another word.

After some careful and nervous resizing of the last whole plank, Viv kept a handle on her strength as she nailed it in place. She held her breath on the final strokes as she knocked the nailheads flush.

When she pulled herself to her feet, she considered her handiwork with satisfaction. The fresh wood stood out, but in time it ought to weather enough to match. Another year, and you'd never know. Gathering her crutch, she stumped over and set her full weight on the plank. Not so much as a creak.

By the time she'd swept away the sawdust, organized the tools, and arranged the junk wood in the street, Pitts was rolling back up to the shop.

He examined the wreckage of Viv's first attempts and the finished product, and she almost expected him to laugh or shake his head, but he simply began loading the wood and his tools onto the cart.

"So, what do I owe you?" she asked.

"What do *I* owe you?" came a high voice from behind her. Fern had approached silently, with a long loaf of bread cradled in the crook of her arm, her red cloak fluttering in the breeze.

"Wood was just scrap," said Pitts, without turning around.

Somehow, Viv didn't believe him.

Apparently, Fern didn't either. "Come on up here, Pitts. You're not getting away without some damn lunch." She fixed Viv with a glare that seemed entirely unwarranted. "And neither are you."

Potroast only had eyes for the fresh loaf of bread as Fern led the way inside. Viv followed, feeling awkward about it, but not as awkward as Pitts looked when he tentatively ducked under the doorframe, flinching as though the shelves might topple over on him in an avalanche of paper.

Fern bustled to the counter, shoved a stack of books aside, and set down the loaf she'd bought. She went into the back and returned with a long knife and a muslin-wrapped bundle. Unfolding it beside the bread, she revealed a hard length of sausage and a yellow wedge of cheese that smelled of cream and salt and summer grass.

Without a word, she sawed off slices of bread and piled them with hunks of cheese and discs of sausage, handing them to the two orcs without really looking at either of them. Then she cut a portion for herself and flipped a rind of cheese to the gryphet, who gobbled it down and wagged his tail for more.

Finally, she met their eyes. "Well? Eat!" She took a bite herself and chewed defiantly.

"Uh, are you—" Viv began.

"*Eat.*"

"Okay, fine." Viv tore off a corner with her teeth. The bread was, predictably, incredible—sour and soft with a chewy crust that flaked away in the mouth.

Pitts wolfed his down with a slightly hunted look.

Fern cleared her throat. "Thank you both," she said

carefully. She stared hard at Pitts. "Can I interest you in a book?"

Viv didn't think he *looked* interested, but Pitts also seemed to recognize the path of least resistance. He reached tentatively for the smallest one he could find, and held it up between thumb and forefinger. It looked even tinier there. "This one?"

"*Thorns and Pinions*. A very fine book of poetry. It's yours," said Fern with a regal nod.

"I . . . gotta be goin'," said Pitts. He made a halting bow and backed out of the shop.

Viv watched him depart, smiling. "I don't think I've ever seen anybody that terrified of a free lunch."

Fern was staring at the closed door. She glanced down at her meal, tossed the whole thing onto the floor for Potroast to savage, and promptly burst into tears.

~

"Fuck," sobbed Fern. "What am I *doing* here? I'm relying on charity to fix a *broken board*."

Viv had never felt less equal to the needs of a moment. She ushered the rattkin onto her stool, whereupon the girl folded her arms on the counter and buried her face in them.

"Come on, it can't be that bad . . . can it?" mumbled Viv.

Fern's sigh was watery. "I can't keep on this way. Not for much longer. *Maybe* a month."

"This place has been around a while, right? I'm sure it can last a *few* more than that."

The rattkin raised her head to fix Viv with a bleak gaze. "Fifty years. That's how long it's been here. My father opened this place. I grew up here. Used to sleep in that shelf over there when I was little." She pointed to the far corner. "He left it to me when he died, and it's going to be *me* that runs it into the fucking ground. Gods, what would he say if he could see?"

Viv awkwardly patted her shoulder. "I don't know a lot about running a shop, but . . . what's changed?"

"*Nothing* has changed. It's all the same. Well, that's not true. It's all shabbier. Half falling apart. And I guess *I'm* the main thing that's different."

"Uh. Maybe . . . maybe that's the problem, then?"

Fern's eyes narrowed. "You're not very good at consoling, are you?"

"Oh, no, I don't mean *you.* I mean . . . doing things the same way." Viv winced apologetically. "Sorry, this is *really* not my area."

The rattkin laughed a little. "Don't sell yourself short. You're the most interesting customer I've had in a month."

"Wow, that *is* bad."

Fern's weak laugh turned into a hitching snort. When she recovered, she said, "You know, it's not because I haven't thought about it. About changing things. But it always seems like there's no time or money to patch the holes. Just enough to keep tossing water overboard."

Viv rubbed the back of her neck. "Well, one less hole today. I guess I made that one, though, so it probably doesn't count as progress."

Fern shrugged, resting her chin on her crossed arms.

"If you *could* change something, what would it be?" asked Viv.

The rattkin was quiet for a long time. Viv guessed she wasn't going to get an answer. Then, "*So* much. The inventory. Those fucking sea charts. Newer printings. Some paint on the walls. Magically transport the whole place to a city full of bibliophiles." She glanced at Viv. "What would *you* change? You've got a recent first impression."

Viv tried to look apologetic. "Uh, the smell? Probably that carpet too."

"The *smell*?"

"Yeah, it sort of smells . . . yellow. And not a good yellow." She eyed the gryphet. "Kind of like somebody dunked him in a bucket."

Potroast hooted indignantly and nipped at her boot.

Fern laughed again, then lapsed into silence. After a while, she quietly said, "Thanks for your help today. Thanks for listening to me complain."

"You're the only thing keeping me sane around here," replied Viv. "I've got a vested interest."

The rattkin perked up and her expression cleared. "How's *Heart's Blade* treating you then?"

"Well, I'm . . ." Viv started to hedge, then thought better of it. "I'm just getting started. I'll let you know when I finish."

"Not enough swords for you?"

"I'm reserving judgment, okay?"

Fern pressed herself back up from the counter and shook out her whiskers. She cut another couple of slices of bread and passed one over.

While Viv chewed, the rattkin surveyed her shop again. "The carpet? Really? I'm so preoccupied with all the bigger problems, I don't really think about the small things. I guess it could use a good beating."

Viv swallowed and shook her head. "No. It could use a good burning."

8

"What in the Eight are you doing here?" Highlark seemed half-way between annoyed and thoroughly surprised. "It's two days until I'm due to see you at your room." He glanced up and down the street, as though someone had spirited Viv to his doorstep.

She gave a half-shrug, leaning fully on her crutch. "I figured I'd get out and see the rest of Murk, and once I was here, I thought I'd kill two birds with one stone. Not really hard to find the place."

Highlark's surgery sat near the center of the town snugged within the fortress walls, and everybody knew where it was. The building was tall, narrow, and neatly kept, with flower boxes in both the upper and lower windows, which Viv found oddly amusing. An iron sign in the shape of a healer's staff and crescent was mounted above the lintel.

He narrowed his eyes at her. "What do you want? You're caring for the wound daily like I showed you, yes?"

"Yeah, of course. But . . . well, maybe you could take a look. That callis oil seemed to work pretty well. Maybe I should do that again?"

"*Again?*" He looked shocked.

"Yeah. Wouldn't that get me off this crutch faster?"

"It doesn't work that way," he said with an exasperated tone.

Now that he wasn't wearing a rain cowl, Viv could see the elf cut a fine figure in a crisp white shirt and finely tailored trousers. For some reason, she'd expected him to appear at his door in a bloody smock. She was glad to note that the bruises on his neck were nearly gone.

"I doubt very much that I can offer any other advice until you've healed further. And even if I could, it's clear you wouldn't pay it any mind. Come in, if you must." He opened the door the rest of the way and ushered her in with a resigned air.

As Viv entered Highlark's office, she was surprised to find that it looked more like a bookshop than the real thing. One wall was nothing but floor-to-ceiling shelves, complete with rolling ladder. The spines looked to be in excellent condition, gleaming as though oiled.

"Wow," she said.

A small desk sat before the shelves, piled with notes, folders, an appointment book, and an unlit lantern. She must have interrupted him in his work. It didn't look much like surgery, as far as Viv was concerned.

Highlark strode past a staircase leading up, and through a white door into the back. Astringent smells assaulted Viv's nose as she followed into a very different room. Modern flick-lanterns lit the area brightly, their low hiss filling the air. A pair of long, padded tables stood in the center, and the walls were covered in charts, notes, and illustrations. Vast counters with rows and rows of drawers below them ran along every wall. Bottles, boxes, neatly folded linen, and jars of blue fluids stood ready. She even spied several small—but exceptionally detailed—wooden skeletons of various races suspended from metal arms by thread.

"Up," said Highlark, gesturing to the furthest table. "I suppose you're saving me a trip. And if you can make your way here once, you can do it again, if the need arises."

As Viv slid onto the table—she didn't even have to push herself up—she grimaced and pulled *Heart's Blade* out of her back pocket to lay it beside her. Highlark lifted her injured leg and rested her heel on the table opposite.

Without another word, he deftly unwrapped her bandages. When the flesh was exposed, he made an involuntary sound of consternation.

"What?" asked Viv.

Highlark didn't answer, instead bringing his spectacles up to examine her wounds. He prodded the flesh, and while it was still *very* tender, her head didn't go all swimmy at the pressure, as it had during his last visit.

"It's getting on fine," he said. He straightened, letting his spectacles dangle back against his chest.

It *did* look a lot better. Her leg was still very swollen, but it wasn't actively oozing, and the hot blush of red had receded to a fainter and less far-reaching pink.

Highlark glanced at the book, and his expression registered a different shade of surprise. "A little light reading?"

"Yeah, I think Fern has made a project of me."

"Fern?"

"You know, at the bookshop. You must have been there before?" She gestured vaguely in the direction of Highlark's library.

"Ah! No, I've not made her acquaintance."

"Huh. Where'd you get all the books, then?"

Highlark squinted at her. "They're mostly specialty volumes. Reference texts. I'd be surprised if those were the sort of books she carried. A shabby little place, isn't it?" He opened a drawer, removing a tub of salve and a length of gauze.

As he applied the ointment and rebound her thigh, she asked, "Does that matter? It's all words in the end, right?" Quite apart from her wound, she felt a mild sting of indignation on Fern's behalf.

The elf stared at her quizzically, as though she'd suddenly been replaced with someone else entirely. "Why so interested?"

"I dunno. I guess I've gotten more out of the place than I expected, and I figured that people who already *have* books would go to . . . book places."

"She recommended *this* book to you?"

"Yeah. Although I think she's maybe trying to get a rise out of me at the same time."

"Russa Tensiger. An elven author. Quite accomplished." Highlark picked up the volume and examined it thoughtfully. "And *you're* reading it?"

"I'm half through. So you *do* read things that aren't . . . what did you call them, reference texts?"

"From time to time." He handed the book back.

Highlark had her make a circuit around the room, watching as she moved on the crutch and asking her to apply more weight to her heel. Then he had her stand without support, shifting her weight on and off her wounded leg.

It still hurt like hells, but maybe not all eight of them.

Finally, he observed her thoughtfully, tapping his spectacles against his chin for what seemed like a long time. Then he swapped the crutch for a walking staff he produced from a tall cupboard in the corner.

"Your associates have already paid for your care. I'd like to see you back in a week, yes?"

"Yeah, sure."

"And when you do, I'll be interested to hear your thoughts on what you've read."

His lips held just the hint of a smile as he closed the door and left her alone on the street.

⌁

Viv reveled in the freedom of movement the walking staff afforded. Unfortunately, her bare heel and toes, while callused and tough, were already getting battered on the cobblestones of the town proper now that she was walking more ably.

After collaring a few townsfolk for directions, she found a cobbler and convinced him to sell her a single large sandal, although he had to lengthen the thong to accommodate her swollen foot. The result was an enormous improvement, and Viv was immediately thankful.

The area within Murk's fortress walls was considerably more crowded than the beachfront rows, both in terms of buildings and people. Even the seabirds seemed to bunch too close on the rooftops, and Viv found herself longing for the open air and clean dunes outside.

A market street ran straight through the heart of the city, packed on all sides with merchants, net-menders, another inn or two, a mishmash of trades, and a stable near the gate. There was even an open lot with jumbles of furnishings, clothing, and miscellanea on trestle tables packed into its boundaries. A pair of young gnomes that looked like brothers appeared to be trying to liquidate an estate.

She came across a familiar sight midway back to the

beach—a bounty board checkered with requests. None of the scant postings were big jobs, but they were a stark reminder that she wasn't fit to take on even one of them. Precious few beast hunts or brawls lay in her immediate future. Her mouth thinned, and she cursed her leg under her breath.

As she was closing the distance to the fortress gate and looking forward to the quiet of the beach, she suddenly stopped short. The skin at the back of her neck crawled, and the wood of the walking staff creaked as her grip tightened.

It took her only an instant to spy him between passersby. He almost completely blended into the shadows of a small courtyard beside the chandler's shop.

His cloak was the gray of fog and travel-frayed, and the skin of his exposed hands was pale, nearly white. An overstuffed pack weighed down one shoulder, and his hood was up, so that only the blade of his nose was visible. It twitched her way, and she sensed a galvanic tension in his stance, a wariness.

That dangerous promise in the way he held himself made Viv scan him for a weapon that wasn't there. She almost let go of her staff as her hand involuntarily jerked toward the saber that used to be belted to her waist.

Then a group of three sailors broke her line of sight. When they'd passed by, he was gone.

She searched the crowd for him, but in the end, it wasn't like she could mount a pursuit in the state she was in. Viv gave up and carried on, but the image of him nagged at her, prickling her survival instincts in a way she'd learned not to ignore.

As she passed through the front gate, Viv glanced to the side to find Iridia the Gatewarden in conference with others in the same blue uniform. There seemed an awful lot of Wardens in Murk, but Viv supposed a garrison was kept against the unlikely event of trouble from the west again. Or maybe they'd gotten word of Varine's progress up the coast and were taking precautions. Stories of the wreckage left in her wake had to have trickled here by now.

Almost as though she could sense her presence, the head Warden interrupted their conversation to fix Viv with her golden eyes. The tapenti eyed her up and down and Viv could feel the challenging weight of that regard. She returned the stare in kind, but only one of them needed a staff to get around, and she imagined she saw that knowledge reflected. Viv felt like she was fleeing the field of battle as she passed out of sight.

She came to a halt a few yards outside the fortress walls, heedless of the traffic flowing around her, and took a long breath of briny air.

For the first time in several days, Viv regretted leaving her sword in her room.

~~~

As she made her way up the slope and past the bakery, still trying to shed an anxious mood, a bell tinkled and someone called out to her.

"Viv!"

Maylee emerged from Sea-Song Bakery, the scent of sourdough arriving with her. There was no line out the shop door, so the day's rush must have been over.

"You're gonna make a lady think she's lost her touch," accused the dwarf, dusting the flour from her apron as she stepped down. In her other hand she held a folded paper sack.

"Huh?"

"Well, you haven't been back since, hon." She flipped her

thick braid back over her shoulder, her cheeks still rosy from heat, or hard work, or both. "A baker could take offense."

"Oh! Oh, no, those biscuits? They were great. Amazing, even! But I'm surprised you even remember my name."

Maylee rolled her eyes, as though that was ridiculous. "I see you've got some new transportation?"

Viv banged the staff against the ground. "Moving up in the world."

The woman offered the sack. "You're at The Perch, ain't you? Here's a little somethin' for the hike up the hill. Had a few spares."

Viv took it, raising her brows at the dwarf. Then she peeked inside. Four or five muffins filled the sack, crusted with nuts and sugar.

"Seems like the Eight granted you a second chance." Maylee winked at Viv and reentered the bakery without another word. The bell tinkled after her.

"Uh, thanks!" Viv called belatedly to the closed door.

She withdrew one of the muffins and took a bewildered bite. An involuntary moan escaped her lips. The rest of the muffin didn't survive long.

"Second chance?" she mumbled through the final mouthful. Then she licked her fingers clean and walked on, shaking her head.

9

"So, for about half the book, I couldn't stand either of them," said Viv, her voice slightly raised. "I thought for sure I wouldn't make it to the end, and I'd owe you twenty bits."

She dealt Fern's carpet a terrific blow with her walking staff. A cloud of dust, dander, and down erupted into the air. Gripping her end of the carpet firmly, she flicked it upward, and even more filth drifted out.

Fern coughed and waved a hand, both feet on the other end of the rug where it was draped up and over the boardwalk railing. "But?"

"But then, I don't know. I'm pretty sure it was when they were stuck in Red Rule House with Pruitt and the rest of them. Everything flipped. It was the two of them back-to-back against a bunch of liars. They didn't even *talk* to each other differently, all sarcasm and nasty jabs. And sleeping back-to-back too, with the sword between them . . ."

She motioned to Fern, and they flipped the threadbare rug before Viv delivered another savage crack. Amazingly, there was more of Potroast to be dislodged. The gryphet in question hooted in his sleep as he dozed in the sun in front of the door.

"The framing changed everything," finished Fern. "Like one of those trick drawings that become something else when you turn them upside down."

"I think I saw something like that once on a tavern sign. The Coney & Gull. Looked like a bird straight on, and a rabbit if you tilted your head."

"Yeah, exactly that. But you did finish?"

"I did." Viv pulled the rug taut and dusted the surface with one hand, examining her fingers. Not *too* filthy.

"And?" Fern sounded impatient.

Viv smiled and held her peace a moment longer, making a big show of inspecting the carpet. She folded it in quarters until she'd gathered it all in, moving slowly with most of her weight on her left foot. Stacking it up in front of the door, she could feel the rattkin's impatience burning on her back.

She very carefully withdrew four five-bit pieces from her wallet and offered them to Fern. "I don't think *I'd* ever want to care about somebody the way those two did. Seems kind of dangerous."

Fern didn't take the coins, crossing her arms instead. "But you did *like* it? Even with the distinct lack of sword-fighting?"

Viv thought for a moment, idly moving the bits with her thumb. "Well, there was plenty of fighting, I guess. Just not a lot of bleeding. And I might have *more* than liked it? I'm having a hard time saying why, though." She cleared her throat, embarrassed. At the same time, there was something about Fern's attentive, almost *hungry* gaze that made her want to satisfy it.

"It's like . . . they were so terrible together in some ways, but . . . they still defended one another? I'm pretty sure they even loved each other. I mean, if you count chapter thirty-five, they *definitely* loved each other." She rolled her eyes. "But past that, in a way that mattered more."

The rattkin was studying her face with a half-smile. Viv thought she remembered her Pa looking like that when she was first able to heft a steel blade. A little rose of warmth bloomed in her chest to see it one more time with fur and whiskers.

Awkwardly, she finished, "And I guess it makes me think that if I'm willing to call *that* love, then . . . a better kind might not be so impossible." She blushed and looked away. "Love. Gods. C'mon, I feel like an ass here. Take the damn money."

Fern did so with a knowing look.

~

While they were at it, they swept out the shop, which required moving the stacks of books nested in the corners. Viv traded her walking staff for Fern's bristle-broom. Potroast seemed to object, nipping at it and growling at her. He waggled his tiny vestigial wings, but she nudged him gently out of the way with the broom. Well, mostly gently.

Fern unclasped her red cloak and tossed it across the counter. "Damn. With you in here too, it's like working next to a furnace!"

Viv shrugged. "Orcs burn hot. You always want to sleep in an orc's tent in winter. That's just a fact."

The rattkin snorted and hefted a stack of flaking, leather-bound tomes to cart them out of the way.

The clouds of dust were prodigious, and at one point, they had to stop while Viv flapped Fern's cloak toward the open doorway to clear the air. Potroast scrabbled across the floor-boards in alarm, hiding behind a shelf.

When they were done, Viv dropped the carpet on the

threshold, gripped the doorframe, and used her good toes to lift one corner and flip it open. Fern grabbed hold of the end and stretched it out to its full length.

Viv looked past her at the towers of books still unshelved, crowding the back hall and the area beside the counter. The front of the store was so much less claustrophobic with them out of the way.

"Are all of those important?" She gestured with her head.

Fern looked affronted. "Of *course* they're important! They're my books!"

"I mean, do you think anybody is going to *buy* them if they're just in piles around the place?"

The rattkin puffed in exasperation as she straightened, dusting herself off. "If a customer tells me what they want, then I'll find it for them. That's how a bookshop works. They have to be stored *somewhere*."

"Well, if they can go anywhere then . . . why not in the back? If you know where they are?"

Fern squinted at her.

Viv hurried on. "It's just, when they're all out and everywhere, I'm sort of . . . afraid to touch anything. Or look at anything. Or move."

There was a long pause while the rattkin nibbled at her lower lip.

"And," ventured Viv, "you could probably toss all the sea charts back there, too."

"Those gods-damned sea charts," Fern said with remarkable savagery.

"So why not hide them? And see how it feels?" She saw the look on the rattkin's face and held up her hands. "I mean, it's not my place to say, but . . . seems like maybe a hole you can patch that doesn't cost you anything?"

"Fuck!" muttered Fern.

"Yeah, I'm sorry, I really shouldn't—"

"No, it's not that." The rattkin sighed and didn't look at Viv. "It's that it's easier to do this when you're here. And that makes me feel stupid. Have I been sitting on my tail all this time? Doing nothing because I was *pretending* I couldn't? Am I so pathetic that I couldn't muster the energy to do this without . . . without a *chaperone?*"

Viv stayed quiet. Sometimes, that was just what you had to do.

"I'm not blaming you," Fern said. "I'm *thankful*. I'm just . . . angry. At myself. And I don't understand why I didn't see any of this before. Maybe it means I never wanted it to work out in the first place."

"Or maybe you just needed to be back-to-back with someone."

The rattkin blinked at her.

"To reframe it," continued Viv.

"To look at it sideways," said Fern.

"So. Let's find out if it's a rabbit or a gull, yeah?"

❦

With the "floor books"—as Viv insisted on calling them— tucked away in the back room where Fern handled binding repairs, they stood together in the front and surveyed their handiwork.

"It feels twice as big in here," said Viv. "And since *I'm* twice as big as *you*, I have to say, that feels pretty good."

"I'll admit, it's a lot . . . airier."

Potroast promptly curled up on the carpet in the pool of sun streaming through the open door. He fluffed the feathers of his ruff and closed his enormous eyes in obvious contentment.

It was a far cry from the oiled and gleaming ranks of volumes in Highlark's office library, but it was a little less shabby. Not exactly organized. Not precisely inviting. Overstuffed shelves still ringed the room, and the central pair still threatened an avalanche, but it was remarkable what some open floorspace achieved. Even the peeling paint and cracked lamp chimney seemed less desolate.

"Doesn't smell so yellow anymore, either," Viv said to herself.

"What was that?"

"Nothing."

The creak of the boardwalk outside preceded the arrival of a bandy-legged gnome in salt-crusted clothes. His hands had the hard, callused look of a man who spent his days on the deck of a ship.

Fern sighed, then mustered a smile. "Afternoon, sir! Looking for a sea chart?"

Two long creases below his cheeks deepened with his surprise. "Naw. Ain't been sleepin' lately. Just figgered I'd get somethin' to occupy the hours. Whaddaya got for that?"

"How do you feel about swordfights and jailbreaks?" asked Viv, before Fern could say another word.

The gnome gave her a considering once-over. "You got a suggestion?"

"Yeah, I do," said Viv.

The leathery little man ambled out a few minutes later with a copy of *Ten Links in the Chain* folded under his arm.

When he had gone, Fern turned to Viv and stroked her whiskers.

"So, do I get a commission, then?" Viv leaned on her staff with a challenging cock of the head.

"I have another proposal for you," began Fern, timid for once.

"Another wager?"

"Not exactly." She hesitated further.

"Well, I'm not going to bite. Go on. I want to hear."

"What would you say to spending more time here? During the day?" Then, haltingly, she added, "And in exchange . . . I'll . . . keep you in books."

Viv considered that.

Fern rushed on. "It'd be like your library. You could read whatever you like and bring it back when you're done. As many as you want at a time! Books can be expensive, of course, and this way you could—"

"Would you suggest them for me? The books?"

It was Fern's turn to consider. "I . . . Yes, of course. I'd be happy to."

Viv tapped the door with her walking staff and then winced, checking to make sure she hadn't dented the wood. Potroast glared at her sleepily. "Yeah. Consider it done, then."

The rattkin looked relieved, but also a mite guilty.

Something inside Viv twisted at that expression. There was a kind of need buried in it. And maybe she saw a possible distraction while the Ravens marched off with the life she should have been living. Something to fight against, at least. "I've got a counter-proposal, though."

"Oh, really?"

"I don't want to just sit here reading your books. What if you tried to do more than bail water? And what if I helped make that happen?"

"So you want to do battle with the bookselling business?" Fern's mouth quirked in a smile that was almost, but not quite, skeptical. "I guess you could maybe intimidate somebody into buying a book."

"I think you're underestimating how charming an orc can be when they're not pissed off. Besides, total ignorance never stopped me from trying anything before. I've got one other condition though."

"What's that?"

"We've got to figure out someplace to sit in here. There's no way in all eight hells I'm standing all day."

10

A place outside The Perch to spend the balance of her day was growing increasingly attractive.

When Viv descended to the dining area in late morning, a familiar figure reclined in her favorite chair, her heels up on the table. It was a very awkward angle, given Gallina's height, and from the look on Brand's face, he didn't much appreciate the placement of her boots.

The gnome's eyes followed Viv, even though the tilt of her chin affected disinterest.

Gallina had taken up very regular residence there since blowing up at Viv a few days before. Viv thought the gnome really ought to have more to do with her day.

Shaking her head, she went to the bar and paid no mind. "Morning, Brand."

"Viv," he said. "Breakfast, same as always?"

She eased onto a stool with a relieved sigh, resting her walking staff against the counter. "I gotta ask, is that the *same* mug you're always cleaning, or do they all get a chance?"

The sea-fey's gray brows rose. The tattoos on his forearms boiled as he scrubbed. "Didn't think you'd notice. Old tavernkeeper's secret. Wash one, everybody assumes the rest are clean, too." He grinned at her. "Oatcakes and eggs today. Got some fresh honey too."

Viv massaged her right thigh. She'd overdone it with the flurry of cleaning and rug-beating the day prior, because her leg was stiffer and more tender. Or maybe it was the fact that she was wearing her spare and un-ruined trousers today. The swelling in her leg was down enough that she could fit into them, but they still squeezed uncomfortably.

And while she was cataloging vexing feelings, it was hard to ignore the prickling weight of Gallina's eyes on the back of her neck.

When Brand returned with a plate of soft eggs, griddled oatcakes, and a slathering of raw honey, she leaned in. Cocking a thumb close to her chest, where it wouldn't be visible from behind her, she whispered, "Is she in here all day?"

Brand grunted. "Used to be an old tomcat around here. Never saw him unless I had scraps too rough for stew. Soon as I stepped out to toss 'em, there he'd be, like he'd been watching through the window. That one over there's the same way." He cleared his throat and lowered his voice. "'Cept, *you're* the scraps."

Viv rolled her eyes and picked up her fork.

"Cat didn't put his boots on the *tables*, though," called Brand.

"What?" the gnome asked sharply.

Viv swallowed a mouthful of egg and turned to her. "Not sure what you're waiting for. I don't have Rackam in my back pocket, so there's not much point in hanging around, expecting him to fall out of it."

The gnome glared daggers at her, then pointedly drew one

from her bandolier and began trimming her fingernails with an expression of disgust.

It shouldn't have bothered Viv, but when she'd eaten and paid, she got out of there as quickly as she could without looking like she was in a hurry.

~⁓

Low, soft banks of fog piled up over the dunes, obscuring the beach and stacking against Murk's walls. The spectral shadows of a ship at anchor could be spied through the pearly gray. Above, the sky was scraped clean of cloud, flat and faded blue.

Leaving Gallina behind was a relief, although Viv checked over her shoulder to make sure the gnome wasn't following, feeling ridiculous about it.

She hoped to collar Pitts on his morning rounds, because she'd been sitting on an idea overnight and was anxious to see if it could be done.

The fog lent the trip down to the boardwalk a peculiar, muffled quiet, where near sounds seemed to come from far away, as though the world had been stretched in all directions and only mist filled the spaces in between.

Viv didn't see anyone until she reached the bakery, which was reliably busy. At this point, she figured that if enemies from across the sea lay siege to the fortress walls, there would still be a line at Sea-Song. And some of the besiegers would probably be in it.

When she reached the front of the line, Maylee planted both hands on the counter and leaned forward with a welcoming smile. "It was the muffins, huh? That's what tipped it." She winked. She seemed to do that a lot.

"I did eat all of them before I made it up the hill, so, maybe?"

"How long are you in town, hon?"

Viv shrugged. "A few more weeks, I guess. I've got a, uh, crew that's coming back through. I should be fit to travel by then." She patted her leg more enthusiastically than she should have and then regretted it.

A dockworker leaned around Viv to see what the holdup was, opening his mouth like he was about to say something.

Turned out, Maylee had a remarkably effective glare. Viv was glad it wasn't directed at her.

"So you're a soldier of fortune sorta gal then, huh?" the dwarf continued brightly. "I mean, to look at you, I'd figured as much. How d'you like it?"

Viv was increasingly aware of the line growing behind her and shifted her weight uncomfortably.

"Oh, well. I guess it's what I always wanted to do? Get out there and raise a little hell. Right wrongs, that sort of thing." She shrugged. "Although there's a lot more spineback-hunting than I expected. A *lot*."

"Mmm. Yeah," said Maylee dreamily. Then her eyes narrowed at the man behind Viv, and she stabbed a finger toward him. "Rolf, you'll get your buns. Hold on to your ass!"

When Viv left with a sack of lassy buns, she tried to make her expression apologetic for the benefit of all the impatient folks in line.

～

She continued onward to the city proper, the fog growing denser as she went. The slap of waves echoed strangely through the mist, and the ghostly creak of ships acquired a dreamlike quality. If she didn't stumble across Pitts, at least she could see if what she wanted could still be had.

But Viv *did* run across him. She spied his cart first, drawn to the side where the sand piled in little humps against the salt-streaked fortress wall. Pitts sat on a dune amidst long grasses, his scarred shoulders hunched forward.

He was reading the little book Fern had gifted him.

She came very close before he noticed, looking up at her with that same mild expression he'd worn the first time Viv met him.

"Guess you liked it then?" she said.

He glanced down at the tiny orange book, then back at her, pursing his lips. "Guess I did." He looked into the mist, as though he could see through it. "Good day for it, too. Sometimes, I just read one page and think about it. Kind of turn it over in my head like a stone and look at it from all sides."

Viv blinked at him. That was almost more than she'd ever heard him say, and words she didn't expect. "Hey, I had something I wanted to ask. But I've already gotten more of a favor out of you than I wanted already, so you have to let me pay you this time."

She held the sack out toward him. "First though, these are for you, either way. Just wanted to thank you again. I *know* that wasn't scrap wood you brought."

Pitts accepted the sack, looked inside, and gave it an appreciative sniff.

He withdrew one of the buns, took a surprisingly delicate bite, and chewed with his eyes closed. The orc held his place in the book with one enormous finger.

After he'd swallowed, he nodded, waiting.

She indicated his cart, which was mostly empty, and told him what she wanted. He thought about it, nodded again, then stood to dust the sand from his trousers and tuck the book carefully into a pocket.

He ate another bun before they went anywhere, though.

~⁓~

The gnome brothers had haggled, as she'd known they would, but maybe the clammy morning air worked to her advantage, because they didn't seem that tenacious about it. During her previous trip along the market street, she'd spied a couple of chairs in the jumble of furnishings for sale. Nothing fancy, but they had bradded green velvet cushions, and most importantly, they were big and sturdy enough that she could sit in them without danger of collapse.

Lighter a silver and two bits, she stumped along behind Pitts's cart with the chairs in back. She'd also negotiated her way to a small matching side table.

On their way out of the fortress walls, she glanced toward the courtyard beside the chandler's. The man in gray with the overloaded pack was nowhere to be found. She shook her head and huffed an annoyed chuckle at herself. Viv hadn't forgotten that prickling sense of danger when she'd spied him, but he was hardly worth the vigilance.

A Gatewarden watched the comings and goings, but it wasn't Iridia. Viv supposed even the tapenti couldn't find fault with a wagonload of furniture, though.

When they arrived at Thistleburr, Pitts helped her unload her purchases onto the boardwalk. Then he rolled his cart away one-handed. He held a bun in the other, chewing placidly as he went.

~⁓~

"No fucking way. There can't be enough room, not for *both* of them," said Fern, frowning doubtfully at the furniture in front of her door. She drew her red cloak tighter against the misty chill.

"Never going to know 'til we try. At *least* one has to come in, though. It's one of my conditions, after all." Viv grinned at her.

Potroast unhelpfully peppered her with irritable hoots as she dragged in the first chair with an awkward shuffle-gait that favored her injured leg.

Fern fussed with the positioning while Viv brought in the other two pieces. They fit remarkably well under the east-facing window, and the light from the hurricane lamp pooled around them in a cozy golden glow.

Viv lowered herself into one with a grateful sigh. The cushion was a little damp, but when she stretched her leg out fully and leaned back, it was remarkably comfortable. She laced her hands across her belly. "That's more like it."

Fern slid up onto the matching chair, flipping her cloak and tail out behind her as she did. She drummed her claws on the arms. "How much did these cost, though?"

Viv closed her eyes. "Doesn't matter. Let's just say they're mine and pretend I'm taking them with me when I go. Besides, your customers might want to sit and read something, too?"

"I'll admit, it is . . . *nice*," allowed Fern. She leaned back and cocked her head at Viv. "You know, it's odd, but I've never actually asked you any real questions. That's pretty gods-damned rude of me, isn't it? I've told you more about me than I've told anyone in ages. I guess I haven't had much time for . . . acquaintances the past few years. I'm out of practice."

Cracking an eye at her, Viv said, "You're in the tunnel. I know how it goes."

"The tunnel?"

"You're just trying to make it to the other end, and while you're in it, there's nothing to either side. Only the way forward. You know, the tunnel. Maybe when you find a way out, you can look around, but until then . . ." Viv shrugged deeper into the chair.

"Huh." Fern was quiet for a long moment. "All right, well, let's pretend I'm not in a fucking tunnel right now. What *are* you doing here? I don't even know what happened to your leg!"

So Viv told her about Rackam and Varine the Pale, rushing as quickly as she could past the bit where she was stabbed in the thigh.

"A fucking *necromancer?*" exclaimed Fern. "Around here?"

"Oh, she's miles and miles north. They'll probably already be into the snowy foothills by now. You don't need to worry about her. The Ravens will catch her eventually."

"So you're only here until your leg mends?"

"That's about the size of it. Well, until Rackam shows, really, which is probably weeks, at the rate they were moving. Might not be fully mended by then, but I can join back up even if I can't run a footrace." Viv tried hard to make herself believe that.

"And so you *like* it? You're anxious to get back to it?" ventured Fern.

"Why wouldn't I be?" asked Viv.

"So far, it sounds like sleeping rough and getting stabbed a lot."

Viv laughed, but then considered, and said, "Being one of the Ravens is living all the way to the edge of things. One second in the thick of battle is like a whole day anywhere else.

Once you step back from that"—she shrugged—"everything else seems like a waste of time."

Just as Fern started to reply, Potroast ambled in, making a show of glaring at Viv and ruffling his feathers at her. She withdrew a chunk of bun she'd saved and held it up, and he regarded it suspiciously. Then he pointedly averted his gaze and curled up under the rattkin's feet. Viv sighed and tossed the morsel to Fern.

"He'll warm up to you eventually," she said with an apologetic shrug. She let it fall, and the gryphet extended his neck to snap it out of the air. Viv tried hard not to feel spurned but wasn't very successful.

As Fern trailed her toes along the ridge of Potroast's spine, he burbled happily and snuggled closer. The rattkin stared out the window into the fog, and then the only sounds were the gryphet's vocalizations and the soft hiss of the hurricane lamp.

Eventually, Viv said, "So, that next book. Any ideas?"

Fern returned from somewhere far away. She looked . . . *calm*. "Actually, I do." She slipped down from the chair, careful not to step on Potroast's sleeping form. She retrieved something from behind the counter and presented Viv with a hefty volume.

The title of the book was *Sea of Passion*. "Zelia Greatstrider" was printed in bold serifed letters below a fairly racy woodcut print of two frantically entwined sea-fey and a crashing wave that was *very* strategically positioned.

Viv mumbled a doubtful, "Huh."

"You know, now that I think about it, I *did* ask you questions about yourself. Because that's exactly what *this* is," Fern said with a surprised laugh. "I can't wait to hear your answer."

11

Raleigh fumbled a quick cantrip, and light kindled. It branched across lichen clinging to the ceiling of the cave in which they rested.

Beneath the blue glow, they both looked even colder than she felt. Leena's cheeks were flushed rose, but she shivered uncontrollably, the exposed flesh of her shoulders pale and delicate. She winced in the fresh light.

Raleigh's magestone warmed at her hip after the casting, and she cradled it in her fingers, absorbing what little heat she could.

"Wish there was anything here for tinder," she said. She tried to make room for the smaller woman to sit and drew a sodden cloak from her pack to spread across the rock for comfort. It was a wonder she'd held on to the pack during the frantic swim. A wonder they both hadn't been battered to death on the rocks.

"We'll make do," murmured Leena. She managed a wan smile. Even bedraggled and clinging to her cheeks, her hair was radiant. Her smile too. She scooted onto the cloak, and after a bare moment, leaned into Raleigh.

For a while, Raleigh sat still, inhaling the scent of her hair and salt and wet cotton. She might not have been able to conjure a fire, but a warmth grew between them, and as the frantic energy of their flight abated, it was replaced with something else.

"Raleigh," whispered Leena, and moved against her, just barely.

But in recent days, Raleigh had found new meaning in the simplest of gestures, a complex underpinning that terrified and thrilled her.

"Yes?" she said, and the sounds of Leena's motions were loud in the sea cave as she turned slowly. A single hand rose, tentative.

Leena's fingers found her collarbone, and slipped beneath the wet fabric to trace its length, intimate in a way that Raleigh could hardly bear to endure.

The fingers stopped, just so, and then . . . Raleigh's mouth was on hers. At first, she closed her eyes, but when she opened them, she found Leena looking back with a gaze made of hunger and need.

Their hands moved down, and their bodies nearer, heedless of the rocks beneath the cloak, every sense attuned to what they could touch and taste. Farther down, and—

Viv abruptly looked up and found Fern watching from her perch at the counter.

Dawdling around the shop all day would've been easy if it weren't for this specific reading selection. Not that Viv wasn't enjoying the book, because she was. Unfortunately, certain passages, pages, and whole *chapters* made her flush all over. Moreover, she caught Fern eyeing her progress, and the rattkin seemed to know *exactly* when those moments might occur. It made her uncomfortable, like someone was watching her bathe.

"I think I'm going to read this in my room," Viv declared, marking her page number and setting *Sea of Passion* on the side table.

"Hm. Need some private time?" Fern smirked, which Viv didn't think she'd ever seen her do before.

"No. But you're watching me like you expect me to steal something."

The rattkin shrugged. "Just . . . gauging your interest."

Viv hoisted herself to her feet with the help of her staff. "In the . . . the *moist* bits?"

Fern burst into laughter, startling Potroast out of his nap.

"What are you up to? This really doesn't feel like I'm helping at all." Viv hobbled toward her.

The rattkin was going through a massive printer's catalog and making marks in her inventory book. "Well, just having you here is keeping me—"

At that moment, a tall sea-fey woman opened the door and stepped cautiously inside.

Viv preempted Fern. "Sea charts?" she asked with a broad smile.

The customer looked startled and furrowed her brow in confusion.

"What can I do for you?" asked Fern, shooing Viv to the side.

~⌒~

When the woman departed with three books in hand—a long journey ahead of her, apparently—Viv stood watching out the door, drumming the frame with her fingers.

"What?" asked Fern. "It looks like you're about to suggest furniture again."

"Just want to sort out how to help more. I feel . . . itchy. At least, when I'm not reading." Viv interrupted Fern before she could say anything. "And yeah, I meant it. *That* chapter is a 'my room' chapter."

"You know, there have been more customers in the last two days than in the previous week—not counting you," said Fern.

"Really? Still seems pretty quiet."

The rattkin wrinkled her nose. "Yes, well, welcome to the life of a bookseller in gods-damned Murk. Maybe they see you in the window and figure the place isn't about to close? Or *collapse?*"

Viv ran a finger down the remnants of red on the front door. "Could be a little paint would give them the right idea."

"It just wears so fast in the salt air. Seems like throwing money away to repaint it, when there's so much else around here that needs the silver."

"Like what?"

"Like new books." Fern tapped the catalog. "Most of my inventory is old. Nothing wrong with classics, but . . ." She shrugged. "The stuff coming out of Azimuth these days is just fresher. Kind of daring. Also, there are a lot of series coming out, and if you buy one, then you need the *next* one. I could definitely do with more repeat customers."

She closed the catalog with a snap. "Gods-damned expensive, though. And then there's the space problem."

Viv studied the packed shelves. "Too bad you couldn't make more room . . ."

"Hm?"

"Just thinking. Don't mind me. Look, I need to limber up.

Leg's getting stiff, and I haven't been staying fighting fit the way I need to. Going to head back for a while and see if I can do something without falling on my ass this time. Okay with you?"

Fern flapped a hand at her.

"Back in a bit." Viv waved and headed back to The Perch.

~⁓~

Strapping her saber to her waist was like pulling on a pair of comfortably broken-in boots. How many days had it been since she'd worn it? Viv had lost count.

Instead of venturing down to the dunes and potentially running afoul of Iridia, Viv headed around back of The Perch. No tomcat awaited scraps. Fortunately, Gallina didn't seem to be in evidence either.

The area behind the inn was mostly flat, with crates and barrels stacked against the wall, and a small burning pit. Sand and rock rumpled into a hillside behind it, tufted with sea grass. Thankfully, it was all mostly sheltered from sight.

Viv leaned her stick against the crates and gingerly stepped into the center of the flattened area. It was a damn sight better than the dunes for form work, and the fact that she hadn't bothered to look here the first time vexed her.

Drawing her saber, she eased carefully into a guard stance. She even let a little extra weight settle onto her right leg, and while it burned—fiercely—it didn't feel like the pain that preceded a tear or a collapse.

She deliberately and slowly cycled through high and low forms and then extensions. Her entire upper body felt stiff at first, but fluidity returned more swiftly than she expected. The ache in her leg continued to build, however, and she only lasted about fifteen minutes before she had to call a halt.

Sweat slicked her back and under her arms, and a thudding pain in her temples told her she was right to have stopped.

Wiping her forehead with one arm, she sheathed her saber and headed back inside to see if she could wrangle a basin of water from Brand.

With her hair washed and wrung out in wet curls down her back, and the rest of her bathed with a basin and a rag, Viv made her way back to Thistleburr. The afternoon sun was hot and angry as it plunged toward the sea, eager to be extinguished.

After the prior exertion, she favored her leg heavily, making more use of the walking staff than normal.

When she stepped into the shop, she ran her fingers through her wet hair, clawing it out of her face. "Well, not the *worst* practice I've ever—" she began, and then stopped abruptly.

The man in gray was there.

In the shop.

He had no pack, but it was him, she'd swear on all the Eight. That pale blade of a nose, the tattered no-color cloak. His hood was thrown back, and his hair was white and receding, gathered into a queue. Something about his eyes—pale and rheumy—made her skin prickle, and the wet hair against her shoulders felt like ice. She could see a blue vein pulsing in his cheek as he glanced at her.

His gaze was speculative. After a long look, he dropped his hand from the shelf and tucked it inside his cloak.

"Oh! I didn't hear you come in," called Fern as she hurried down the hall, refastening her cloak. "I stepped out back to—"

Potroast exploded into the room. His sharp, hooting barks

had a ragged edge to them as he barreled toward the gray-clad man, who whirled in surprise.

The gryphet leapt, and almost quicker than Viv could follow, the stranger slapped the creature alongside the head, dashing him to the floor.

Potroast fell in an ungainly tumble, feathers and fur flying, and his hoot strangled into a startled squawk. Viv immediately moved toward the man, shifting the stick higher in her grip.

"What in the *fuck* do you think you're doing!" cried Fern, storming up to him.

"Apologies, ma'am," said the man, bowing his head. "A startled reaction. I was only surprised." His voice was calm and drier than desert sand. He gestured to the gryphet as he struggled to his feet. "It seems no harm was done. Again, my apologies."

"I don't give a flaming—" began Fern as she hurried to check on Potroast. The man was already turning toward the door. He glanced up at Viv again, noted the grip on her staff, then smiled, and his smile was wrong in every tooth.

Every instinct in her snapped awake, like a burning beneath her skin.

She almost *growled* at him, a buried, primal urge that she couldn't recall feeling outside of battle. Her arm wanted nothing more than to crack the man across his chin with her staff and lay him low. But she bested it, and by the time she did, he was past her and out onto the boardwalk, as if time had sped him on by.

"Who in the eight fucking hells was *that*?" spluttered Fern.

Viv leaned out the door and discovered that the man was already twenty feet down the thoroughfare.

"I don't know," she snarled. "But I sure as hells am going to find out."

12

Maybe it was the sword forms she'd practiced earlier. Maybe it was a pent-up need to move, to *act*, after so many idle days. Maybe his casual cuffing of the gryphet, or the way he made her every instinct sting. Maybe it was all of those things and more.

Viv emerged onto the boardwalk, staff clenched tight. She bitterly regretted leaving her saber in her room, but she was weapon enough on her own. Or she used to be.

She'd seen no blade on the man, but she knew well enough how little that could mean. Everything about him had screamed *threat* from the first moment she'd seen him, and she'd never been more than passingly acquainted with hesitation in the face of such a thing.

She strode after him, shedding idleness and physical fragility like an ill-fitting coat. Viv felt herself filling her own skin for the first time since she'd come to Murk, near bursting out of it. Distant thuds of pain echoed in her thigh, but they got farther away by the second.

Part of her mind reminded her of the headlong charge that had landed her in Murk in the first place, but caution was even farther away than the pain.

The man in gray was several shops down, but her strides were much longer, even using the walking staff. She chewed up the distance between them in moments.

Viv's breath came sharp through her nose, and her lips drew tight against her fangs. For the first time in too long she felt powerful and purposeful in the way she was accustomed to.

He sensed her before she reached him and came to a casual stop. His hands were buried in his cloak.

"Hey," she said. She let the head of the staff drop as she towered over him.

Slowly, the man turned, that white wedge of a nose swinging around like a knife blade. "Ma'am," he said, with toneless politeness.

"Don't fucking *ma'am* me," she snarled.

"Have I done something to distress you?" he asked, his pale eyes amused.

"What were you doing in there?" Her voice came out grim and flat.

"My dear, I believe you're letting your baser nature rule you." He withdrew both hands from his cloak—Viv tensed as he did—but they were empty, and he splayed them in supplication. "I was only browsing. Hardly a crime. The beast caught me unawares. An honest reaction, and no harm done. Now, you must excuse me, as I—"

"I can *smell* it on you. Something . . ." There *was* a scent. One she recognized. She couldn't seem to place it, but—

As she uttered the words, something in his eyes changed. The light went flat, like a fog rolled over it. His hands disappeared inside the cloak, and Viv knew with absolute certainty that when they reemerged, they wouldn't be empty.

She eliminated the distance between them in two strides,

casting the walking staff aside. It would only get in the way. Planting her left foot, she reached for him. His false smile fragmented into a snarl, and the icy glint of a blade was already half uncovered.

Viv jammed one forearm against his and brought her other hand looping up behind it, twisting sharply until the dagger spun away. From the corner of her eye, she spied the bloom of his cloak where his other arm was rising, doubtless with another knife at the ready. She brought her hand back to intercept it, curling the fabric in her fist to foul his strike. But his left foot kicked out, hooking around the heel of her damaged leg.

Before she'd been stabbed, it would've been like trying to move a mountain, but her knee folded, and she stumbled against him. She gave up all attempts at deflection and seized him around the middle with both arms as they fell, crushing him so flat against her that he'd not be able to bring a blade to bear.

Then they were on the ground in a spray of sand and a tangle of cloak, and the agony in her thigh burned bright again. Even so, she spun him over and straddled him, pressing his arms flat, ignoring the sizzle of pain all through her leg. She growled at him, and that *smell* assaulted her—cold and wrong and so familiar. Not *precisely* the same, but a cousin to something deadly, if only she had a moment to place it.

The man in gray bared his teeth at her in savage effort, and she felt his hand twisting, his fingers contorting. With his cloak flared to the side she could see a magestone belted to his hip, and her eyes widened as it glowed with heat. A sudden impact hammered into her, as though she'd slammed into a lake spread-eagled. Viv was blown back and across the street, smashing against the edge of the boardwalk.

Now she wished she had the staff.

This was the moment where hesitation meant the end of things. She felt the wound in her leg pull and tear, along with a rush of warm wetness as she scrambled to him on all fours. Before he could recover, Viv lunged for the magestone in his cloak. Her fingers caught in his belt and yanked as they both went over again. A satchel went flying from his shoulder and tumbled across the sand. When he struck the earth, she heard the breath blow out of him, but his hands were moving again, and she couldn't get the belt off him.

"Stop movin' that hand or this goes through your gods-damned throat," came a sharp, high voice that Viv recognized.

She didn't know if it was meant for her or the man in gray, but they both froze.

One of Gallina's fists tangled in the man's hood, and the other pressed a poniard against his Adam's apple.

"Get the belt off him," said the gnome, cool as you please. "Can't have him castin' again, can we?"

If someone had told Viv that morning that she'd be pleased to see Gallina, she would've questioned their sanity.

The man's eyes remained fixed on Viv, wide and hateful. She grunted, shifting her weight away from the leg now oozing through her trousers, and managed to find the buckle on the thin magestone belt. Her thick fingers fumbled to open it, and she whipped it out from under him, the silver teardrop stone twinkling with flecks like mica.

Viv became dimly aware of their surroundings, as though she was emerging from a heavy mist. Figures gathered on the boardwalk. Fern must have been there, too.

Then another voice spoke, far from welcome.

"You'll *all* stop, or it won't be just one of you bleeding on my street," said the tapenti. Iridia the Gatewarden circled them, her scaled hood flaring from temples to throat. She held her longsword effortlessly point down, but Viv recognized the capability in that grip.

The woman eyed all three of them, but her gaze lanced into Viv. Four more Gatewardens moved into view behind her, lanterns gleaming at their belts, hands on their undrawn weapons.

"I told you I liked it quiet."

~

Viv's third trip inside the fortress walls of Murk was the least auspicious of the bunch.

There was only a pair of cells in the old stone building the Gatewardens occupied. Viv and Gallina ended up in one, the man in gray in the other. They'd let Viv reclaim her walking staff for the long and exceptionally painful walk, during which her trouser leg became saturated with blood. Once they'd arrived, Iridia had plucked it from her hands and stowed it at the watch desk along with Gallina's daggers and the stranger's weapons, satchel, and magestone.

The ceilings were so low that Viv couldn't stand fully upright, but at least there was a pair of cots. She sat gratefully on one with her leg extended, and her heartbeat echoed in booming waves throughout the wound.

Gallina stood clutching the bars and muttering under her breath.

Across the way, the man in gray sat with his hands clasped between his knees. They'd taken his cloak, and underneath it he wore a long, loose, gray shirt and ragged, colorless trousers. He gazed at the floor with a serene expression on his face.

The tapenti stood in the slim passageway between the cells

and surveyed her captives with narrowed eyes, which gleamed a startling, luminous gold in the dim light.

"I'll have word sent to Highlark you're here," she said to Viv. "Try not to bleed all over my cell until he arrives." The tapenti made a disgusted sound deep in her throat. "I'm not interested in speaking with any of you at the moment. You can keep until tomorrow."

"We gettin' somethin' to eat?" asked Gallina. "Gnomes got a high metabolism."

Iridia's eyes narrowed even further. "No."

Then she swept out of the corridor. A young dwarf with a close-cropped beard settled at the watch desk and began whittling something with a pocketknife.

Gallina blew out a breath. "Well. This is a shit-show."

Viv grimaced and examined her leg. She thought the bleeding was stopping but wondered how much worse she'd make things for herself if she *did* leak all over the cell. When she looked up, she found the gnome watching her expectantly. She sighed. "So. Uh, *thank* you."

The girl's face split into a wide smile. "Told you people like us gotta look out for each other."

Viv couldn't help a weary laugh. "Still angling for that recommendation, huh?"

"You brought it up, that's all I'm sayin'. Besides, if I'm gonna starve in here overnight because you let this guy get the jump on you, I figure I earned it."

"Get the *jump* on me?" Viv stared at her disbelievingly.

"How else do you figure you needed my help? Look at the size of you!" Gallina glanced over her shoulder at the cell opposite. "Hey, you got the jump on her, right?" she called.

The man in gray didn't so much as twitch.

"Creepy bastard," said Gallina.

Viv looked at the man. He hadn't moved *at all* since he'd sat down. She imagined if she tossed a pebble at his forehead, it would bounce off like he was carved from stone.

She couldn't smell him, not at this distance, but she could still remember the scent. Something like blood under snow, cold and dry and coppery. The forest east of Murk had been rank with something very like it. She'd had plenty of time to notice while she'd bled against a tree trunk.

"Who the hells are you?" she called to the man. Viv figured she had to try at least once.

No response.

Gallina hopped onto the other cot and lay back, folding her hands behind her head.

"Now that you don't got a book to read, I guess we can get to know each other. Lot of hours 'til sundown. How 'bout Rackam's crew, then? Wanna tell me about 'em?"

"Not really," said Viv. Gallina really *had* saved her ass. That was the second time in the last ten days that she'd acted when she should've considered. What would Rackam say about her odds now?

She wondered if Highlark would show soon, or if she should tear her trouser leg up and inspect the wound herself.

Viv sighed resignedly. "But I guess I owe you. You already seem to know a lot about Rackam though, so I don't know why you're so keen."

"Knowin' *about* somebody is on the other side of the Territory from knowin' 'em."

She'd fully intended to be grudging about it, but thinking about the old warhorse, Viv couldn't help but warm to her subject. She was anxious over every growing mile between her and the Ravens, but in something of a surprise, it turned out she missed the man too.

"Well," she began, "he's obviously a brilliant fighter, but he's also like this uncle of mine. The man talked my ear off when I was five, showing me how to chop kindling in one stroke, but if you asked him what he did yesterday? He'd answer in one word or less if he could get away with it."

"All business, huh? I can respect that."

"I guess. But an *uncle* who's all business. If things get hard between you, you're still family."

"Stoic uncle. Got it. So, who else? C'mon, what's it like to share a tent with the Ravens?"

Viv huffed a laugh. "Just don't share one with Tuck."

"Oh yeah?"

"Trail rations don't agree with him. Let's leave it at that."

13

"Absolutely ridiculous," groused Highlark as he finished unwrapping the bindings around Viv's thigh, exposing her now-messy wound.

"Eight hells," said Gallina, leaning over from her cot to examine it with interest. "You're *walkin'* on that?"

"She shouldn't be without a staff," said Highlark, snapping open his black valise to rummage inside. "Which of course means that she's getting into street fights instead. I really don't know why I bother. I thought you'd been spending your spare moments *reading?*" he asked pointedly.

The surgeon didn't seem the right audience for her growing suspicions, so Viv settled for an apologetic shrug. Highlark made a disgusted sound, and she did her best to keep her expression level as he swabbed the wound with something powerfully astringent. She was very aware of Gallina studying her face for a reaction. Whatever the tincture was, it had nothing on the callis oil, so she remained stoic. Mostly.

The elf peered through his spectacles at the long cuts, gently squeezing either side with his fingers. Given the brilliant bolt of pain, he might as well have jammed them inside. A hiss escaped Viv, and she didn't miss the beginnings of a grimly amused smile on his lips. "Torn open, obviously. Although I'm surprised at how quickly the deeper tissues have healed."

"Is this going to take much longer?" Iridia waited outside the cell, wearing a look of extreme impatience.

Highlark sighed. "No. I won't bother dispensing any advice, since I don't imagine anyone would listen. I'll just clean and bind the wound and pretend that my expertise is valued."

When he'd finished wrapping and pinning fresh bandages, the elf rose, hoisting his bag with a clink of glass. "Do you want anything for the pain?"

Viv shook her head. "No. And thanks, again. I *am* sorry to drag you down here."

The surgeon glanced across to the figure in gray, still sitting with his hands clasped before him. His lips thinned as he studied the man. Viv thought he might have sniffed the air as he did so. "Is *that* one any the worse for wear? If he's going to tip over in a pool of his own fluids later, I'd just as soon attend to it while I'm already here."

The tapenti shook her head and opened the cell door. "Nothing worth mentioning."

Highlark glanced between Viv and the man one last time, an unreadable expression on his face, then departed. Iridia locked up behind him and strode out of sight without another word.

~⌐

As per usual, Viv didn't really fit on the cot, so she ended up sitting with her back against the wall, increasingly uncomfortable while her leg throbbed under the fresh bindings. The man in gray stayed stock-still, but his very presence seemed to settle on

Viv's skin, and she had the irrational urge to brush it off. She could only think about what would happen after Iridia let them out, when this man got his magestone back and was out of her sight. The very idea made her want to bare her teeth. You just didn't leave a threat wandering around when you were at a dis- advantage. Not if you wanted to keep breathing, anyway.

But there was nothing to do at the moment but stew over it.

After Gallina blew out a third or fourth theatrical sigh, Viv rolled her eyes. The gnome's hands were tucked under her head as she studied the ceiling, tapping one boot against the other.

"Why are you still here, really?" Viv finally asked. "You can't honestly be waiting for Rackam to ride back into town. I can barely stand waiting myself, and I have no choice."

Gallina didn't look at her. "So what if I am? Hells, you should be happy about it right now."

"There has to be a better use of your time. You have to have something else lined up, right? What did you do before you got off the boat?"

Gallina frowned. "You got any idea how tough it is to get an outfit to give you a chance when you're me?"

"Well . . ."

"Course not. They probably see you a mile off and sign you right the hells up. You're a walkin' justification. Nobody doubts you can crack a skull, do they? Just look at you!"

"Hey, I still have to pull my weight and put in the work. I spent an hour limping through sword forms today, trying not to fall on my ass, because if I don't—"

The gnome blew a raspberry. "Spare me. What'd you think when you first saw me? *Really?*"

Viv opened her mouth but discovered she had no idea what she was going to say.

"That's what I thought." Gallina ran her fingers over the front of her shirt, where her bandolier of knives would have crossed over.

They lapsed into an awkward silence, and the man in gray only magnified it.

Viv couldn't even tell if he was breathing.

~⌒~

"You have a visitor." Iridia's husky voice startled Viv from a fitful doze. Adrenaline washed through her in a nauseating wave, the low tide of bad sleep. Weak light still filtered through the slit windows at the back of the cell, but the hurricane lamps in the hall had been lit.

The tapenti appeared annoyed. Viv wondered if that was just her resting expression. The fine scale patterns on her face didn't exactly seem conducive of a welcoming smile.

A rattkin stepped into view, one paw clutching the clasp of her red cloak and the other carrying a paper sack with a familiar aroma.

"Fern?" Viv was astounded that the Gatewarden had allowed her in. Iridia had made a show of grudgingly admitting High-lark, but Viv had assumed that had more to do with the mess she'd have to clean up otherwise. She couldn't help glancing quizzically at Iridia, but her face remained unreadable.

Fern glanced worriedly at the tapenti and approached the cell, thrusting the sack through. "I wanted to make sure you were all right. And I may have suggested she wouldn't have to feed you if she let me pass these along."

Viv hauled herself off the cot, pressing a steadying hand against the wall, and hopped toward the bars. "Highlark patched me up. I'm fine."

"From Maylee," said Fern. "And you might want this as well." She removed *Sea of Passion* from under her arm.

"I don't recall agreeing to *that*," said Iridia, moving as though to intervene.

"It's a gods-damned book," snapped Fern, with surprising heat.

The tapenti's lips thinned, but after a moment, she stepped back.

Taking both, Viv wrinkled her brow. "Maylee?"

"Yeah, she seemed awfully concerned. She saw the whole thing."

"Enough in there for two?" piped Gallina.

Viv waved a hand to quiet her. "How's Potroast?"

"He's pretending he ran off an intruder. Very proud of himself right now. He's fine." Fern glanced at Iridia and then at the man in gray, who hadn't acknowledged her entrance in the slightest. "No thanks to that bastard."

"I'll bear that in mind," said Iridia, looming behind Fern. "As you can see, she'll survive the night just fine."

"*That's* the one you need to keep an eye on," replied Fern, stabbing a finger at the silent man.

"He's cooling his heels, isn't he? If there's more to be said, we won't say it here."

Fern shot Viv one last searching look and let herself be ushered out.

Viv settled back on the cot with the book and examined the contents of the sack. Huge, flaky biscuits and lassy buns—still warm and smelling of molasses and ginger and butter.

There was a beat of silence.

"So, did I ever tell you about my metabolism?" asked Gallina.

~

The biscuits and buns didn't last long. Viv split the sackful evenly between them.

Gallina licked her fingers for the last crumbs. "Eight hells, how'd you rate delivery of those?"

"Be damned if I know," said Viv.

"Lemme see that book."

Viv hesitated but then handed it over.

The gnome's eyes widened as she scanned the cover. "Wow. Pretty lucky with that wave, weren't they?"

"Give me that."

"I will!" She lifted it away from Viv's reaching hand. "So, you've been readin' this? Any good?"

"Why, you planning to pick up a copy?"

Gallina grinned at her. "Nah, I get antsy when I read. You could read it *to* me though. What else we got to do?"

Viv thought about the chapter she'd left off on. "Uh, yeah, I don't think I'd be any good at that."

"I'll make a deal with you."

"Again with the *deals*," muttered Viv.

"You read me some of this, and I won't mention this whole thing again. Ever."

She gave Gallina a speculative look. "This whole thing? As in . . . ?"

"As in me savin' your ass from a bony little guy in gray."

Said bony guy didn't twitch at the mention. By now, Viv had almost forgotten he was there. Almost.

After careful consideration, and a quick mental review of when things got really spicy, she said, "One chapter."

"Three."

"Two."

"Deal." Gallina tossed the book back, and Viv snatched it out of the air.

"I'm warning you, I'm not much of a storyteller," said Viv.

"You gotta actually try though. I'll know if you don't."

Viv waved the book airily. "Deal's already made. Can't add terms now."

Gallina blew another raspberry at her, and Viv couldn't help cracking a smile.

She settled back against the wall and arranged her wounded leg as best she could.

Clearing her throat, she began, haltingly at first.

"Raleigh spent most of her life at sea until she was tall enough to grip the wheel. Even then, she was so willowy that—"

"Willowy?"

Viv made an exasperated sound. "It means thin. Are you going to let me read this?"

"Are you gonna do voices?"

"No."

"Huh. This wasn't a very good deal."

"Do you want me to read it or not?"

Gallina grunted but gestured for her to carry on.

Viv resettled. "She was so willowy that her mother feared she'd be washed overboard in a bad squall. She was beautiful, like the first sight of land after a hard journey. She'd never be a proper seawoman, though; everyone knew that. It wasn't until Tesh boarded with his books of magic that the weather turned for Raleigh. The seas were never calm afterward, not for her, but they took her to interesting places indeed."

The gnome was softly snoring before she'd reached the

fourth page. With a hard glance at the man across the way, Viv flipped to where she'd left off earlier in the afternoon and began reading to herself.

It'd been an exhausting day, though, and she was wrung out. It wasn't long before sleep dragged her down as well, and the book fell open across her lap.

14

"Where the hells is he?"

"Wuh?" Gallina mumbled groggily.

Viv grabbed the edge of the gnome's cot and shook. That woke her up fast. "He's gone."

"Wh—who?"

"Who do you think?"

Gallina ran to the bars, peering into the hall. "Nobody at the desk neither!"

It was still dark out, a predawn indigo just visible through the windows. The door of the cell opposite remained shut tight, but Viv couldn't believe she would have slept through the commotion of releasing him. No matter how exhausted she was, the throb in her thigh hadn't let her sink too deeply into unconsciousness.

"Hey!" shouted Gallina in the direction of the watch desk. "Who let him out?"

There was no response.

Viv lurched to her feet and stumped over to join Gallina at the cell door. The gnome stared up at her wide-eyed. "Think he killed the guard?"

"And we didn't hear it?" Viv shook her head grimly. "I dunno. Don't smell blood either."

"Then they gotta have just . . . let him *out*?" Gallina screwed up her face and hollered through the bars again. "Hey!"

Viv's voice was considerably louder. "Anybody up there? Warden!"

They bellowed until they were both going hoarse, and then Viv held up a hand to forestall Gallina, cocking her head to listen.

A breathy groan issued from out of sight, followed by the scuffle and slap of someone struggling to their feet.

The dwarven nightwatchman staggered into view, holding himself upright against the wall. He stumbled into the hallway, glancing between the cells and gawping at the empty one.

"Oh, shit," he rasped. "Where'd he go?"

"You better find Iridia," said Viv flatly.

~∿~

"Who was he?" asked Iridia, her voice dangerously toneless.

"I guess you should have asked him yesterday," replied Viv, every word dripping with disgust.

Gallina shot her a warning look.

"He wasn't forthcoming," replied the tapenti, though she was clearly loath to explain. "A hungry night in the cell usually rectifies that. In my experience, patience and time solve most problems."

"Except *this* one," said Viv, slamming a hand against the cell door and rattling it on its hinges. She felt hot all over, and a fierce urge to try her strength against the bars.

The dwarf nightwatchman sat on the floor, breathing slowly

and evenly and looking very green. Iridia had already directed a few sharp words his way, and Viv didn't know if his current state owed more to that or whatever had knocked him senseless in the night. He hadn't seen anything, though, and couldn't remember much before his unconsciousness. He complained about an all-over headache, but the tapenti wasn't much interested in his excuses.

Iridia considered the bars, and then Viv. She did not appear concerned.

"Let's start at the beginning, shall we? If you help me make sense of this, then maybe I'll take a less dim view of your continued presence in my city, given the trouble you have clearly invited."

Viv barely kept her frustrated oaths behind her teeth as she paced in her cage. She glared at Iridia, and then with an effort of will, unclenched her hands and swallowed her curses.

She sighed and settled back on the cot. Kicking her leg out, she tried to find something to do with her hands that didn't put pressure on it and didn't crush anything else. "I was at Thistleburr—"

"The *bookshop*?" interrupted the Gatewarden incredulously.

"Yes. The bookshop."

Iridia blinked slowly at that, and then gestured for her to continue.

"Anyway, he was messing around in there, and then Potroast—"

"Pot—?"

"He's a gryphet. Fern's gryphet. Anyway, he comes tearing out of the back, absolutely losing his little mind, and leaps at the guy. Who just . . . casually slaps him aside." Viv replicated the motion. "And yeah, that's not great. Who hits little ani-mals? I'd toss him out on his ass for that alone, but—"

When Viv didn't continue, Iridia prompted her. "But?"

Viv sighed. "I don't know how to say this so you'll care or pay attention. Look, I smelled him, and he smelled like . . ." She returned the tapenti's fierce gaze. "You know who Varine the Pale is? You've heard of her?"

Iridia pursed her lips, and her gaze became more consider-ing. "The necromancer?"

"That's who we were after, before I ended up here."

"Oh, shit, really?" asked Gallina. Her eyes were round. "Rackam is hunting *Varine*? The *White Lady* Varine?"

The Gatewarden hissed at the gnome's interruption and returned her attention to Viv. "What are you getting at?"

"You ever been around a wight?"

The tapenti shook her head.

"Well, I have. Lots, at this point. They smell like death. You'd figure that part, right? But there's something else, like . . . frozen blood. The way your nose goes all dry in winter and you can taste copper when you breathe. If you get right up on them, they smell just like that."

Viv gestured at the empty cell. "That's the way *he* smelled."

"He was no wight. He definitely had a pulse."

"Yeah, I know. But I know that smell, and I knew something about him was *wrong*. All the way through me, I knew it. And if he has anything to do with Varine . . . ? Well, I was going to find out if that was true, one way or another."

"That's why the city has Gatewardens."

Viv snorted. "Didn't see any close at hand, or I would've flagged one down." She patted her leg. "And I wasn't going to run inside the fortress walls to find one, was I?"

"It didn't stop you from leaping into the fray."

Viv tossed her hands up. "And if I'd had my sword, maybe things would've gone different. What do you want from me? He slipped out of *your* cell, knocked out *your* guard, and it didn't seem to cost him a lot of trouble. He's a threat. If not to us, then to somebody else. You leave a snake in your tent, you're asking to get bit."

"Pretty shitty analogy," hissed Gallina as Iridia's expression darkened.

"How *did* he get out?" asked the tapenti, with a precision that bespoke a temper held in check.

"How the hells should I know? We were asleep!" Viv couldn't help raising her voice. "Neither of us saw a gods-damned thing, but now he's out there, and we're in here, and I figure he has his stuff back to boot, yeah?"

"He does," grunted the dwarf, massaging the back of his skull. "That satchel, the magestone, the daggers . . ."

"He didn't swipe *mine*, did he?" asked Gallina anxiously.

The dwarf shook his head, and she breathed a sigh of relief.

"You're both still alive. So is Luca here," Iridia observed bitterly. "If our nameless visitor could escape, then he could've killed you in your sleep. Whoever he was, vengeance wasn't on his mind."

"Maybe we're not as easy to kill as you think, and maybe he figured that too," said Gallina, obviously feeling left out of the conversation. "And there's two of us! Still in here, by the way. With him gone, what are you even holdin' us for?"

"I don't have to come up with a new reason," said Iridia. "The first was perfectly sufficient." But Viv could tell that something was shifting inside her.

"You wanted us to help you make sense of it," said Viv, in as reasonable a tone as she could. With her leg screaming at her, it was harder than it should've been. "You know what we know. So? What's the verdict?"

"I'll tell you when I decide," replied the Gatewarden. She spun on her heel to stalk out of sight.

~~

Iridia let them stew another hour, but Viv thought that was just some bullshit show of dominance. It was Luca who released them, still looking pale and unsteady. He returned their things and passed on a muttered warning to stay out of trouble, but Viv thought he looked relieved to see the back of them. Gallina stroked the hilts of her daggers fondly as they left the building and stepped into the morning light. The scents of damp, smoky morning cookfires and boiling oats and bacon threaded through the air. The gnome's stomach made loud, longing noises of protest.

They were otherwise silent leaving the walled enclosure of Murk, but each kept a watchful eye out. Predictably, there was no sign of the nighttime escapee. Viv would've been amazed if there were, but it didn't stop her from looking.

The Gatewardens were looking, too. Iridia clearly hadn't taken the man's disappearance lightly, and they saw women and men with lanterns on their belts at nearly every corner. They all had a watchful, distrustful look about them, hands on hilts as often as not. Viv had supposed the well-garrisoned fortress was a precaution against an unlikely sea invasion. Now, the bored Gatewardens finally had something pressing to demand their attention.

Several even patrolled the sandy thoroughfare leading

down from Murk's massive stone gateway, although what they expected to find there, Viv couldn't imagine.

A pair of schooners rolled at the dock in the morning mist, and waves roared in hard and loud. The sun gleamed on the sea, promising real heat later in the day.

She supposed the man in gray might be on one of those boats, but somehow, she doubted it.

With the aid of her staff, Viv limped her way up the slope toward The Perch. Gallina matched her pace, and Viv decided she didn't mind that much.

"Think he's gonna kill us in our beds, then?"

"Not where I plan to die," Viv replied with a grunt. Although the fact that he'd disappeared from right under her nose disturbed her more than she cared to admit. She was going to sleep with her saber close at hand, that was damned certain.

"That's where you're spendin' all your time?" Gallina asked as they passed Thistleburr Booksellers.

Viv snorted. "Planning to haunt that, too?" She saw the darkening look on Gallina's face. "Joking. Yeah, I guess I like it. Especially now that there's a chair. A *comfortable* chair."

"Comfortable, huh?"

"Can't fit your boots on the table though."

Gallina stifled a chuckle. "I mean, I got things to do."

"Uh huh."

They were quiet for a while longer.

"You never did hear those chapters, though," Viv mused aloud.

"Hm. Guess we *did* have a deal."

"Yeah."

"Suppose if I ever need to fall asleep again, I'll call in the rest of it. Maybe in that comfortable chair."

Viv didn't dignify that with a reply. But she was still smiling as they mounted the steps of The Perch and headed gratefully toward collapse in their own beds.

15

Viv *did* lay the saber on the floor beside her that night, the hilt only inches from her fingers. Her imagination was unfortunately pretty good, and she even fancied she caught the man in gray's scent once or twice. It was all too easy to picture him right outside her door, casting some cantrip on the lock, a silver blade in his fish-belly hands.

The day was hot, too, a real scorcher, and the wind had breathed itself out. She lay on the straw-tick mattress, sweating and bone weary, leg afire, and running a thumb along the wrapped leather of her blade's grip.

She was fed up with being injured, and furious with herself for setting back her recovery by doing something as stupid as brawling in the street. Viv resolved to try to follow Highlark's instructions. Mostly.

While she was wrestling with herself over that, sleep crept up and seized her unexpectedly. When she slept, she slept hard.

Viv didn't wake until late the following day.

"It looks good," called Viv as she made her way carefully down the slope. A fresh breeze from the sea teased heat away from her skin, and her saber was back on her hip.

Fern held a broad bristle-brush in one paw, and crimson flecked her fur. Fresh paint covered half the door—the lower half—and a rope-handled pail sat beside it on an old scrap of sailcloth.

"Oh," she replied, wiping her brow and leaving a faint smear of red behind. "Good. You can save me balancing on something to get the rest. Gods, I hate being short." She blinked when she saw Viv's scabbarded blade, but she didn't say anything.

"Can't promise I won't muck it up," said Viv, wincing as she climbed onto the boardwalk.

The rattkin made a hissing noise as though the wound were her own. "I'm surprised Iridia's already let you out. How's the leg?"

"It'll mend if I ever let it." She leaned against the newel, blew out a big sigh, and let the pain subside like the tide going out. When she looked up, she saw Potroast staring at her goggle-eyed through one of the windows.

Fern glanced around sharply. "And . . . if *you're* out, then what about *him?*"

Viv frowned. "Well, that's a longer story. Why don't I tell you while I paint, yeah?"

She unbuckled her sword-belt and leaned the saber in easy reach against the wall. Taking possession of the brush, she did her best to be neat about the work, with long, sure strokes. Her undamaged leg was sturdy enough that she could keep most of her weight off the other one as she worked, and Fern held up the bucket so Viv didn't have to lean down to reload the brush.

Viv relayed all that had happened during her night behind

bars and the following morning. When she got to the part about the man in gray's disappearance, Fern squeaked and almost dropped the pail.

During Viv's explanation about the necromancer and her suspicions about their connection, Fern couldn't hold her peace any longer.

"So, he disappeared from a locked cell, and he's just out there with his knives and his . . . his fucking *magic?*" she spluttered.

Viv didn't like it either but was surprised at how incensed the rattkin was. "That's about the size of it, yeah."

"Then he could come back at *any time?*"

Viv gestured at her sword with the brush. "I don't think Iridia is going to give me any trouble about carrying that around right now, and if she does, I'm not sure I care."

Fern eyed her doubtfully.

"This is what I do." Viv shrugged. "I'm menacing for a living. Hey, it just makes me twice as useful taking up space in your shop during the day, right?

"It was . . . odd to see you in action. I don't like your company because you're *menacing.*"

Viv frowned. "Well, only when I need to be."

Fern glanced back at her. "That's not what I mean. I saw his eyes when he . . . when he hit Potroast." She swallowed. "They were so *dead*. It made me cold all over."

"He's wrong, for sure. All the way through."

"I just mean to say I don't doubt you. Don't doubt what you did. At first, I was upset, because I'll be honest, I haven't seen a lot of street fights. Not very common in Murk!" She laughed weakly. "I suppose Iridia makes sure of that. Now, I guess I'm a different sort of upset. And not at you."

They were quiet for a moment while Viv painted around the

top edge as best she could. She wasn't sure her brush technique could even be called workmanlike, but the door was definitely red.

"Last night, Potroast woke me. Hooting and barking, just like before. Do you think . . . ?"

Viv finished the last stroke with the brush and carefully placed it in the pail. She looked at Fern seriously. "I don't want you to worry about it. If he's coming for anyone, he's coming for me, and he won't do that here. What could he possibly need from the bookstore? Or have to fear from you?"

"I'm not sure that makes me feel any better."

"Like I said, this is what I do," replied Viv. She grinned a little. "Now, you'd better take care of that paint in your fur. You look like you've been murdering chickens."

~⁓~

"Aw, shit," said Gallina, shaking her open hand. "Was that wet?"

Viv was so astounded to see the gnome in the bookshop, she almost forgot to be annoyed. "Didn't you see the sign about the paint?"

The gnome braced the door open with her back—on the unpainted side—and glanced over at the window, and then up, where she finally spied it. "Outta my eyeline."

Viv pushed away from the counter, where she'd been leaning in conference with Fern. "If that's got fingerprints in it now . . ."

"Don't get all touchy. I'm sure it's fine."

"If it's on your hands, it's not on the door," groused Viv.

"What do you care? It's not your—Oh, hey." Gallina wiggled her fingers at Fern. "Nice to meetcha."

The rattkin put her chin in her paw and sighed. "It's fine. I guess I should be thanking you for helping Viv. Some prints in the paint are a small price to pay."

Gallina beamed, and Viv thought she might've puffed out her chest, too, though it was hard to tell under all the knives. "See, yeah, that's what I'm—Wait, *helping?*"

"Saving my ass. Is that better?" asked Viv. "I'm still checking the door." She stumped the rest of the way over and gave it a careful inspection while the gnome ventured into the shop, looking around with a critical eye.

"Fern," said the rattkin. "And you must be Gallina?"

The gnome cocked a brow at Viv.

"Yes, I told her about you," she said patiently. "You're *very* appreciated."

Gallina settled into one of the chairs.

Her chair, Viv noted. Gallina appeared to be developing a habit.

"Hey, you're right, this is pretty comfortable."

Potroast trotted into view, promptly leapt onto the chair, and curled against the gnome's leg.

"Aw, who's this?" Gallina stroked the feathers between the gryphet's eyes, and Potroast snuggled even closer.

Viv was more nettled by that than she would ever admit.

"That little gentleman is Potroast," said Fern.

Gallina made a face. "What'd he do to deserve *that?*"

The rattkin laughed. "His real name is Pallus. My father named him after the Great Gryphon in *The Fourth Wish* as a literary joke, but I was little and couldn't say the name right, so . . ."

"You deserve better," the gnome stage-whispered to Potroast.

Fern directed a curious glance at Viv, who shrugged

helplessly and asked, "Anything we can help you with?" Oddly, that "we" felt perfectly natural.

"I think you owe me another chapter or two," Gallina said.

"Looking to fall asleep this early in the day, huh? Well, I don't have the book with me."

"Sounds like welcher talk. Are you, like, *workin'* here, or what?"

Viv shrugged. "I help out."

"For free?" The gnome seemed shocked.

"Oh, no, she's got the run of the store. Whatever she wants to read." Fern regarded her with amusement.

Gallina made a face. "So, *basically* for free. What exactly do you *do* in here all day?"

"Well, when customers come in—like you, for instance—we sell them books," supplied Fern.

Gallina studied the rattkin as if trying to decide whether her tone was patronizing or not. Fern did an admirable job of providing no clues.

The rattkin continued, "We were just discussing a book for someone in particular. A gift. That's the bookseller's art, choosing just the right one for the person in question."

"Who for?"

Viv cleared her throat. "Uh, just . . . a friend."

"You've got friends here?" asked Gallina incredulously. "Oh, wait, is it me?"

At that, Viv burst out laughing. She couldn't help it.

~⁓~

"What's this?" Maylee asked as Viv handed over a parcel wrapped in brown paper and secured with string. Fortunately, Fern had tied it, or it would have been a hopeless tangle.

"I just, uh, wanted to thank you." It was the first time Viv had seen Sea-Song without a line. The baskets and shelves sat nearly bare, and the heat and humidity weren't quite as thick as she recalled. No fires roared in the ovens, and the slim girl with her hair in a bun industriously scrubbed pans at a deep basin in the back. The whole place seemed to be sighing in relief after a day of relentless energy.

The smile on the dwarf's face was huge but also softer than Viv remembered, as though genuine surprise had caught it halfway to forming.

"Aww," she said quietly, running a finger under the string. Flour edged her nails. "Can I open it, then?"

"Sure! Yeah, of course." Viv stood there awkwardly, simultaneously wanting to make a quick exit and hoping to catch the expression on Maylee's face when she realized what it was. She and Fern had talked things over, and while Viv had worried the choice was a little too on the nose, in the end, she trusted the bookseller more than she did herself.

The dwarf snapped the string with a brisk tug and carefully folded back the paper, withdrawing a large volume bound in wood and sturdy lacing. Her brow furrowed at first. No title graced the front, but as she opened it and her eyes scanned the first few pages, her smile returned and journeyed all the way to fullness.

"Well, if that . . . aw, Eight . . ." She glanced up at Viv, eyes wide. "Is this what I think it is?"

"I felt a little weird, giving you a book of just recipes, because, well . . ." She waved around her. "Do you really need them? But—"

"*Just* recipes? This is a book of *gnomish pastry* recipes." Maylee laughed. "Hells, I don't even have to *make* 'em. Just readin' 'em is a treat. Some of these . . . gods! The steps! And look at these woodcuts! I *love* it, hon."

"I'm glad," said Viv, although at the same time she felt a spike of embarrassment that she hadn't thought of this particular book on her own. "And thanks for thinking of me. Uh, in prison. You didn't have to, but it was . . . it was nice." She flushed. Giving gifts involved a lot more careful navigation than it ought to.

"Thinkin' of you?" Maylee leaned on the counter. "Hon, I ain't stopped since you got here."

"Oh. Um." Viv's thoughts were obliterated as surely as if she'd been brained with a cudgel.

The dwarf watched Viv's expression, her own a mix of amusement and something else besides.

"Take care of that leg, Viv." Maylee winked, gave the book a loving pat, and went back to cleaning up.

Viv left the shop confused, but not unpleasantly so.

16

Viv maintained a state of heightened suspicion for the first few days following her night in prison, but those feelings ebbed into a background alertness not far from her usual state of being.

No furtive men in gray were in evidence. Still, she kept her blade at her side, Iridia be damned.

She tucked it behind the counter when she was at the shop, though, after Fern pointed out that it wasn't the most welcoming thing to spy through the front windows.

And for once, there were actually customers to deter. Neither Viv nor Fern could decide whether it was the fresh paint or the slightly less chaotic interior or some other nebulous perception of activity. It was hardly a flood of traffic, but a steady trickle wandered in throughout any given day—sometimes curious browsers who left empty-handed, but actual buyers too. Once or twice, even two people at once. A few shot curious looks Viv's way, but when that happened, she made sure to pick up her own book, and their gazes wandered elsewhere.

Gallina dropped by off and on, usually on the pretext of visiting Potroast. More often than not, though, she ended up hanging around for a while on one of the chairs.

The inactivity was good for Viv's leg, which regained some of the ground she'd lost after her inadvisable tussle in the street. Highlark even seemed grudgingly satisfied with her progress. But the quiet did nothing to relieve her restlessness over the whereabouts of the Ravens, and a hundred imagined scenarios where she missed their return, or they didn't return at all. Rackam surely wasn't the sort to break his word, but Viv was hardly a veteran of the company. She couldn't silence a nagging voice that said he'd be happy to be well shut of a reckless orc that got herself into trouble she couldn't get out of.

Words were the best distraction she could hope for.

"All right," she said, entering the shop. "I finished the book." The fog was piled high up the slope in front of the building, and it curled behind her like cold smoke.

Potroast regarded her with narrowed eyes and hid behind some shelves.

"Oh, really? Took you long enough. Too many chapters only suitable for your room?" Fern smirked at her from behind the counter.

"Hm," replied Viv.

"You know, she's local."

"Who is?"

"Zelia Greatstrider, the author. She lives around here."

"In *Murk*?" Viv asked incredulously. She unbuckled her sword-belt and hid her blade in its accustomed place. She slid *Sea of Passion* onto the counter.

"Yes, well, some of us *like* it here," replied Fern, pulling the book toward her and running a paw down the front. "She's got a family estate a little north. I've seen her once or twice, but I don't think she gets down this way very often. Probably sends somebody else. She's very . . . very *regal*."

For some reason, the concept of an author being a real person you might bump into on your way down the street seemed impossible to imagine. "And she just . . . writes books?"

Fern gave her a funny look. "Got to happen some way. And she doesn't just write books—she writes a *lot* of books."

"Like, how many more?" Viv asked, as indifferently as she thought she could get away with.

Fern's lips curled into a grin that was positively feline, no small accomplishment given the circumstances. "You know, for a bookseller, it's *very* satisfying when you finally set the hook."

Viv rolled her eyes.

"Let me see which ones I have on hand. I've been trying to finish this restocking order, and—"

The door creaked open, and it was hard to say who was more surprised when Pitts ducked in from the fog, moisture beading on his shaved scalp.

He stood awkwardly just inside the doorway, then held up the little orange book of poetry between two fingers. "Was wonderin'," he said slowly, staring intently at a spot far above Fern's head, "if you had another like this?"

~

"Hey, hon!"

After Pitts's unexpected appearance at the shop, Viv thought she was done with surprises until Maylee slid into the chair across from her in The Perch.

"Hey . . ." Viv set her mug down slowly.

Maylee wore plain clothes, and for once, she wasn't gleaming with sweat and heat, although her cheeks hadn't lost their rosy flush. Her braid draped like a rope of flax over her shoulder, and in the lantern light, her eyes were luminous. It took Viv a second to recognize it, but as a warrior accustomed to the hunt, the shiver of being pursued was novel.

"Brand!" hollered Maylee. "I'll have the beef! And you got any of those little red potatoes? You know the ones I mean."

Brand raised a tattooed arm in acknowledgment.

"And somethin' to drink!" she added.

Viv slid her plate to the side and crossed her arms on the table. It seemed polite to wait. "Don't think I've ever seen you in here." She lowered her voice and added, "And this is kind of embarrassing, but it feels weird to see you outside your bakery. You just seem to . . . I dunno, *belong* there." It had knocked her back to imagine Zelia Greatstrider marching around Murk, but seeing Maylee out and about seemed equally improbable. And yet, here she was.

"Hm, well, if that surprises you, you shoulda seen me a couple years ago."

"Oh, yeah?" Viv's brows rose.

"I guess you wouldn't know it to look at me these days, but I used to raise some hell myself." Maylee curled one arm. "I didn't get these just punchin' dough."

"You're serious?"

"I swung a mean mace. Big, flanged thing. Mostly mercenary stuff and only for a few years, but yeah."

Viv leaned further forward. "Who'd you run with? What happened?"

Maylee laughed, a more delicate sound than Viv expected to hear coming from her. The dwarf might have been short, but everything about her seemed like it should be big. "Oh, nobody you'da heard of. And I guess it just got so I wanted to spend more time fussin' over my campfire biscuits than trompin' around some damp cave. You ever cooked biscuits on a campfire? Pain in the ass. I got pretty good at it, though. And at some point . . ." She shrugged.

Viv was mystified. She immediately thought of the Ravens, and something like homesickness flared up in her chest. "And you're . . . happy doing that? You don't miss it?"

"Sleepin' on roots? Nah."

"Here you go, miss," said the tavern kid, sliding a steaming plate and a copper mug in front of Maylee. An inch-thick slab of heavily peppered beef crowded a bunch of salted, diced potatoes. Viv had already half finished her own meal, but her stomach snarled at the smells of hickory, rosemary, and hot, crispy fat.

"Thanks, Ketch." So, the tavern kid had a name. Viv noticed he didn't rate a "hon."

Maylee's eyes sparkled as she arranged her plate before her, and her delighted expression made Viv smile. The woman was definitely enthusiastic about her food.

Viv dragged her own plate back in front of her and picked up the fork. "Eight hells, I can't even imagine. I'd go crazy. I feel like I've got an itch I can't scratch waiting around here, and it gets a little worse every day."

The dwarf enthusiastically sawed off a bite and popped it into her mouth, closing her eyes as she chewed. "Oh, that's the stuff." She sighed contentedly. "Anyway, nah, not really. I keep myself busy, and there's a lot less bleedin'." She pointed her fork at Viv. "And a lot better food."

They ate in silence for a few minutes, only the clink of knife and fork on the tin plates marking the time. It was comfortable.

Eventually, Maylee put down her utensils and steepled her fingers over her plate. She was still smiling, but there was something serious about her gaze, too, and Viv had the sense of a curtain being swept aside.

"Look," said Maylee, and her voice was softer, pitched just for Viv. "I like you."

Viv cleared her throat as that comfortable feeling evaporated, replaced with a jumble of emotions she couldn't sort out without time to claw through them. Time she suddenly didn't have. "Uh, I guess I sort of figured that out," she said, lamely. And then lower down, "Don't know why, though."

Maylee arched a speculative brow. "Well, I *woulda* said it was when I first saw those arms, 'cause . . . eight hells! But really it was when I saw you waitin' in line. Watchin' the careful way you moved around the other folks."

Viv's cheeks went hot, and she couldn't find any words. She suddenly didn't have the breath for it.

"All real cute. And okay, then I talked to Fern, too." At Viv's widening eyes, Maylee laughed. "She didn't spill any secrets, hon. But maybe I got a peek at you. Enough to know I'd like to know you better."

Her smile slipped, and there was something distant and sad in her eyes. "You know, there's a lot of people out there. Lot of noise. I love what I do, love it every day, but none of us sees more than a tiny piece of all the world, like we're lookin' out a little-bitty window. And I saw you through mine, and somethin' inside me said, 'That's somebody you oughta know.' Simple as that.

"I know you're gonna be gone," she said. "Maybe in a couple weeks. You know what, though? Doesn't matter to me. I'm just gonna make it real simple for you. Do you think you oughta know *me*?"

Maylee tried to say it casually, but Viv wasn't so dull she didn't feel the thread of tension running through those words.

Viv stared at her entirely too long as words turned to vapor in her mind, and all the while she felt that line of tension grow tighter. And when she couldn't bear for it to break, she suddenly had to answer.

"I'd like that," said Viv. And while that was true, part of her knew it was a truth with an edge to it. One that might cut them both later.

17

"You own a *boat?*" Viv looked bemusedly at the dinghy moored to the smallest of the four piers, which benefited from the sheltered, stiller waters off the cove. A long sandbar curled out in a narrowing arm, and the promontory with the unrecognizable structures overlooked it all.

Seawater slopped along the hull of the tiny boat as it seesawed gently back and forth. Viv eyed the size of the vessel with trepidation, having some difficulty mentally fitting herself into it. "I've gotta say, I figured it would be . . . bigger."

Other watercraft, none terribly large, bobbed in a ragged line down the length of the jetty, which was mostly populated by gulls and terns toward its end.

"I just borrow it when I feel the need to. This old sailor who comes by every day for biscuits lets me use it as I please. Don't know why he even keeps it, since he's out on a trawler all day." Hanging on to one of the pilings, Maylee stepped into the belly of the boat. "Hand that over, hon," she said, gesturing at the wicker basket on the boards.

Viv obliged, passing along the basket with a soft clatter and clink.

The dwarf tucked it behind the plank seat near the prow and glanced back, brows raised. Viv's doubt must have been plain on her face, because Maylee laughed that delicate laugh, sparkling as the seawater. "C'mon, you know how to swim, don't you?"

"I know *how*," said Viv. "But it doesn't seem to matter much. I still sink like a stone. And with a bum leg? I'm definitely headed straight for the bottom."

"Well, I never learned, so if we capsize, we're goin' down together. It'll be very tragic and very romantic."

"You don't know how to swim, and you like to go out on this tiny boat?" Viv made a show of eyeing her from head to toe. "Guess you didn't give up the mercenary life for lack of bravery, huh?"

"Enough stallin'. Untie that, all right?"

Viv laid her walking staff against a piling where she was reasonably sure it wouldn't roll off, then unmoored the ship, tossing the rope into the boat. Maylee held it steady to the pier with one hand, then leaned to the side to make room and said, "You can do it. Left leg in first."

It had been a few days since their dinner together, and Viv had managed to walk down to the pier with only a moderate limp and the aid of her staff. Still, she couldn't help hissing and wincing as she made her ungainly way into the boat. There was a bad moment when she hiked her wounded leg after her, wobbling precariously, and then Maylee's hands were on her waist to steady her.

She slowly lowered herself onto the stern seat, next to the shipped oars. Cool air billowed out from the shadowed water under the pier.

"You know how to row?" asked Maylee.

"Seems like something I could figure out."

The dwarf gave her a considering glance, then held her hands out. "Eh, pass the oars to me."

Maylee rowed them away from the pier toward the center of the cove. The sunlight shattered to pieces on the gentle, scalloping waves. A brace of terns followed them, scolding with their harsh, burring voices.

The gong of the tolling hour glanced off the cliffside to the north, and in the distance a galleon forged southward, sails belling in the offshore winds.

The baker's sturdy arms kept up steady, powerful strokes as she charted a course along the sandbar, heading north and around the cape.

For the first while, Viv clutched the sides tightly, sensitive to every sideways swell and feeling entirely too big for the boat. Visions of toppling overboard—and taking Maylee with her—crowded her mind. No matter what Maylee said, Viv didn't think there was anything romantic about drowning in sight of land. Eventually, she relaxed, though, and enjoyed the feeling of the sun on her skin and the growing hush as they drew farther from shore. The water glinted blue as sapphires, but Viv could see in the distance where it blackened over unknowable depths.

As they rounded the northern promontory, another small cove came into view, this one shaded by the bluff. When they coasted into the shadows, Maylee dug the oars in to slow to a stop.

The cool of the shade was shockingly sudden, and Viv's arms broke into gooseflesh. Maylee flicked the end of an oar to catch her in the salty spray and grinned mischievously.

"I'll remember that," said Viv, with a slow grin of her own.

She looked at the exposed rock of the cliff wall above them, a thousand layers sandwiched at an angle. Gulls twirled before it in a whirl of white, but surprisingly kept their voices to themselves, as though reluctant to ruin the hush. "You come here a lot?"

"It's quiet. Cool. Pretty much the opposite of the bakery," said Maylee. She hoisted the wicker basket into the center of the boat, between Viv's legs, which occupied a lot of the room. Unfolding the linen, she withdrew a full loaf of bread and knocked on it with a knuckle. It sounded almost hollow. "Old and stale. And not for us."

Viv raised her brows at that.

Maylee tore it in half with a brisk crackling sound, and shards of crust sprayed in all directions like wheat chaff. She handed one piece to Viv, who held it up with a quizzical expression. "Not for us?"

With a secretive smile, Maylee plucked a chunk from the center of her piece and flicked it overboard to float on the water.

Viv started when the bread almost immediately disappeared. A silvery form breached the surface with a sound like a stone dropping into a still pond. "You come here to feed the fish? Feeding Murk isn't enough?"

"These customers are quiet," replied Maylee, her voice low. "And look." She pointed, and just beneath the surface, a swirl of pink and silver made broad, sinuous curves before doubling hopefully back.

"Oh," breathed Viv. The fish moved like a single organism, and as they turned, the sunlight scattered across their sides in a gleaming flash. "There must be a hundred of them."

"Peachgills. Yeah. Well, what are you waitin' for?"

They took turns picking the loaf apart, tossing morsels to the fish and a few brave gulls who swooped down to inspect the proceedings. The slap of the water against the hull and the *glips* and *glops* of the hungry peachgills lulled them both.

Viv sometimes paused to watch Maylee's face and the way her cheeks squeezed her eyes nearly closed whenever one of the fish received her offerings. The ache in her leg drifted far away.

When they'd satisfied the appetites of the undersea diners— or at least run out of stale bread—Maylee rummaged in the basket again, withdrawing a green bottle and a pair of glass tumblers.

"When we fed the stale bread to the fish, I figured you'd have a fresh loaf in there for us," observed Viv.

"Oh, you thought this was a *picnic*? Nope. I just got you alone so I could liquor you up." Maylee pulled the cork without visible effort and poured something clear into both of the glasses where they balanced on the seat between her knees. Viv caught a whiff of juniper that made her think of solstice wreaths and snow.

With cheeks rosy, Maylee offered a toast. "To chance meetings."

"To chance meetings." Viv knocked their glasses together and sipped. The dry taste unfurled across her tongue into what seemed a hundred different herbal flavors, followed by a tide of warmth that crept down into the center of her. "What is this?" she asked.

"Gin," replied the baker, sipping her own. "Smells like winter. Tastes like summer."

They drank companionably, and the warmth of the gin overtook the cool of the shaded cove. Viv could imagine it slowly heating every part of her like hot water poured into cold. She felt loose and easy in a way she hadn't in some time.

She gazed at Maylee while liquor burnished the edges of everything. At the dwarf's bare knees below tucked-up skirts. At a soft stretch of flesh beside her neck that made Viv think of Raleigh and Leena in the sea cave and what it would feel like to slide her fingers under the fabric and trace Maylee's collarbone.

The flush of the gin became a different sort of flush altogether.

Then she noticed she was staring and flushed hotter.

"So," she said, clearing her throat. She settled in and let her back rest against the stern. The boat canted a little in that direction, but not dangerously so. "Years out on the road, you said. You still got that mace lying around?"

Maylee sipped idly at her second glass of gin, and the corner of her mouth tucked up. "In a box upstairs. Couldn't get rid of it."

"So you *might* go back."

"Nah. I never will. But just because I'm done doesn't mean I have to forget, right? I can be a little sentimental sometimes."

"Okay. So, tell me a *good* memory. Something you miss. Obviously, not sleeping on roots and burning biscuits."

"You're makin' me feel old," said Maylee, gesturing with her glass. "You *baby* mercenary."

Viv laughed at that, and Maylee swirled what remained of her drink, pursing her lips in thought. After a few long moments, she said, "This goblin girl. Red hair, sharp teeth, the whole thing."

She paused again, and Viv was about to press for more when the dwarf continued. "Anyway, we were south of Cardus. There was this bandit, Voss, causin' a lot of trouble, and we were mostly in this little nothin' of a village tryin' to track him down and collect on the bounty. We're camped on one side of this little hill, a river on the other, and it's mornin', and I'm takin' the pans over to scrape 'em in the water."

"Burnt biscuits?" asked Viv, smiling.

"Who's tellin' this? Anyway, the river's kind of wide there, but shallow at the edges, bushes all along the shore and mornin' mist sittin' on the water. And I'm scrubbin' this pan with some sand. Then somethin' tells me to look up, and when I do, there she is on the other bank."

"The goblin?"

"Yeah. And she's one of Voss's, I can tell. They wore these red armbands. Real silly. And *she's* scrubbin' a pan."

Viv barked a laugh.

"She looks up at the same time, and we're both crouched there, wet to our elbows, cleanin' up after the cookin'. Voss had to be over the next hill, not quite shoutin' distance. And we just sat there. The river's too wide and deep in the middle. No way we can get across. There's no bridge for miles up or down stream, and we've got no horses."

Viv gazed at her through half-lidded eyes, warm and content. "And what happened?"

"We stared at each other for maybe a minute, which doesn't seem like long, but it is. And then, like we both agreed at the same time, we just went back to washin' our pans."

Another long pause, during which Viv studied Maylee's face and her wistful expression.

"I think that was when I knew I was done," she said. "But also, I wouldn't trade that moment either. I can still see her face right now."

Viv nearly asked whether Maylee had seen the goblin again—perhaps when and if they caught up with Voss's crew. Had their campaign been successful? She found herself wondering what that goblin's ultimate fate was.

But in the end, she thought better of the question.

18

As Viv's leg healed, she began gradually rebuilding her endurance. The speed at which she'd sensed her body soften and slow was a source of real anxiety for her, and she'd be damned if she'd put her conditioning off further. She kept at her sword forms in the lot out back of The Perch, but she had also commenced longer and longer hikes into the hills behind Murk. She was careful and pressed only as far as her mending wounds allowed, but she was methodical and persistent, and thoughts of the man in gray hardened her resolve.

Now, for the first time, she planned to make her way to the top of the bluff that overlooked the city, the one with the small structures she hadn't been able to discern when she first spied it. A sandy path ribboned over a series of stacked humps covered in long grasses, clusters of thistle with bright purple flowers, and windblown, scrubby trees.

Viv settled a good bit of her weight onto her recovering leg as she stepped, and while the ache was unpleasant, it was a far cry from the sharp jags of pain she'd endured only days earlier. She kept her walking staff in play but leaned on it less and less.

Sweat made her shirt cling to her back, and she had pinned

her hair up in a mass of dark curls to let the breeze cool her shoulders.

She'd planned to make the trip alone, but it hadn't worked out that way. With Viv's limited strides, Gallina didn't even have to struggle to keep up.

"Not a bad view," said Gallina, shading her eyes against the sun. She had her sleeves rolled up and her boots slung over one shoulder by their laces, feet bare and sand-caked.

The ringing of a bell echoed around the cove, sounding incredibly distant. Well past noon, the sky was flat and clear, the morning fog long burned off, and all of Murk seemed to doze in the heat. A schooner drowsed against the pier as though too exhausted to sail. The remote tumble of the waves hushed into nothingness.

Viv saved her breath and kept moving. She'd finally had the good sense to rig up another solution for carrying her saber around. The scabbard lay belted slantwise across her back, where it wouldn't foul her gait.

As they crested the top of the bluff, she stopped to take in the hilltop. Her leg quivered but held. Some of the burn was even pleasant, although that sick throb of a deep wound was hardly absent.

"It's a graveyard," said Viv.

A low iron fence surrounded the old cemetery. The grasses grew just as long within it as without, rustling around stones and pillars. She even spied a few dwarven graves marked by hunks of quartz.

Viv made her way through the gate and found a stone to rest her weight against. Any inscription was long since scoured away by rain and salt, so she didn't feel too bad about it. Her leg thanked her too.

Gazing off to the north, she could see an estate on a high hill. It was surrounded by real, old-growth trees—not the scrubby, tenacious things that flourished everywhere else—and what looked like hedges. Manicured hedges. Fern had mentioned that Zelia Greatstrider lived near Murk. Viv wondered if the place was hers.

Gallina surveyed the cemetery skeptically. "Seems like a bad idea, you ask me."

"You've got a problem with *burying* people?"

"I've got a problem with buryin' em way up *high*. Look at this place. It's all sand! One bad washout and somebody's grandpa comes slidin' down on top of the city."

Viv glanced at the markers. "These have been here a long time. I figure if that was going to happen, it already would have."

"Still. Anyway, that's not what I wanted to talk about."

"Oh, you have an agenda? Here I thought I was coming up here to train, and you were tagging along to take the air."

"Aw, you *know* you need a trainin' partner. You just gonna wave your sword around in the air by yourself? And who else are you gonna ask—Iridia?" The gnome tested the firmness of the open ground outside the fence, which was ringed by thistles that curved down the soft edge of the bluff.

Viv thought about explaining *exactly* how much time she spent training on her lonesome, but the circular conversation that would follow unspooled in her mind, and she decided to avoid it entirely. "Fine, I'm curious. You've got something you needed to ask me out of everybody's earshot, so let's hear it."

"Maylee."

Viv blinked. If she were listing subjects of interest to Gallina, that would've been at the bottom. "Okay. That's not a question."

"You're sweet on her, huh?"

"I . . . Where are you going with this?" Viv pushed away from the stone, her wind recovered. Her thigh no longer twitched beneath her like an animal set to flee.

"Well, are you?"

"What if I am? Are you *jealous* or something? I don't get what you're after here."

"Jealous? Nah." Gallina turned to look at her, her hands on her hips. She took a deep breath and then launched into it. "I'm just tryin' to figure you out. You hang around in a bookshop, diggin' in real good as far as I can tell. Paintin' doors. Sellin' books. And you're out on evenin' walks with the baker, real cozy-like. Are you plannin' to *stay* here or somethin'? Settle down?"

Viv frowned. "I just hiked to the top of this bluff to sling a sword around. What do you think?"

"That's why I can't figure it. Does she know you're leavin'?" She tried to ask it offhandedly, but there was a keenness to her gaze that Viv didn't miss.

"Of course she does. Why are you so interested in this? Worried you're going to lose your shot at joining up with Rackam if I decide to stick around?"

The gnome stared at her. "Just thinkin' about what it feels like to be left behind. That's all. She seems nice."

Viv returned her look soberly. "Maylee wasn't something I planned on. She knows what I am. Where I'm going." She thought about what the dwarf had said about tiny windows and the people you could see through them, but didn't think she could do it justice by repeating it. "It's two people with both eyes open having a little fun for a few weeks. Hells, I'm hardly ever around *anybody* for very long." She shook her head. "You know, this is not a conversation I figured I'd be having."

"Yeah. Yeah, well." Gallina cleared her throat and kicked at the sand. "Just thought I'd ask."

Viv was nonplussed. She understood what she was doing, and so did Maylee. No lies, no secrets. So why did Gallina's words unsettle her?

Well, the fastest way to get to the other side of unsettled was to muscle it out.

Leaning her stick against the fence, Viv slid out of her sandal, and removed her boot. She drew her saber from its scabbard and, keeping it low, stepped gingerly onto the open area of sand. "This place looks like it should work. Did I answer your question?"

Gallina pursed her lips. "Sure. None of my business anyway, huh?"

"Hey," said Viv. "Look at me."

The little gnome did.

"I'm a lot of things—gods know—but I don't think I'm an asshole. And I think that's the answer you really want, yeah?"

Viv made sure that Gallina met her gaze, and after a few moments, the gnome nodded. Viv had the strangest sensation that they'd both snapped into focus for one another, like blinking away sleep from a slow waking.

Dropping carefully into a defensive stance, Viv began the deliberate dance of the blade, feeling her muscles bunch and relax, the weight of steel balanced by a hundred contractions of flesh.

After a few seconds, Gallina drew two of her knives and began a parallel dance, different in a thousand ways but, underneath it all, with steps much the same.

19

"No staff today?" Fern's brows rose in surprise.

"I wasn't going far," said Viv. "I brought lunch."

"Isn't it sort of early?" the rattkin asked skeptically.

"For lunch? Oh, the *leg*." Viv shrugged. "I trust my body to tell me what it'll put up with. Got to listen to that before anybody else." She set a wrapped paper parcel on the counter and a stack of books beside it. "Besides, I talked to Highlark yesterday. He rebound it and made a lot of grumbling noises, but this time I think he was annoyed because it's healing *well*."

"And why would that annoy him?" asked Fern as she examined the parcel.

"Nobody likes a showoff," Viv said with a grin that she knew would annoy the elf if she were fool enough to flash it in his presence. "Especially not surgeons."

"And what's in here, hm?" Fern fingered the twine binding the package.

"Maylee said she tried something from the gnomish cookbook. That's all I know. Open it."

Fern needed no further prompting and untied the neat bow. Unfolding the paper, she revealed several flaky pastries, scored across their tops, oozing preserved fruit. She picked one up and took a bite. "Eight hells," she breathed. "If you were sweet on Maylee for nothing but the food, I'd hardly blame you."

"Everybody's got an opinion on that, don't they?" grumbled Viv, coloring slightly.

"Kiss who you want. You're grownups. *I'm* just grateful for the side benefits." She patted the books with a paw. "You're done with these?"

Fern withdrew a book from under the counter and set it next to Viv's pile. "I've been meaning to spring this on you, and I think you're ready."

Viv ran a thumb over a rich green clothbound cover. "*The Lens and the Dapplegrim?*"

"It's a mystery."

"You mean you don't know what it's *about*?"

"No, it's a genre. The book is *about* a mystery and how it gets solved."

"And they need this many pages to do that?"

Fern laughed. "Well, it's also about the investigator, and he's one of my favorites. You might relate. He's this grizzled old mercenary who lost a leg. And he's got this clever companion, who's a chemist."

"I should relate to grizzled and old, huh?" Viv pretended to be affronted.

The rattkin stuck out her tongue and slapped Viv on the arm. "Have I steered you wrong yet? And if you like it . . . well, there's more where that came from." She took another huge bite of the pastry and closed her eyes in dreamy pleasure as she chewed, then swallowed. "Fuck," she said appreciatively.

Viv undid the buckle across her chest and slung the saber behind the counter. Fern hadn't said so, but she seemed more comfortable having the weapon around, which made Viv feel a complicated mix of pride and guilt. They didn't speak of the man in gray often, but neither had they forgotten him.

When Viv straightened, she fidgeted some curls out of her face. "Look, I've been meaning to talk to you."

Pausing before her next bite, Fern said, "That sounds serious."

Viv sighed. "I don't feel right about this, the longer it goes on. Sitting in your shop. Borrowing your books. Sweeping and painting the things you can't reach. How much of that is there to do? I don't like feeling useless."

"But you're *not*—"

She held up a hand. "I know what you're going to say. I get it. But tell me seriously, how are things *really* going around here? When I met you, you were positive the ship was going down. I feel like I'm scrubbing the deck while you bail water. And I don't like it."

Fern stroked the clasp that pinned her cloak in place. It was a nervous gesture that Viv recognized.

"The shop . . . will last a *little* longer. It's been better lately. A *bit*. More visitors. A few more books." It seemed to pain Fern to say this. There was a long pause while she marshaled further thoughts. "But in another way, it's the best it's *ever* been. It's been better for *me*. Having you here is connecting me to why I do this. To why I used to love it. I don't know if I can explain it, but watching you read what I give you, putting a book in your hands and seeing what happens to you once you put it back down . . . I can't make you understand how that gives me something I didn't know I had to have."

When she fell into silence, Viv was wise enough not to fill it.

"You help me remember why I bother," concluded Fern, almost in a whisper.

Another long silence.

Viv nodded. "Okay. I'm glad. Feels like I'm taking advantage, but I guess I'm not stupid enough to disbelieve you. But another couple of weeks, at *most*, and I'm gone. So . . . maybe I help with something else, too, so the boat sails on even longer? I'm used to making a difference with my hands. Let me *do* that."

"I know that's what you're used to," said Fern, "but you don't have to use your hands to matter."

"Maybe not." Viv smiled faintly. "But it's nice when you need to paint the top of the door."

Fern shrugged resignedly. "Fine, I'll—"

The door slammed open and Gallina dashed inside.

"Oh thank the Eight, you're here. C'mon, Viv, you gotta see this," she said breathlessly.

"See *what?*"

"It's him," replied the gnome, her eyes wild.

Viv didn't need further clarification. She grabbed her saber by its scabbard and didn't bother to belt it on. She caught Fern's gaze. "Stay put," she said, as every angle of her sharpened.

~

He was dead. Very dead.

It was the man in gray all right, sprawled between a dune and a slowly disintegrating clapboard storage building behind one of the rows. If his tangle of colorless clothing hadn't been enough to mark him, up close, that cold smell prevailed, dry and metallic in Viv's nose.

"Did *you* kill him?" She strapped her saber onto her back and squatted beside the corpse, scanning the sand, but it was a muddle of inconclusive traces. The wind wasn't helping the situation much either.

"Gods, no!" said Gallina. "Found him this way. Okay, I didn't find him. It was that orc with the wagon."

"Pitts?"

"Hells if I know his name! How many orcs with wagons have they got in Murk?"

The sand drank in the man's blood, and his ashen cloak writhed along the churned earth like a living thing. Overhead, the sky darkened, and the smell of a landbound storm rode the breeze.

"Where did Pitts go?"

"Didn't ask. Ran off that way." The gnome flung a hand toward the fortress walls.

Viv sighed. "Off to find the Gatewardens then, and that means Iridia. Shit."

"Well *we* didn't kill him, so I don't know why that's a problem for us. Hells, we should be relieved, right?"

Viv glanced at her. "That depends a lot on who killed him—and why—doesn't it? And whether he was alone? After all, who broke him out of that cell?"

On a hunch, she stood, hooked her good foot under one of his armpits, and flipped him over.

His face was expressionless, pale eyes staring sightlessly. He might as well have been out for an evening stroll from the set of his mouth.

She squatted again, grunting at the thrill of fire along her thigh, and twitched his cloak aside. His magestone was belted at his waist. There was a money pouch, too, both conspicuously left behind. Viv shucked his sleeves up to the elbow on each arm.

"Whatcha doin'?" Gallina moved to get a better view. She had a dagger in hand, as though he might scramble up and lunge for them. Given what Viv was looking for, she thought it was a worthwhile precaution.

She didn't answer, instead pulling his bloody and torn shirt up to his neck. The hiss of indrawn breath had nothing to do with her leg this time.

A few inches above the stab wound that killed him, etched into the skin below his clavicle, was a diamond with branches like horns.

Varine the Pale's symbol.

"Oh, shit," said Viv.

"What?" Gallina's voice thrummed with anxiety. "You're freakin' me out."

Viv rose and looked down at the gnome. "Was there anything else here? A pack? His *satchel?*"

"No, nothin'! What's that symbol?"

Viv sighed. "It's Varine. He's one of hers."

"The necromancer? But he's not *dead*, though! Uh, I mean, he *wasn't* dead. He—" Gallina huffed in exasperation. "You *know* what I mean!"

"Her followers aren't *all* wights," said Viv grimly. "Kick around in the sand. See if that satchel is buried around here." Viv climbed awkwardly up the dune and peered over the crest toward the fortress walls. She didn't see any Gatewardens headed their way, not yet anyway. "If it's still around, I want to find it before Iridia gets here."

"Because . . . ?"

"Because I don't think this is over, and I don't trust her to listen to a gods-damned thing I have to say."

They searched the immediate area, combing the sand and

clumps of beach grass, before Viv stopped to consider the out-building. It was leaning as though in a stiff wind, gaps yawning at the corners where the wood had pulled free.

She circled the structure, peering into the shadows and hidey holes until she drew up short. A soft gleam beckoned from the blackness.

"Find somethin'?" called Gallina, coming around the other side of the building and looking harried.

"I think so," said Viv, getting down on one knee again and regretting the stiffness all this was going to cost her tomorrow. She reached into the darkness and withdrew the battered leather satchel, its copper fittings winking in the light. "He hid it in here from *somebody*."

The sound of approaching voices rose above the hiss of the grass and sand.

Viv shoved the bag back into the shadows and quickly rose.

Gallina opened her mouth to say something, but Viv saw her figure it out before the words came. The gnome nodded.

"Later," she said.

"Later," Viv agreed.

Together they moved toward the approaching Gatewardens.

20

"Of course I'd find you two here," said Iridia. She looked at the both of them from the other side of the corpse. Storm clouds clotted the sky above, and flickers of lightning licked at the sea in the far distance. A brace of Gatewardens flanked her, while Luca the dwarven nightwatchman examined the body and checked the man's pockets.

Viv crossed her arms and glared back. "I know how this goes. Now you'll decide we had something to do with it, rattle your saber about trouble in your town, and toss us back in a cell, right?"

The tapenti regarded Viv stonily. "No. In fact, this is one less problem for me to deal with. And you clearly didn't kill him."

Viv had to admit she was surprised at that, and some of the tension in her shoulders unwound.

"*Clearly?*" said Gallina, with her hands on her hips. She sounded offended.

Iridia snorted. "He still has his magestone. An orc definitely didn't sneak up on him from behind, and the wound that killed him is too high on his body for *you* to have dealt it. Besides,

I don't think either of you are stupid enough to hang around the corpse of someone you murdered." She arched a scaly brow. "Should I revise my judgment?"

Gallina seemed like she was going to answer that, but Viv jumped in first. "This might be one less problem, but I'm pretty sure there's more to follow."

The wind kicked up higher, sending frills of sand down the lee of the dunes. Gulls squalled and fled for the fortress walls. Iridia knelt behind the corpse to examine him. "Obviously, I mean to find whoever killed him, if that's what you're getting at."

"Check under his shirt."

The Gatewarden captain nudged Luca to the side and slid the garment all the way to his neck. She examined the symbol inscribed in his flesh, eyes narrowing. "Should I recognize this?"

"That's Varine's mark."

Iridia snapped her gaze to Viv, instantly more present. "Then he is one of hers?"

"No doubt in my mind. So, why was he here? Is he a scout? Does that mean Varine is headed this way? Who the hells knows? But if you like Murk quiet, it might get real noisy real soon."

"Could as easily be a deserter," said Iridia, but she didn't sound convinced. "Was there anything else here? He had a satchel before."

"No," Viv lied with a flicker of misgiving. "Why, was there something special in it?"

Iridia hadn't been as dismissive as she'd expected, but Viv still didn't actually trust the tapenti. Once she and Gallina had a chance to investigate the satchel's contents, they could unexpectedly "find" it again, if need be.

Iridia studied her. "Nothing that seemed important at the time."

One by one, heavy raindrops stippled the sand, and the wind skirled through the gaps in the outbuilding.

"Hells," said Iridia with real feeling, clapping her hands on her knees and rising from her crouch. "Fold his cloak around him and let's haul this mess back to the walls before the rain worsens," she directed the wardens.

Glancing between Viv and Gallina, she said, "My turn to anticipate what you're going to say, I think. You're assuming I'll ignore the possibility of Varine showing on my doorstep. Pretend this never happened. Like some sort of bad bard's tale, yes? The pompous, stupid Gatewarden that can't see past her own nose?"

Viv's surprise must have shown on her face, because Iridia smiled for the first time since either of them had met her. It wasn't exactly a pleasant smile, but it wasn't without humor. "I'm happy to disappoint you. I take threats to my town *very* seriously. But let me fulfill at least one of your predictions." She leveled a finger at them. "I want both of *you* to stay the hells out of it. In fact, it's best if I don't see you at all."

The tapenti snapped her fingers at the dwarf, who was apparently still paying the price for his supposed dereliction of duty. "Luca, search the area more thoroughly. I want that satchel. It might get fouled by the rain."

He squinted into the oncoming storm. "Uh, how long should I . . . ?"

"Until you think I'd be satisfied," Iridia replied dryly.

Then she turned and followed the other two wardens back toward the fortress walls.

The rain whirled in, icy and earnest.

Luca began miserably searching the dunes and grass, while Viv and Gallina hurried for shelter, praying to all the Eight that the dwarf was no better at this task than he had been at the night's watch.

~~⌒~

They waited on the boardwalk outside the perpetually closed junk shop, watching the road to Murk as the storm built and blew inland. Ribbons of moisture whipped up under the eaves, licking their faces and bare arms. The ocean and docks dissolved behind the curtains of rain and the mist it drummed up out of the surf.

"Luca's gotta be half drowned," said Gallina. "Kinda feel sorry for him."

"I'll feel sorrier if he finds that satchel," replied Viv, her hands gripping the boardwalk railing tight enough to creak.

At last, Luca stumbled into view from between a pair of dunes, hurrying toward the fortress walls, head bent. His lantern flashed at his hip, where the weak flame gleamed against the glass.

"Can you tell if he's got it?" asked Viv anxiously.

Gallina shaded her eyes as though that might improve her vision. "Nah, can't tell. Too far. Only one way to find out." She glanced at Viv. "You stay here, stumpy. I'll go check."

Viv opened her mouth to protest, but the gnome bolted off the boardwalk and hurried through the wind, her hands over her head to deflect the pelting rain.

Gallina disappeared around the opposite row of buildings, leaping nimbly between the growing puddles where hard-packed sand didn't swallow them up.

Drumming her thumbs on the railing, Viv leaned out,

letting the rain catch her more fully. She considered her leg and contemplated following Gallina, but she controlled her impatience as best she could.

Still, it was taking entirely too long.

"Hells, don't you remember where I stowed it?" said Viv under her breath.

Then Gallina rounded the buildings again, and even at a distance, Viv could tell she was grinning, with the satchel held across her belly, both arms clutching it to protect it from the rain.

At last, as she stood dripping on the boardwalk, Gallina unslung it and brushed away wet sand. Combing locks of wet hair out of her eyes, she groused, "If this thing is filled with a change of clothes, I'm gonna be real pissed."

❦

"Oh, thank the Eight!" cried Fern when they entered the shop together, Viv dripping and Gallina sodden. Potroast hooted anxiously and ran in little circles before them both, fluttering his vestigial wings. "What the hells happened?"

"Well," said Viv, "you don't have to worry about any trouble from our friend in gray anymore. And neither does anybody else."

"Dead?"

"Couldn't be deader," supplied Gallina, doing the best she could to stamp clots of wet sand from her boots.

"What took so long?" Fern hurried over to them. "And what is . . . Is that *his*?" She pointed at the damp satchel.

"It's a long story," replied Viv. "We had to dance around Iridia a little first."

"And yep, it's his," said Gallina, smiling triumphantly. "I

gotta know what's in this, and as the wettest gal in the room, I should get to do the honors." She trotted over to the pair of chairs and set the bag on the side table. The gryphet followed, his stubby tail practically vibrating with interest. The hurricane lamp on the wall seemed to hiss louder, as though stoked by an errant breeze.

"Just be careful!" warned Viv.

Gallina shot her a reproachful look.

With a flourish, the gnome unclasped the front of the satchel and tossed the flap back with a creak of leather. She pried the top open further and peered inside, and then her brow wrinkled in consternation. "What the hells?"

"What is it?" Fern moved to get a better look.

Gallina shoved her arm in and drew out something long, knobbly, and cream in color. "It's just a bunch of damn *bones*."

21

"That's it?" Viv loomed over the proceedings. "You're sure?"

"Hang on," replied Gallina, and Viv could swear she was up to her shoulder in the bag, which shouldn't have been possible. "Definitely other stuff in here . . ." She grunted as though stretching out her fingers to barely reach something, bit her lip, and then withdrew her arm with a glass bottle clutched in her fist.

Fern examined the bone the gnome had first retrieved, squinting as she tilted it in the light of the lamp. "Is this what I think it is?" she said.

Gallina held up the corked bottle and shook it. "Somethin' in it. Looks like sand? Who carries around bones and a bottle of sand?"

"Well, a necromancer's involved . . . Maybe the guy used them for . . . necromancer things?" suggested Viv lamely.

The rattkin noticed the bottle. "I don't think that's sand."

"I thought Varine was the necromancer." Gallina handed Fern the bottle, then groped around in the satchel some more. "Did the dead guy just wander around carryin' her *bones* for her? Pretty crap job. Maybe he *did* run off. Probably bored. Hey, here's another one," she said, pulling out the bottle's twin.

Uncorking hers, Fern sniffed delicately, whiskers twitching. She carefully tilted a few grains into her paw and prodded them with the claw on her thumb. "I was right, it's not sand. It's bonedust."

Viv sighed. "Well, this was a waste of time, wasn't it? All that trouble for a sack of garbage."

Fern carefully poured the grains back into the bottle, recorked it, and then peered around her shop with a thoughtful look on her face.

"What?" prompted Gallina, pushing her wet hair out of her eyes again. "Obviously, you got some kind of idea, huh?"

The rattkin ignored the question, lost in thought as she disappeared around the end of one of the shelves with the bottle still in hand.

Viv and Gallina peeked after her and found Fern on tiptoe, running her claw along the spines of a set of big leather-bound volumes shelved in a back corner.

"I'm sure it's here somewhere . . ." muttered Fern. "Aha!" She pinched one and slid it from between its neighbors, catching it awkwardly with the arm still occupied with the bottle. "Shit! Heavy!"

As she carried it to the back counter, Viv caught Potroast gnawing on one of the bones, his beak clacking loudly against it. She rolled her eyes and left him to it. At least they were of use to *someone.*

"Now . . . where the fuck are you . . ." whispered Fern as she leafed through pages thin as onion skins. Viv had noticed she got even more foul-mouthed when speaking softly. Gallina and Viv looked at one another, shrugged, and waited quietly until at last Fern stabbed a passage with a claw and said, "Ha! I knew it."

"So . . . it's *not* worthless junk?"

Fern favored Viv with a triumphant smile. "I guess that depends on if it works. Osseoscription!"

"Never heard of it," said Gallina.

"Not surprising, but—Fuck! Potroast, no!" shouted Fern, noticing his chew toy for the first time.

The gryphet hooted longingly around the bone jammed crosswise in his open beak and then very grudgingly set it down. He licked it once before backing away a step.

"Bring it up here," Fern briskly ordered.

Viv moved to grab it, but Gallina made it there first. "Your leg probably got you in enough trouble today already, yeah?" Her expression curdled into one of disgust. "Aw, hells, it's all slimy."

Fern took it in paw and dried it with the hem of her cloak, then held it up again, rotating it in the light. "You see this? Look closely. They're incredibly tiny."

Viv leaned in, squinting. "Are those . . . words?" Tiny scratchings were engraved into the bone in long, swooping lines that curled around the length and flourished toward the knobby ends.

Gallina tried to tiptoe high enough to see but gave up and went to grab another bone from the satchel. "Huh. There *is* somethin'."

"Osseoscription," said Fern. "It's sort of . . . an enchantment of animation, permanently inscribed into the bones. Incredibly challenging to create, or so it says here."

"Doesn't seem real animated," observed Gallina, tapping what looked like an ulna against her palm.

Fern held up the bottle. "It doesn't function without a

catalyst. Bonedust. A powerfully invested powder that activates the scripts."

"And then what?" asked Viv. "You sprinkle it on some bones and you get . . . a *wight*? So, what you're saying is, we should keep the two things as far away from each other as possible?"

"Not a wight. At least that's not what it sounds like. A . . . well, the book calls it a bone homunculus. It's an . . . assistant of some sort?"

Gallina frowned. "What does it assist with? Stabbin' things?"

Viv's eyes widened. "Or maybe it's the sort of assistant that breaks you out of your prison cell."

"Huh, that'd explain a lot," said Gallina.

"Well, I say we fucking try it!" cried Fern, her eyes ablaze with excitement.

Viv and Gallina shared another look. "Ain't *we* supposed to be the reckless ones?" said the gnome.

"Are you telling me you're going to just pretend you don't want to fucking *know*?"

Viv frowned. "Well . . ."

"Isn't this what you do?" demanded Fern. "And if it does turn out to be a wight? Can't you just, you know"—she swung an imaginary blade with both paws—"use your sword to bash it apart?"

For a few moments, Viv felt a nagging need to be the voice of reason, but in the end, there was no way in all eight hells she could leave well enough alone.

"All right," she said, trying to maintain a tone of patient deliberation. "But we're going to prepare first."

In the end, they cleared a space in the shop, shoving the chairs and side table into a corner, rolling up the carpet, and locking Potroast in the back room. He made his displeasure known with a series of forlorn hoots.

The satchel sat open in the center of the room. It seemed more prudent to keep the bones clear of the walls, in case it gave them an advantage if things went horribly wrong.

Viv and Gallina argued over which of them would apply the dust, but in the end, the choice was obvious, since Viv had actually fought the things before.

"So, how much should I sprinkle in there?" Viv asked in a quiet voice.

"Why are you whispering?" hissed Gallina.

Fern shrugged. "No idea. The book isn't an instruction manual. Start small?"

"Start small," echoed Viv.

She stood back as far as she could and tilted the bottle, tapping with her forefinger to sprinkle dust into the open satchel as though she were salting a bowl of soup.

Stepping away briskly, she held her breath and waited. All of them did.

For a long time, nothing happened.

Viv was just about to apply another dose when the satchel rustled, and they all jumped.

The leather sides flexed and contracted, as though the luggage was breathing. A delicate clatter arose from within.

Questing like pale caterpillars, the phalanges of a skeletal hand crept over the lip of the satchel, wriggling in the air until the bones of a wrist and forearm clicked into position behind them.

Viv's hand tightened on her saber's hilt.

Thunder rattled the windows, and wind howled hard under the eaves.

Viv and Gallina both readied their blades as the hand curved over the side to probe the floorboards. It patted around, then dug its fingertips in and pulled. The satchel tumbled onto its side, spilling an improbable number of bones onto the wood—far more than the bag should have contained.

Fern gasped and drew back, as Potroast began hoot-barking even louder.

With a gentle clatter, the spray of bones wriggled up until they formed legs, ribcage, and arms. Even as the metacarpals of the left hand slithered into place, the homunculus was reaching into the satchel to pluck out a skull, which it settled onto its shoulders. Two nubby horns rose from its forehead.

The bones were pearly and clean, and a tracery of blue lines veined them, glowing briefly before vanishing. Curls of cobalt flame licked the interior of its orbital sockets.

A long sigh escaped from somewhere in the neighborhood of its jaw. It examined its left hand, which was missing a finger, and massaged the air where its right ulna should have been.

Viv's sword arm remained tense, but this creature was half the height of the wights she'd battled, and delicate. More than anything else, though, it didn't *smell* the same. The room was filled with the scent of lightning strikes and burnt dust, but that cold odor of winter blood was nowhere to be found.

"What the shit?" breathed Gallina.

The homunculus stared at each of them in turn before

settling on Viv. It tilted its head in a gesture of curiosity, then bowed. "M'lady."

Its voice was hollow, like it was speaking down a chimney, and wholly, inexpressibly *sad*.

"I exist to serve."

"I fucking *knew* it!" cried Fern.

22

"What are you?" asked Viv, although he was clearly no wight, so small and weaponless. Still, she didn't lower her blade an inch.

He stared back at her with the unreadable blue flames in his sockets. "I am the Lady's homunculus." He invested the word with something like reverence. Or maybe fear?

"The Lady? You mean . . . Varine?"

The creature dropped abruptly to one knee and snapped the bony knuckles of one hand to his forehead. "The Lady," he hissed in an eerie, echoing whisper.

"Guess that answers that," muttered Gallina. Then, louder, "You gonna jump us or somethin'?"

The homunculus unfolded. "I . . . exist to serve," he repeated hesitantly.

"Serve *who*?" Gallina waggled her dagger meaningfully in his direction, although Viv couldn't imagine it would be much use against a bunch of bones with no blood to draw. Her saber at least might smash him to pieces if he decided to turn threatening. Somehow, though, she didn't think he was going to.

He extended a hand toward Viv. "The one who wakes me," he replied.

Fern stepped boldly toward the homunculus, and Viv held up a hand to try to stop her. "Hang on! Wait until—"

The rattkin waved her off. "He's not going to hurt anyone, can't you tell?" Then to the skeletal creature, "You aren't, are you? Going to hurt us?"

He shook his head and clasped his bony fingers before him. He really didn't seem threatening. The sepulchral voice and genteel tone sounded incredibly ancient, but something about his behavior was almost . . . innocent.

"What do we call you?" asked Fern, studying him with keen interest.

"The Lady calls me only Satchel."

"She named you after the gods-damned *bag?*" cried Gallina, slapping her dagger into a loop on her bandolier. Her righteous indignation signaled a shift in the atmosphere.

Viv sheathed her blade as well and looked the poor creature over. "You serve me then? But *also* the Lady?"

Satchel's fingers vibrated together—in nervousness? "I shall endeavor to do both, m'lady, to the very limits of my ability."

"You have to do what I say?" asked Viv.

Fern's expression clouded at that, and she glanced sharply at Viv.

"Yes. And also . . . no," said Satchel. His nervousness increased.

"What do you mean by that?" Fern asked.

Satchel pointed at the bottle of dust which Viv still held in her off hand. "Without the dust, I do not exist. To defy the one who wakes me is to cease to be. It is the truth that binds me, and thus binds my will."

"So, you *can* disobey, but if you do, you won't wake again?" Viv examined the bottle's contents.

The homunculus nodded.

"That's awful," said Fern, and the lack of colorful language spoke to the depth of her revulsion.

"Why are you here? Why aren't you with Varine?" pressed Viv.

"I was taken." Satchel acquired a hunted look. "Balthus stole me away from the Lady, and I was not all he stole. She will be most angry when she finds him."

"Balthus?" asked Gallina. "Wears gray, real pale? Somebody already saved her the trouble." She drew a finger across her neck and stuck her tongue out. "He ain't breathin' anymore."

"Dead?" asked Satchel—hopefully, Viv thought. "I don't doubt she sent a thrall to apprehend him."

"Oh, whatever it was apprehended the *hells* out of him," said Gallina.

Something nagged at Viv. "You've seen us before, haven't you?"

"I have, m'lady. I did not imagine I would again."

"*You* must have let the guy—Balthus—out of the cell. This explains a hells of a lot," she mused aloud. "Still, why was he here in the first place?"

"Fleeing the Lady. Hiding. He spoke of the sea," replied the homunculus.

"He should've been quicker about catching a ship, then. If he hadn't wasted time browsing bookstores, he might still be breathing. Feels off."

Satchel remained mum.

Viv shook her head. "Here's what we really need to find out, though. She sent someone after Balthus. Does Varine know where *you* are? Is she coming here?"

Satchel raised both hands in a distinctly human gesture of helplessness. "I cannot say, m'lady."

She frowned. "You don't know . . . or you can't say?"

"I cannot say," he repeated miserably. "I must keep the Lady's secrets."

"Did she bind you in some way?" whispered Fern.

His skull turned to regard her. The glow of the hurricane lamp turned it the color of ruined cream. "Fear is binding enough," he replied.

~

After that, Viv wanted to speak more privately with her friends. "So . . . can you go back to sleep, then? Just for now?" she asked Satchel. "I promise, we'll wake you again later."

"At your command, m'lady," he replied resignedly. He carefully placed his skull into the bag before a waterfall of bones followed. The sides of the satchel didn't even bulge at the skeletal inrush.

Viv couldn't convince herself he wasn't listening. She folded the flap over and latched the bag shut, then handed it to Fern. "Maybe tuck this away in the back? Just in case?"

Fern opened the door in the rear to do so, and Potroast burst from his confinement, paws scrabbling on the bare wood as he snuffled and hooted around the room while Gallina and Viv put the chairs and carpet in their original positions.

Viv leaned against a bookshelf while the other two took the chairs. They sat quietly while rain chattered against the east-facing window. The entire building creaked in the breath of the storm.

"Well," said Fern, breaking the silence. "What now?"

"What *can* we do?" asked Viv. "You heard him. He serves Varine and keeps her secrets. We don't know anything about him or what he might do. It's a risk to have him out and about. Maybe even to have him here at all."

"So we just *leave* him?" Fern was aghast.

Gallina chewed her lip. "I dunno. I feel *bad* for him."

Viv tossed up her hands in exasperation. "I guess I do, too. He's like a *slave*. It's terrible. But also, he's something *she* created. How much can we trust him? How much is he like us, really?"

"Enough to be frightened," Fern said sharply.

That was hard to argue with, so Viv didn't even try. "Okay, you're probably right, but still. Do we want to chance him running to Varine in the night? Or sending her a message or . . . I don't know." She made a vague gesture. "Doing something . . . untoward?"

"Could hand him over to Iridia," mumbled Gallina. When they both looked at her, she shrugged uncomfortably. "Maybe he *should* be her problem?"

Viv was surprised at how vehemently she rejected the notion. But not as strongly as Fern, apparently.

"We will fucking *not*." The rattkin's voice was firm. "You don't pass people around like . . . like luggage. Even if they're *inside* luggage."

Sighing, Viv stepped away from the bookcase. "Well, we don't have to figure it out tonight. Let's sleep on it."

They were all too tired to argue, and nobody had a better idea. After awkward goodbyes, they left Thistleburr, each of them thinking of the creature folded up in the bag—waiting or asleep or gone to some netherworld they couldn't imagine.

Viv and Gallina hiked the slope to The Perch as fast as
they could through the lashing rain and whipsawing wind.
Lightning scattered between the churning clouds, and in the
distance, the mournful cry of some creature in the hills made
them hurry even faster.

23

"It's a lie. All of it," said Beckett. He gestured with his snake's-head cane at the disarray: the overturned table, the lens shattered across the floor, the debris spilling from the window, and even the splash of blood that trailed up the wall.

"A lie?" Leeta's expression was dubious as she capped a phial and shook it vigorously, examining it for changes in hue.

The old man raked his fingers through tangles of gray hair, and his grim smile was half admiring. "This is Aramy's work. She's giving me just what I want to see. Of course we'll believe it's the groundskeeper, and of course we'll believe Lady Marden is dead. I'd warrant that's even her blood."

The gnome narrowed her eyes at him, searching his face for signs of fatigue or misgiving, but there was only certainty chiseled there. "How can you be so sure?"

"Because it's all too obvious. Because she's toying with me. She said as much in that damned cryptic letter." His expression soured. "But that's what vexes me most. She's been *too* obvious. Which means there's something else I've missed, and we have to find it before it's too late."

"So you believe Lady Marden is alive?*" exclaimed Leeta.*
"Then that's what we—"

"Hey there, hon. Thanks for waitin'. Got another one, huh?"

Viv glanced up from her seat on the boardwalk in surprise. Maylee closed the door behind her with a jingle, forehead still damp with sweat, cheeks sparkling like fresh-washed fruit.

"Hey." Viv smiled back, glad of the distraction. She'd read the same page at least five times, plagued by thoughts of the bone homunculus sitting in the back of Fern's shop, of Balthus lying dead in the sand, and wondering if Rackam had cornered Varine yet. Maylee's company was much more welcome.

She snapped the book closed and tucked it away. "Yep. Fern's still picking them for me."

Maylee squinted at her. "Somethin' botherin' you?"

Viv shrugged awkwardly. "Yesterday was . . . a lot."

Maylee bumped Viv's left leg with her hip. "Well, let's get movin', and you can tell me about it. I've got an hour before the bakery falls to shambles without me."

Viv grabbed the walking staff from where it leaned against the clapboard. She figured if she had it in hand, Highlark was less likely to use the sharp side of his tongue.

"Back with the stick, huh? How's the leg, then?"

Viv considered the question. "Little stiff today, but on the mend."

They walked together toward Murk proper. In Maylee's company, Viv didn't struggle against her own deliberate pace. The sand was still soaked and hard from the prior night's storm, and the sea had a gray, sullen look about it. The smell of waterlogged wood and spent rain was heavy.

She saw Gatewardens patrolling on top of the fortress wall.

True to her word, Iridia *was* taking the potential threat of Varine seriously. Viv wondered what other preparations the tapenti might be making.

As they strolled, Viv relayed all that had happened the previous day, from the discovery of Balthus to the appearance of Satchel.

"Eight hells," breathed Maylee, eyes huge. "So, what're you gonna do?"

"Wish I knew. You got any ideas?"

Maylee thought about it as they continued, two strides to every one of Viv's. She stared out over the breaking waves, and finally asked, "You think there's any harm in him?"

Viv thought it over as they walked, then sighed. "Maybe not in him. But maybe he drags it behind?"

"So you're tellin' me *you* want to stay out of trouble? Who're you kiddin'? Remember, I used to do this stuff, too."

"Well, it doesn't mean I want to bring trouble down on everybody around me."

"I'll risk a little trouble. I'm a big girl." Maylee looked Viv up and down. "Relatively."

"You *are* trouble. A nice kind of trouble."

"Maybe someday you'll be lucky enough to find out how much. Also, I want to meet it. *Him.*"

"Fair warning. I don't think he eats much."

"Well, half a loaf is better than none." Maylee swatted her arm, but Viv wouldn't have minded if the touch had lasted longer.

~~~

Having Maylee along did more than lift Viv's mood. It also worked a remarkable transformation on Highlark's attitude. Not a single long-suffering sigh passed his lips as he cleaned, examined, and rebound Viv's wounds. Healing appeared to be proceeding well, and the elf administered a new and pungent salve that he said would reduce stiffness and scarring.

As she examined the model skeletons suspended from their metal arms, Viv thought idly of asking if he knew anything about osseoscription, but reconsidered. Instead, she nodded in all the right places, and soon the two of them were back outside his office.

"I should've had you with me from the beginning," said Viv. "I think that's the first time he's treated me like he was getting paid to do this."

"Sourdough loaves," Maylee said in sage tones. "He picks 'em up at least three times a week." She leaned into Viv and said seriously, "Don't mess with your baker."

"Especially when your baker has a mace upstairs."

"Oh, the rollin' pin works just fine, hon."

⁓

"He's out," Viv said flatly as the door to Thistleburr closed behind her.

Satchel regarded her from where he was sweeping the back hallway, his eyes twin blue rings of flame. Fern glanced up from the counter with a start, and a guilty expression stole across her face.

Viv couldn't decide if she was annoyed or not. Did she even have a right to be? She'd assumed they'd talk it over and decide together what to do about him. But it was Fern's shop, and the homunculus—Satchel—wasn't a *thing*.

Still, she felt a prickle of dread. A premonition.

"And you have him *sweeping*? Like some kind of—"

"I tried to stop him," blurted Fern. "I *tried*. I stared at that gods-damned bag all morning. Couldn't keep from looking at it, thinking of him folded up in there, and I just . . . couldn't leave him." She wrung her hands anxiously. "But as soon as he was out and about, he insisted on being useful. Eventually, I gave up trying to get him to relax."

"I'm quite incapable of that," agreed Satchel. He resumed sweeping.

"At least the shades are drawn." Viv sighed. "But I walked right in, and he was the first thing I saw. What if somebody else gets a look at him?"

"Well . . ." Fern said slowly. "What if?"

Viv opened her mouth to reply and then couldn't think of one.

"Right? What are they going to do?" asked Fern.

Still, Viv couldn't bring herself to give up the argument so easily. "What if whoever killed Balthus wanders in? Or somebody like him? What if it's *Varine*?"

Fern made an exasperated noise. "Well, we're fucked anyway at that point, right? What difference does it make? And as long as we keep the bag out of view, nobody else is going to make any connections. All they can do is ask questions we don't have to answer."

Viv looked at Satchel, as though for assistance.

He shrugged.

She couldn't stop a burst of laughter from escaping and tossed up both hands in surrender. "Eight hells. Okay! You win. I guess that means I don't have to put Maylee off meeting him."

Viv made her way to one of the chairs and gently lowered herself into it. Highlark might not have aggressively probed her wound with Maylee around, but it was still tender after the hike into Murk and back, on top of the previous day's activities.

"We have a lot to talk about, though, don't we? I mean . . . ?" She gestured at the sweeping homunculus. "Why don't you sit down, Satchel?"

"If it's all the same to you, m'lady, I have a great deal to do. This place is . . ." He examined the shelves, and somehow managed to look like he was trying to be diplomatic. "Desperately in need of my further attention."

Viv raised her brows at Fern. "Well, he seems to be settling right in."

The door banged open and Gallina trotted inside. "Holy hells, he's out!" she said, in an echo of Viv's entrance. "And he's *sweepin'*?"

"We've already had this conversation," replied Fern, with narrowed eyes. "The housekeeping wasn't my idea."

"Now that we're all here, we have to decide what to do with him though, right?" asked Viv. At Fern's expression, she amended, "Or . . . we have to find out what *he* wants to do. Assuming a necromancer doesn't swoop into town and murder everybody before then."

She caught Satchel's gaze, hoping he'd have a response, but he only looked uncomfortable as he fingered the spines of the books.

"What *do* you want, Satchel? If you could choose?" asked Fern.

The homunculus glanced between them, and the fires of his eyes twirled faster. "It does not matter. I can never be alone. I must always serve a master. There is no other way."

"You don't have to *serve* nobody. We could just, like . . ."

Gallina rubbed two fingers together. "Dust you and let you get on with it. Right?"

Satchel was silent for so long, his broom immobile, that Viv thought he might have seized up, his enchantment somehow halted. But then he slowly replied, "I should like to simply *be* for a while. To . . . serve in the way I choose."

Fern's voice was firm. "Of course. But you don't have to *serve* anybody but yourself. Do you understand?"

He nodded, but Viv wasn't sure that he believed it. Or maybe he just disagreed. At any rate, it wasn't going to do any good to belabor the point.

"Hey, somethin' else you said yesterday," said Gallina. "That guy, Balthus. You said you weren't *all* he stole."

Viv had forgotten about that, and from her expression, Fern had, too.

Satchel bobbed his head but said nothing.

"Well?" prompted Gallina. "What else did he take?"

The homunculus hung his head. "Alas, the Lady's secrets bind me. I cannot say." Then, in an abrupt change of subject, he addressed Fern. "I do so look forward to tidying here. Sorting. Organizing. It gives me *great* peace. I wonder, what do *you* discover when you bring order to things?"

Something about his tone bothered Viv, something plaintive, but he already sounded so eerie that maybe it wasn't worth marking. Still, Satchel *was* regarding one of the bookshelves with strange intensity.

Viv opened her mouth to ask, and—

"Guess that's that then, huh?" said Gallina, clapping her hands to the armrests. "And if Varine does show her face, well . . ." She fingered the knives on her bandolier. "Maybe it won't be so boring around here."

"Let's not tempt the Eight, shall we?" said Fern.

Viv didn't miss the way Satchel stilled at that exchange. His jawbone opened as though he meant to speak, but then it slowly closed, and he turned away.

She watched him thoughtfully, then tilted her staff toward the gnome. "On that note, I'm heading up the bluff to get in a little workout. Are you game?"

Gallina was.

24

Viv's feelings of high alert ebbed slowly over the following days. No invading army of wights appeared on the horizon, and no gray-clad strangers menaced them. In fact, nothing happened to warrant so much as a suspicious glance, much less a bared blade.

In her experience though, things tended to get quiet right before they got loud.

They discovered that Satchel became even more nervous when customers entered the store. Any time the door opened, he collapsed instantly and rolled his component bones underneath one of the shelves, only emerging when Fern reassured him that the intruders were gone.

Potroast also liked to gnaw at his ankles and could not be deterred.

As a result, Satchel mostly kept to his satchel during the day.

Maylee showed up one late afternoon, put her fists on her hips, and demanded, "Well, where is he?"

When Fern sprinkled dust over the bones and Satchel made his rattling appearance, she took it in stride. Viv supposed she shouldn't have been surprised, given her history. When the dwarf extended a hand for the homunculus to shake, Viv couldn't help but think of her long-ago encounter with the goblin across the river.

Fern rigged a box on the countertop with a slit in the front that Satchel could occupy during the day, but for the most part, the homunculus preferred to be up and about outside of business hours. The animating force granted by the bonedust ebbed over the day, and he seemed to sense when it would desert him.

While awake, however, he could not be dissuaded from tidying and arranging, with rag and broom, soap and polish.

"I can't get him to *stop*," Fern said, chin in paw. She looked miserable. "It's not right. I can't let him just . . . *do* things around here without paying him." She dropped her voice to a whisper. "He insists he doesn't want anything. That it's his *choice*. But that doesn't make it any better."

Thistleburr was definitely tidier. The wooden floors fairly glowed, the walls had been washed, and Viv could swear that Satchel must have trimmed away the errant binding threads on some of the older volumes. Even the scent indoors was improved, smelling more strongly of paper and ink and wood wax than dust and salt and gryphet.

"Maybe you need to start lending him books, too," said Viv, only half joking.

"Does he read, do you think?" she asked, glancing toward the box on the counter, currently occupied.

"He has a better vocabulary than I do." Viv unwrapped another of Maylee's brown paper packages. Four enormous, rugged scones lay tucked within, larded with nuts and fruit. The gryphet napping on the floor twitched in his sleep and uttered a drowsy hoot but didn't wake.

Fern selected one and nibbled at it as they watched Addis, the gnome who owned the perpetually closed junk shop, ambling slowly beside a shelf. Addis was a serial browser, and Viv had never once seen him purchase a book. He muttered a lot to himself and often selected a volume, only to open it, nod as though discovering some important bit of information, and then reshelve it. Viv found it maddening, but Fern seemed used to it.

"Must not be any silver in the junk business," muttered Viv as Addis rejected yet another book.

"Speaking of a lack of money, did I tell you I finally ordered that fresh shipment?"

"The one you'd been marking in the catalog?"

Fern sighed. "I guess I forgot to mention it. Although there's been an awful lot going on these past few days." She knocked gently on the top of Satchel's box, and a very quiet bump echoed back from within.

Viv leaned more heavily on the counter, extending her leg and flexing it. It was sturdier by the day. "I thought you said you didn't have the room? Satch—Uh, I mean it's definitely more organized, but where are you going to put the new books?"

"I suppose I'll have to stack them in the back. I can barely get to my bed as it is, though. There are old books *everywhere*. I live under threat of perpetual landslide. Still, I have to try something. I'm doing a little better financially, but if I can't get things to pick up . . ."

"It'd be best if you could sell the old ones though, wouldn't it?"

Fern stopped with her scone halfway to her mouth. "My, what a brilliant fucking idea. Whyever didn't I consider that? Thanks."

"If there are that many books people don't *want*, though, then what's the use in having them around?"

"They're *books*. You don't just *throw them away*."

"I didn't say that! But . . . I mean, if nobody wants them, then . . ."

"They just don't know they want them yet. That's the point. How many have *you* been through now?"

"Well . . ."

"Plenty, that's how many. I just had to get them into your hands. The *right* hands." She put the scone down. "That's the whole gods-damned problem, isn't it?"

Viv considered the unfolded brown paper and the remaining scone waiting atop it. Toying with the string, she murmured, "Yeah, I guess the thing is not knowing what you want. Having to pick it in the first place, when you don't know what's out there . . ."

The rattkin searched her face. "Sure. But some folks don't want to be led. And sometimes, I don't know what they want either. A *lot* of the time, honestly." She cocked a thumb at Addis. "Like *this* one, for instance."

"Well," continued Viv, an idea firming in her mind, "what if they didn't have to know? Or at least, not much?"

"What are you getting at?"

"We didn't know what we'd be getting in this package from Maylee. We might not have picked these at all. But we're eating them, aren't we?"

The rattkin retrieved her scone and examined it thoughtfully. "Go on . . ."

"And the surprise is part of it too, right?" Viv ate one in two quick bites. "It's almost better because we didn't know. So—"

"So what if we wrapped up the books?"

"Yeah. Doesn't have to be fancy."

"Maybe more than one." Fern's eyes lit up as the idea took root in her mind. "Tie them up with string. Like little presents."

"Maybe write a few words on there. Give people some idea of what they're in for." Viv thought about *Ten Links in the Chain.* "Swordfights. Beheadings. Betrayals?"

"Mmm. Maybe *moist,*" suggested Fern with a wicked grin.

Viv laughed aloud. "Wonder how many of those you'd sell? Maybe you should put that on *every* package."

Addis exited the shop without so much as a wave, the door banging shut behind him.

"Bye, Addis!" Fern called after him.

Viv shook her head in annoyance.

From within the box on the counter, Satchel's sepulchral voice issued, brimming with sudden interest.

"Moist books?"

~⌒~

"Use the heels of your hands."

"It's sticky," grumbled Viv, trying to shuck globs of dough from around her knuckles.

"That's why you can't use your fingers," said Maylee, with a laugh buried in her voice. "Yeah, that's the way. Now fold it over and do it again. Keep it up. You got the arms for it."

Sea-Song was locked tight for the day, but according to Maylee, there was still plenty to be done. Viv had offered to lend a hand, with the vague notion that this might mean scrubbing or sweeping or something equally straightforward. The dwarf, however, had other ideas.

She looked at Maylee askance as the shorter woman

sprinkled flour in front of the ball of dough in an easy arc. "Are you trying to domesticate me?"

"You said you wanted to help, and I've got bread to bake. Besides, you seem to be domesticatin' yourself just fine at Fern's place."

Her tone was teasing, but the words made Viv tense, like she expected a manacle to snap onto her wrist. A ridiculous reaction, she knew, and yet she couldn't help but infer something hopeful in Maylee's gaze.

"That's different."

"Oh, yeah? How d'you figure that?"

"Well," said Viv, grunting as she folded the dough and pressed into it. The countertops were built for dwarven stature, and she had to really hunch to bring her weight to bear. "I *did* get tossed in jail over a street fight, there's been at least one dead body, and we have a talking bagful of bones, so I think there's a lot more adventuring going on than you'd expect."

"You seem to be gettin' a lot of aggression out on that poor dough, too. Though maybe it's just you. Either way, flour looks good on you." She tossed a playful pinch.

Viv bared her teeth in a mock growl, only to get a faceful.

"D'you figure he's goin' to bring trouble?" asked Maylee, suddenly serious.

"Satchel?"

She nodded, then touched Viv's hip to move her to the side, taking over kneading the dough. The easy press and release of her hands and the sway of her body were unexpectedly sensual.

Viv tried not to stare.

Dusting flour from her arms, she parked her butt against the counter. "Honestly? Yeah. I do."

The dwarf sighed. "So do I. I've just got that feelin'."

Viv knew exactly the one she meant. Like the sound of a battle three hills over.

She was reminded that Maylee wrestled dough with hands that had once wielded a mace. There was some safety in that which Viv couldn't untangle just yet.

Maylee stopped kneading and gave her a searching look. "That doesn't really upset you, does it?"

"I don't want anybody to get hurt," Viv hedged. But that wasn't really an answer at all.

~

A galleon from the far south was anchored in the deeper waters offshore, and small boats had been ferrying passengers, merchants, and crew members to the beach throughout the late afternoon. Coaches rattled in both directions along the southern road to Cardus. As a result, it was one of The Perch's livelier nights.

Viv was comfortable enough on her leg to be seated at the bar. Her favorite table was occupied anyway. She nursed a second beer while she tried not to race through the last three chapters of *The Lens and the Dapplegrim*. Brand was a blur beyond her vision, and the noise piled up against the walls, leaving her alone in the center of a perfect sphere of story. Each word tumbled into the next, a rockslide of prose that would end in a dramatic confrontation between Investigator Beckett and the deliciously devious Aramy, with Leena's life in the balance. At least that's where she *expected* things to go. The book had a way of confounding her expectations, and every time it did, she experienced a thrill of delight.

When someone sat down beside her at the bar, she paid them no mind, absorbed as she was.

As she recognized her neighbor, though, the raucous sound crashed back in on Viv, and she found herself fully, instantly present.

"I'll confess, I didn't imagine you were the literary sort." The voice was husky, dryly amused.

Iridia.

Viv did her best not to sigh in annoyance, marking her place with a thumb.

The woman tapped the bar-top and nodded at Brand for a drink. She was perfectly at ease. Her longsword was still belted at her waist, lantern on the opposite hip. Viv didn't think it looked very comfortable.

Iridia downed a swallow of her beer before eyeing Viv. "I see you're on the mend. I expect you'll be off soon, then."

"When Rackam returns, yeah," said Viv evenly. "No idea when that will be. I guess you're stuck with me until he shows up."

The tapenti silently considered her.

Viv waited for something further, and when no words seemed forthcoming, she ventured, "What do you want? I was just minding my business. Being *literary*. That ought to make you happy, right?"

Iridia ignored the question. "Varine. Have you seen her?"

Viv blinked. "No. Plenty of her spawn, but never her."

"Would you even know her if you saw her?"

Viv took another slug of her beer. "I've got a description, but even if I didn't, I think I'd know."

"And why is that?" Iridia's tone was hardly warm, but it wasn't as antagonistic as it had been during their prior interactions.

Viv studied her. "What are you after? You don't like me much, you made that plain. So what is this?"

The tapenti sighed. "I don't dislike you. I dislike what you *mean.*" She tapped her mug with a finger. "To be clear, that doesn't mean I like you either."

Viv snorted at that and raised her mug. Iridia cocked a brow and clinked hers against it.

"To annoyed mutual tolerance," said Viv.

It's possible the tapenti's lip might have curled in a smile, but Viv couldn't be positive.

After another drink, something shifted in the Gatewarden's posture. The scaled flesh of her hood relaxed, and she swept the long, dry threads of her hair to the side.

"We've found nothing on whoever murdered our gray-clad stranger."

Viv almost blurted his name but caught herself in time. There was no easy way to explain how she knew it.

"Oh, yeah? I guess I'm not surprised." Then, carefully, "Did you find that bag you were looking for?"

"No." Iridia toyed with her cup. "I pride myself on my practicality. Adaptability. Too many Wardens are set in their ways. Authority gives them an excuse to be lazy."

"And to hassle wounded mercenaries minding their own business?" Viv grinned wryly.

"Oh, no, that's just good sense," said Iridia, and Viv was pretty sure she was joking. Maybe. The tapenti continued, "I told you I'd take Varine seriously, and I have. But maybe not seriously enough, because I realized I haven't spoken to the one person who has recent information."

Iridia actually reminded Viv a little of Madger from *Ten Links in the Chain*, but without Legann's balancing influence. Grudgingly, she admitted to herself that she might not actually dislike the tapenti.

But to be clear, that doesn't mean I like you, *either,* she thought, echoing the Gatewarden's own words.

"Brand," called Iridia, catching the tavernkeep's attention. "Her drinks are on me."

She rested an arm on the counter. "So, I'm here to rectify that. I want to know everything you know. Are you willing to talk?"

Viv drained her mug and set it back on the bar. "I won't even make you buy me dinner."

25

The sign hanging from the handle of Thistleburr's red door read CLOSED. Viv couldn't remember ever seeing it before. She tried to peer through the glare on the windows, but the curtains were drawn. She knocked and called out, "Fern? Are you in there?"

Potroast's answering bark came first. The curtains twitched aside, and then Viv heard the latch being thrown. The door opened inward, and Fern appeared in the gap, clad in a filthy smock, her fur haloed in dust.

"What in the—" began Viv, but Fern ushered her in with an impatient paw.

The shop looked like the victim of a very localized, very selective earthquake.

Most of the shelves were bare, although a few lonely volumes still leaned against one another on some of them, like drunks past midnight. The rest tottered in stacks and small mountains everywhere else.

Satchel stood amongst the wreckage, a tuft of fluff clinging to one horn, the flames of his eyes swirling blue. He clutched a large sheet of brown paper, torn along one edge. A spool of twine sat tilted in his pelvis, the location of which made Viv strangely uncomfortable.

Potroast trotted anxiously between the stacks, sniffing and whimpering, and spared Viv a distracted hoot of indignation.

From a small pile near the door, Fern seized a book-sized parcel wrapped in twine. Scrawled across the front in dark ink were the words TRAVEL, ROMANCE, and HEARTBREAK. "We're going to make some gods-damned *room*," she said fiercely.

"You can't be doing that with *all* of them, though," said Viv, staring around the shop in bewilderment.

"No, but this is the perfect time to reorganize. When the shipment arrives, we'll be ready."

Viv looked doubtful. "I think it's a great idea and all, but how many of these do you actually think you can sell?" She picked up another parcel from the stack, this one marked ADVENTURE, BOUNTIES, and BLOODSHED. Actually, that sounded pretty good. She was seized by an impulse to open it. *That* was promising, anyway.

"Well, Satchel and I were talking," said Fern, hustling back to sort through some of the piles. She checked the titles, sometimes opening them to flick through the first few pages, and then arranged them using an incomprehensible system known only to her.

"You were?"

"Indeed, m'lady," replied Satchel.

Fern handed him three volumes, and the homunculus bent over the side table, which had been requisitioned as a workstation. With deft folds, he wrapped the stack, withdrew a length of twine, and snapped it with his bony fingertips. Then he swiftly tied the package with a tidy bow.

Fern's eyes sparkled with more energy than Viv recalled ever

seeing. "A boardwalk sale. Right outside. There's another passenger vessel due in two days. We'll lay out tables, spread these
across them, and see how many we can get into willing hands.
And what we don't?" She shrugged. "I guess we'll pile them out
of the way, like you said."

Viv thought Fern might be overestimating how many she'd
be able to offload, but the rattkin's mood was so high, her
expression so *hopeful*, that she didn't have the heart to dampen
her spirits.

"So," she said at last, feeling like a giant towering over tiny
buildings of words, fearful of where to tread. "What can I do
to help?"

Fern held up an inkwell and pen. "How's your handwriting?"

⌒⌒

They worked together companionably for most of the day.
Fern fretted over what to package up and began the process of
reshelving volumes that were to remain in the shop. Satchel
tirelessly wrapped the books she passed his way, and at Fern's
direction, Viv inked the paper with two or three words evoking
the stories bound within.

"So, Satchel," said Viv, squinting as she blocked in another
letter, fingertips black with ink. "How long, exactly, have you
been, uh . . ." She deliberated over the right word. "Alive?"

The homunculus gently detached Potroast, who was attempt-
ing to remove one of his fibulae. "I couldn't say, m'lady. I
have—"

"'Viv' is fine, Satchel."

After a brief hesitation, the homunculus said, "Yes, m'lady
Viv. I have seen much, but I cannot track the time when I am
away. There is no way for me to know."

"But Varine created you, didn't she?"

Fern paused what she was doing to listen as well.

Satchel appeared to think about that, as though trying to decide whether an answer constituted breaking the covenant he was bound by. "She did."

"So you're not older than her."

"And how old is that?" asked Fern.

It was Viv's turn to pause. "Hells, I have no idea. I guess being a necromancer makes that harder to answer. And that probably counts as one of your Lady's secrets. I bet you can't tell us either."

Satchel shook his head apologetically.

"You said you've seen *much*, though?" prompted Fern.

"Oh my, yes." His hollow voice took on a wistful tone as he tied off another bow. "Many wonders. Perfect beauties. Great seas set aflame by sunsets. Endless underground lakes in soundless caverns. The winter light on mountain snow that has never thawed." He sobered. "And much that I would forget, were I able."

"Satchel, you have the soul of a poet," murmured Fern.

"So, what did you actually *do* for her?" asked Viv. "Is that something you can say?"

"I served," replied Satchel. "In whatever way the Lady required."

"I'm guessing you didn't sweep and dust, though, am I right? Probably weren't wrapping packages?"

When the homunculus replied, his echoing voice sounded even farther away, a mournful wind in a sea cave. "I did not."

Fern wasn't sorting books anymore. She dusted her paws on her smock and regarded Satchel with a pained expression. "I asked once before, but if you *could* do what you wanted—anything—and you didn't have to worry about Varine—your Lady—what would that be?"

He wound a fresh length of twine around a package, tying it off more deliberately. He stared down at his phalanges splayed across the paper.

"I cannot speak against the Lady," he said. And then would say no more.

～

"What in the hells?" said Fern.

Viv glanced up from blowing on fresh ink. Her hands were cramping, and she'd blocked in about as many words as she could stand. Behind her towered neat stacks of paper-wrapped parcels. "What is it?"

"This book," said Fern. "It was wedged in the back. This isn't *mine*. I wonder—"

"Don't open it, m'lady!" cried Satchel, whirling toward the rattkin, his bony hands outstretched. The spool of thread flew from his pelvis and unrolled across the floor. "I beg of you!"

His tone was so plaintive that Fern stopped in the act of doing just that. The book was exceptionally large, half again the size of most of those in the shop. A real tome. "What—?"

"It is *not* one of your books," said Satchel. "It is . . . it is—" His voice became strangled, choked by a growing distance, as though he were being dragged into a tunnel.

An image of Balthus, his hands falling away from the shelves, sprang to Viv's mind.

"It's one of *hers*," she said, rising to her feet, thigh thrumming as blood rushed to it after so long spent in the same position.

"Varine's?" whispered Fern.

When Satchel didn't correct her, Viv said, "Balthus. He hid it here. I wondered why in the hells he'd been in your shop." She held out a hand for the book. "If there's someone in this room who should be dealing with unholy necromancer nonsense, it's me. May I?"

Fern narrowed her eyes. "Didn't you get stabbed and dumped in this town because of unholy necromancer nonsense?"

"Yeah. But I survived, didn't I?"

The rattkin looked like she wanted to argue the point, but she handed the tome over.

It was much heavier than it looked. And it looked heavy.

Viv expected the book to be ancient, some derelict grimoire of forbidden knowledge, but the black leather cover seemed almost new. No text graced the surface, although tiny embossing wreathed the edges. The patterns reminded her of the fine inscriptions on Satchel's bones. The edges of the pages gleamed a gold-flecked red.

And she could smell it. In her hands, that blood-in-snow scent wafted up from the leather. An involuntary shiver scurried up her arms.

"Yeah," she breathed. "Satchel said Balthus stole something else, and this is definitely it." She looked to the homunculus. "I'm right, aren't I? Now that it's in my hands, there's no secret to protect, is there?"

"It is hers," managed Satchel, although his voice remained weak.

"What happens if I open it?"

He tried to respond, jaw quivering, but again, he seemed incapable.

Viv ran a finger along the edge of the leather binding. It felt wet and slick, like a cave wall beaded with moisture from a dampness deep within.

"Fuck it," she said, and flipped back the cover.

~

The page was black.

Not inked black. Not blank. But *darkness* itself. It absolutely devoured light. A tiny margin of creamy paper bordered the null space. Viv thought she felt the faint kiss of wind on her face, and the smell of lightning strikes.

"Fuck!" cried Fern. "You just *opened* it? You're all right, aren't you? No . . . necromancer nonsense?"

"Oh, there's necromancer nonsense all right." Viv glanced at Satchel, who was wringing his bony hands in dismay.

She hovered an index finger over the blackness, but couldn't bring herself to touch it. The air above the page was *cold*, an icy breath radiating from the paper.

Carefully, Viv peeled the page up by its thin margin and turned to the next.

Another black page. And then another. And another. Hundreds. At the bottom of each, an inked number, increasing in sequence, just like any other book.

"Well?" Fern's voice pitched even higher in anxiety.

Viv shook her head. "I don't know." She carefully carried the book over to the side table and cleared the paper from the surface with a sweep of her forearm.

She gently laid the tome open upon the tabletop and stepped back.

"Gods," breathed Fern, edging toward it.

Viv thought she could hear a sound emanating from the impossible night of that page, the chime of a glass sharply struck. "Hang on," she said. She snatched the pen from the inkwell, knocking off the excess ink.

Satchel continued to observe but didn't try to stop them. Not yet, anyway. Viv took that as a positive sign.

She flipped the pen in her grip, feather down, and dipped it toward the page.

The feather disappeared into the blackness as though it were a pool of ink from which no light could reflect.

Fern covered her mouth with both paws, and Viv withdrew the pen.

It was whole, and unmarred.

"Well, that's the first test done," said Viv.

"The *first* test?" protested Fern. "What's the second—"

Viv set aside the pen and opened and closed her right hand. Then, thinking better of it, she shook her head.

"Oh thank fuck," said Fern. "I thought you were going to put your hand—"

The rattkin squeaked shrilly as Viv drove her left arm into the blackness of the page, all the way up to the elbow, and drew it back out, fast.

Flexing her fingers and staring at the book in wonder, Viv finished, "That's the second."

Fern sputtered, waving her paws in apoplexy, and if she ever regained her composure, Viv figured the language would be pretty spectacular.

26

"I touched something," said Viv. "There's stuff *in* there." She'd done no more than brush a surface with her fingertips, a cold and unyielding object.

Fern approached the book again to stare warily into the darkness of the page, as though something might burst from within and drag her inside. "They're portals," she said. "*Hundreds* of them." She dipped a finger into the blackness and withdrew it with a shiver. "It's like icy water."

"That's right, isn't it, Satchel? This is some kind of storage?" asked Viv.

Satchel nodded miserably. "Yes, m'lady Viv."

"I guess once we know her secrets you don't have to keep them anymore, huh?" Viv began to appreciate the scale of what the book might contain, and her eyes widened. "What's Varine *keeping* in all of these? Eight hells, she has to be furious."

The homunculus remained tellingly mum on the subject.

"I've heard about objects like this, but I never thought I'd see one," said Fern. "And so many pages!"

Flipping a few, Viv sank her left hand in again. Fern tensed, but didn't object this time. The rattkin was right; it was like

submerging her arm in icy water. Subtle currents licked at
her skin, and Viv broke out in gooseflesh all the way to her
neck.

She carefully quested around the edges, finding the borders
of the space, like walls of ice that her fingernails skittered
across. Holding her breath, she pushed deeper and found what
was stored within.

It was moist, fleshy, slick with viscous fluid. She recoiled
immediately, yanking her arm back. She stared at her fingertips, expecting to see them smeared with blood or something
worse. They were clean, though.

"Not that page," she said with a shiver, as her imagination
supplied an idea of what *precisely* a necromancer might want
to store for later use.

Turning to the next, she tried again and was relieved to
touch an object she thought she recognized. Dozens of them,
in fact. Coins? Pinching one, she felt writing against her fingertips, letters or sigils in sharp relief. But when she began to withdraw it, the coin bit into her flesh like razors, and she released
it with a yelp. Pulling free, she found a network of fine cuts
lacing her thumb and forefinger.

"Shit." She moved to suck the oozing blood, but thought
better of that and wiped her hand on her trousers instead.

"Satchel." Fern grasped his ulna. "There's not . . . not anything *living* in these, is there?"

Viv stopped with her hand hovering just above another
page, mouth hanging open. "Okay, that's a question I probably
should've thought to ask."

"Nothing living can survive for long in the underspace," he
replied. "But that does not mean there are no dangers stored
within. Be wary."

"Can't survive for *long*? You mean if I put my arm—"

"A few moments will not harm you," said Satchel, and Viv relaxed. "Not permanently, anyway," he finished.

"Hells with it. One more," said Viv, darting her hand into a fresh page. And this time, what she found made her smile immediately. "Now *this* I recognize."

Her fingers traced a pommel and slipped around a leather-wrapped hilt that fit her palm so well, it might have been made just for her. Tightening her grip, she felt momentary resistance, as though the weapon was lodged in a thin scrim of ice. She imagined she could hear the grinding snap as it broke free and she hauled it smoothly into the open, foot by foot, until she held it before her in both hands.

A greatsword, broad and gleaming. As cold shed from the steel with a frosty keening in the warmth of the room, moisture beaded on the blade and ran down into the fuller.

Viv stared in awe, and a thrill of recognition passed through her, like a scent from childhood. "Gods," she breathed, turning it to catch the light. The forging was exquisite, the balance superb. She ran a thumb appreciatively down the flat of the blade.

She glanced at Fern, who eyed it with a worried expression, and then at Satchel, who was hunched over again in that hunted posture.

Her stomach twisted. "What?" she asked, lowering the blade and taking a step back.

Suddenly, the surface of the page seemed to ripple. It should have been impossible to detect, since no light reflected from it, but still, it could be perceived, a vibration that matched a low thrum issuing from the void, like a horn sounding in a distant valley.

"What was that?" asked Fern, whiskers twitching nervously.

Satchel sighed, a feat he accomplished even without lungs. "The Lady's warning. She knows when something is withdrawn. The book calls to her."

"Why didn't you say so?" cried Viv, but when he gazed back at her with those cold blue eyes, the answer was obvious.

"He has to protect the Lady's secrets," whispered Fern, then shouted, "Put it the fuck back!"

An avaricious flinch made Viv's grip tighten on the hilt, and light seemed to drip along the keen edge of the blade, like sap down a tree trunk. "I don't think that's going to help any," she protested.

"Maybe not, but what if it's cursed, or . . . or . . . I don't know. Evil?"

Viv snorted. "It's a sword. A damned *good* sword." But really, she didn't want to admit how much the blade called to her, how very *right* it felt in her hands, and how loath she was to part with it. Besides, there was a more pressing issue, as far as she was concerned. "What we *should* be worried about is the book. Can she find this, Satchel? Can she tell where it *is?*"

"I cannot—"

"You cannot say," sighed Viv. "Yeah, that sounds like a solid *maybe* to me."

"We could destroy it?" suggested Fern. "Although the idea of burning a book . . . even *this* one . . ."

"You must *not,*" said Satchel, his hollow voice suddenly booming. The inscriptions along his bones bloomed with blue light, which faded almost as soon as it had appeared.

They both startled at the force of his admonition and shared a worried glance.

"Besides," said Viv, "imagine what else might be in there.

When Rackam and the rest do away with Varine . . ." She trailed off. "Maybe money wouldn't be a problem anymore for your bookshop, you know?"

Fern wrinkled her nose and looked thoughtful at the same time. Viv could tell she was considering it. The rattkin surveyed the shambles of the shop's interior: the stacked books, the wrapped parcels, the barely filled shelves. She dropped her paws to her sides, and exhaustion seemed to suddenly overcome her. "What do we do with it, though? We can't keep the gods-damned thing *here* and hope that nothing goes wrong. Not now."

Viv reluctantly admitted, "There's really only one thing that make sense."

~

"It's Varine's?" asked Iridia, examining the book with narrowed eyes. She ran her finely scaled hand across the surface, feeling the tracery of glyphs at the edges.

"Our mysterious stranger hid it in the bookshop. I think he stole it from her."

"And you know this how?"

Viv flipped back the cover. Iridia calmly regarded the exposed black page.

"They're portals to an underspace," she said. "Like a treasure vault, or something."

Viv dipped a hand into the blackness and immediately pulled it back out.

The tapenti hissed an indrawn breath and glanced sharply at the orc. "An *underspace?*"

"That's what Fern called it. She, uh, reads about this sort

of thing. There are hundreds of them." Viv turned the pages. "They contain, um . . . various things."

"A fascinating object. Undoubtedly valuable. And yet I don't see how you can be sure it's *hers*."

"No chance I can convince you that I can tell by the smell?" Iridia chuckled throatily.

Viv didn't take that as an affirmative. She scratched the back of her neck. "Look, I might have pulled something out, and then . . . well, I think there's a sort of alarm? It's *possible* Varine may know I took something, and, uh, maybe even where it is right now. Potentially. *Maybe*."

"And what *did* you take from it?"

"Nothing she needs." She hurried onward. "Anyway, I figured the best thing for it was to keep the book someplace protected." She met Iridia's gaze steadily. "Maybe locked up here."

"So what you're saying is that you'd like to store a potentially dangerous object, which is of immense value to an even more dangerous necromancer, here. In my offices."

Viv shrugged uncomfortably. "Yeah. Yeah, I guess so."

Iridia smiled thinly. She slid the book off the desk and weighed it in both hands. "I do so look forward to your eventual departure."

~✄

The greatsword was impossible to hide when Viv pushed her way into The Perch that evening. With no way to sling it over her back, she held all six feet of it point down before her, hoping to make her way swiftly up the stairs.

"Holy hells!" cried Gallina, immediately scuppering those plans. "Where'd *that* come from?"

"It's, uh . . ." Viv realized she should have come up with an explanation for the sword's provenance ahead of time. "I . . . bought . . . it?" she finished lamely. And entirely unconvincingly.

Brand watched her with interest as well. "Hm. Greatsword, eh? Feeling under-armed?" he asked.

Viv tried to smile, but it felt like a grimace and probably looked about the same. "Really done in for the day. Just going to head up to my room."

She limped up the stairs, tucking the blade under her arm, and hurried to her room, where she closed the door firmly behind her. A damp sea breeze filtered through the narrow window, laced with the sulfurous smell of seaweed.

She laid the greatsword atop the leather straps of the empty bedframe, lit the lantern, and stepped back to examine the blade.

The steel glimmered along its flawless length, clean and perfect, not so much as a nick or notch to mar the edges. The leather wrapping on the hilt might have been bound and shrunk yesterday, and a beautiful but substantial silver ring formed the pommel.

Viv immediately wanted it in her hands again.

She probed her thigh, testing the receding ache there. Had Rackam cornered Varine the Pale yet? Was he still alive? Was *she*? The signal from the book strongly implied she was.

Impatience swelled in her breast. She'd been reading and idling away her days, with nothing but a little indifferent training to keep her reflexes afloat.

Murk seemed to have a sleepy power over her, a seductive song of indolence.

She'd almost let it claim her. Sure, she had to bide her time and heal. And there was no harm in wringing a little enjoyment out of her forced recovery. She thought guiltily of Maylee. *Or a little companionship*, she added mentally.

But her time in Murk must draw to an end. And she needed to be ready when it did.

27

The sky threatened rain all the following day. Viv made a perfunctory visit to Thistleburr but didn't stay. Fern was busy shelving the last of the remaining books and fussing over the wrapped packages, and there wasn't much that Viv could help with anyway. She relayed what she'd done with Varine's book, and Fern seemed caught between anxiety and relief, but the tasks of the day outweighed either in the end.

Viv and Maylee had planned an outing, which had been a pleasant prospect until she'd drawn forth the greatsword. She tried to recapture her anticipation as she knocked on the door of Sea-Song.

They shared a leisurely walk along the beach. Maylee traced a finger up and down Viv's forearm in a very distracting way, and Viv described the plan she and Fern had hatched to find homes for the surplus books.

"Thanks to your baking," she said. Viv gave Maylee's hand a squeeze.

"Everythin' good is thanks to bakin'," Maylee replied with conviction.

As they strolled, Maylee talked about old friends and

adventures past, and Viv laughed and nodded when it was expected. But more and more, her thoughts returned to the blade on her bedframe, drawn as if by a deadly lodestone. Her steps kept speeding up, as though she wanted the walk over and done with so she could get back. Viv had to rein herself in several times.

When they parted, Viv could tell from the bruised smile on Maylee's face that she'd noticed, and a spasm of guilt seized her.

It didn't stop her from hurrying back to her room though.

Behind The Perch and out of view of prying eyes, Viv hefted the greatsword, turning it in the silvery overcast light. The weight of it made the muscles of her arms and shoulders strain in a deeply satisfying way. She felt firm and hard and full of purpose, and when she executed the very different practice forms suited to the larger weapon, it was as though she'd wielded the blade all her life.

Any ache in her leg was forgotten. It wasn't fully healed, not by a long shot, but it didn't plague her in the slightest. As she completed a diagonal chop, the metal sighing through the air, a surprised laugh escaped her lips.

The steel seemed drawn by inexorable purpose, tracing a pathway that led back toward the Ravens. Toward where she truly belonged.

She felt the grin transform her face, a savage, joyful baring of fangs. Sweat pooled in her clavicle and flew from her forearms as she snapped the blade back and up.

Gods, it felt good.

~~~

On the day of Fern's boardwalk sale, Viv descended the front steps of The Perch feeling more herself than she had in days. Her shoulders were tight from the bladework, but it would pass soon, she could tell. The rain that had seemed imminent yesterday was nowhere to be seen, the clouds torn up into ragged white ribbons.

She made her way out of the valley of dunes and seagrass leading from The Perch. Drawing near the bookshop, she was surprised to find Pitts setting up four trestles out front. His wagon waited nearby, loaded with a stack of long planks.

As she approached, Pitts nodded and returned to the cart. He slid out four planks together and easily hoisted them onto one scarred shoulder, then set them across the top of one pair of trestles side by side, forming a rough tabletop.

"Here, I'll grab these," said Viv. She matched him, retrieving the other four to assemble a second table. It felt good to easily handle physical work that only a week ago would've had her leg folding underneath her.

"Thanks, Pitts." Fern stepped out onto the boardwalk, and Potroast trotted behind her, his arrow of a pink tongue lolling out of his beak. He didn't even growl at Viv, for once.

The rattkin clapped her paws together, her eyes gleaming with anticipation. "Let's get to it then, shall we?"

"You're roped into this too, huh?" Viv asked Pitts.

He shrugged. "Got a little exchange worked out. A couple of things just for me in the next shipment."

"More poetry?"

Pitts studied her with a small, calm smile. Then he recited, "A worthy hand at patient rest. An endurance of moments. Contentment blossoms there."

Viv nearly offered a teasing response, but her mind caught up with his words. Instead, she frowned at Fern. "How come you haven't tried me out on any poetry yet?"

"I was just waiting for you to get all contemplative on me. You have to approach these things delicately," replied Fern. "Now's not the time for delicacy, though. We've got a load of these packages to shift outside, and the passenger ship arrives in a few hours."

"Yes, m'lady," said Viv, imitating Satchel's solemn tone.

Fern brought a paw to her mouth to suppress a laugh, and Pitts gave her a quizzical look but didn't say anything.

As they stood surveying the two tables and orderly ranks of neatly wrapped book bundles, Fern clapped a paw to her forehead. "Shit! I almost forgot!"

She hurried into the shop and returned struggling under the weight of a chalk sandwich board. Printed on both sides in white chalk were the words . . .

mystery
book
sale

. . . with a neat arrow beneath.

"I need to get this down to the beach," she panted.

Potroast hooted supportively.

Viv went to relieve her of it, but Pitts beat her to it.

"Got to head that way anyway," he said, taking the sign easily with one hand and carrying it over to his cart. "I'll set it up. Good luck to you."

With a wave, he stepped into the traces of his cart and got moving, heading downslope.

"Well," said Fern, fiddling with her clasp. "I guess . . . now we wait?"

"I'm sure it'll be fine," said Viv, although she wasn't sure. Not exactly.

~

The frigate debarked close to noon, and for the hour afterward they waited. And waited.

And waited.

"Oh hells, this isn't going to work, is it?" fretted Fern. "They're off the boat by now. *Fuck.*" She plucked nervously at the twine bow of a package that read FAMILY, BUSINESS and DWARVEN POLITICS.

"Give it a little time," said Viv, although she worried Fern was correct. "Anybody coming ashore probably had things to take care of first. Lodgings. Food. You know . . . stuff."

"Maybe you're right," replied Fern, but she didn't sound convinced.

Then, in the distance, a few scattered figures appeared. Fern shaded her eyes and watched anxiously, but they turned into Sea-Song. "Oh," she murmured, and it broke Viv's heart a little to see the slump of her shoulders.

When the figures reemerged later, though, they continued up the slope, angling in their direction. Viv was worried the couple—a pair of stone-fey in finely cut clothing—would pass right on by for The Perch, but they approached the tables with interest.

"A mystery book sale?" inquired the lady, whose white hair was pinned in high coils. "I've never heard of such a thing."

"Well," said Fern, her words tumbling out fast. "I've selected several books that fit a theme and gathered them together. And we've hinted at what's inside but . . . well, it's a sort of surprise."

The gentleman hefted one of the packages, his thin brows rising as he scanned the words inked on the paper. "Why wouldn't I select them myself?" he asked doubtfully.

"Because she's a genius at picking them," said Viv, leaning against a boardwalk pillar with her arms crossed. "Never steered me wrong yet. Besides, everybody likes a surprise, right?"

"And you won't find a better deal," added Fern. "Only thirty bits for three books." Her whiskers twitched with nervousness. Even if Viv was pretending to be at ease, she shared the feeling.

"*Knitting, murder,* and *wine,*" said the lady. And then she laughed. "Well, that sounds delightful, doesn't it, Fellan?"

"Mmm," he replied noncommittally as he moved to examine another package.

"Oh, hush. I'd like this one." The lady smiled at Fern as she held it up. "We've got a four-day journey north to Stellacia after this stop, all the way around the cape. I nearly went mad with boredom on the previous leg. I won't say I'm desperate, but it's a near thing."

"Knowing what's in that one, I don't think you'll be disappointed," said Fern, as the lady nudged her companion for their purse.

"*Treason, clockwork,* and *horticulture?*" said the gentleman, blinking at the bundle he held.

Then a dwarf edged in beside him, examining the table as he tugged on one side of an enormous walrus mustache.

As Fern chattered animatedly with the lady, Viv grinned and

stepped up to address the dwarf, forgetting about greatswords and necromancers and Rackam for a while.

She might have only hitched along on this wagon for a few weeks, but there was no reason not to get out and push.

And that was the beginning of a very full day.

28

The procession of customers and the curious wasn't exactly steady, ebbing and flowing as the sun tracked across the sky, but it never faltered for terribly long. Some bought, some just browsed, but the stacks of packages were slowly nibbled away.

It was clear they were getting more than the passengers from the frigate, as Fern greeted some folk by name. Viv supposed word must have spread, and to be honest, what else was there to do in Murk? Novelty was novelty.

A few hours in, Maylee appeared with a large basket of lassy buns. Her skinny assistant hauled another in her wake.

The dwarf grinned at Viv as she set the basket on the end of one of the tables while Fern scrambled to make room, a look of distracted confusion on her face. The scent of molasses and ginger wafted through the air.

"Thought I'd donate a little somethin' to the cause," said Maylee, before the rattkin could ask. She surveyed the tables of wrapped books. "I figure nothin' predisposes people to stop and look like their stomachs."

Fern stared back at the dwarf, dumbstruck, until Viv mumbled, "I, uh, *may* have said something about your plan."

"I . . . *thank you*," said Fern, as Maylee's assistant shoved her own basket in beside it.

"Don't mention it, hon." Maylee winked at her. "I've got this real fine book on gnomish pastries that I think you might've had a hand in." She squeezed Viv around the hips. "Only fair to return the favor."

"Thanks," whispered Viv, feeling another stab of guilt. She could still picture Maylee's hurt expression after Viv's obvious distraction during their last walk.

"You bet, hon," said the dwarf, although she didn't meet her eyes.

Viv was in the process of formulating some kind of stealthy apology when a voice piped up from the far table.

"Spicy? *Moist?*" Gallina held a parcel at arm's length with a bemused look on her face.

"You *didn't* put that on there!" exclaimed Fern, with a sharp look at Viv.

Viv shrugged. "I think you said I should write 'passionate' and 'love,' but I thought it was worth the experiment."

"Oh, hells, yeah, this sounds *way* more interestin'," said Gallina. "And I don't even read."

"What are you doing here, then?" Viv gave her a flat look.

"Browsin'. Also it looks like you got sweet buns, so . . ."

"For *paying* customers," said Viv.

"One bun with every sale," added Maylee with a grin.

"See, you still owe me that story though, remember? So, it's kinda like I already paid."

"You won't sit still for me to read it to you. So now it's *my* turn to propose a deal. I'll pay for what's in your hands, and then . . ." Viv plucked one of the lassies out of a basket. "You get your bun. And we're square."

Gallina looked from the parcel to the bun with a speculative expression. "Fine. But mostly for the bun." She shifted her gaze to Maylee and said in a loud stage whisper, "She's shit at reading out loud. Put me right to sleep."

Viv sighed and fished thirty bits out of her wallet, dropping the coins in the cash box. She tossed the bun toward Gallina, who whipped a dagger from her bandolier and speared it with a sassy smirk. She took a deliberate bite out of it and waggled the package at Viv. "I can prob'ly come up with a use for the paper, too," she mumbled through her mouthful.

"Rackam likes the literate!" Viv called after her as the gnome hiked toward The Perch.

"It's a good bun, Maylee!" hollered Gallina over her shoulder.

~

"Highlark!" exclaimed Viv.

"Ah, Viv, what a relief to see you idle and not leaking all over everything."

"Uh, this is Fern." She laid a hand on the rattkin's shoulder. "Thistleburr is her shop. I don't think you've met."

"Pleasure to meet you," said Fern as she finished depositing some coins into the cashbox.

"He's got almost as many books as you do," said Viv.

"A bibliophile?" asked Fern, brows rising with interest.

"She exaggerates my collection," replied Highlark, inclining his head. "Mostly reference texts. I confess, this is a charming idea." He ran a forefinger down the front of one of the bundles. "*Treachery, alchemy,* and *brotherhood.* Intriguing."

"Pretty literary stuff in that one," said Fern.

"You've read them? All of them?" asked Highlark, in apparent surprise, as he gestured across the tables.

"Not exactly. But I've read all of *those*. Do you like Tensiger?"

A more genuine smile bloomed on Highlark's face than Viv had ever seen. "You might even consider me a bit of a fan."

Fern tapped another bundle. "Then this one might be of interest, too."

When the surgeon finally departed, he had three bundles under his arms and a bun in his teeth.

As the horizon began to burn red out over the sea, the tables were well and truly picked over. They hadn't sold everything—maybe only half—but Fern had needed to take the cashbox inside to empty it when it became overstuffed with coins. The entire endeavor had been wildly more successful than Viv had imagined it might be.

Maylee had left shortly after delivering her contribution, and now the baskets sat empty on the tables, nothing but crumbs lining their bottoms.

Viv carried them down to Sea-Song, returning them to Maylee with Fern's thanks, a murmured sweetness, and a promise to visit the following morning. She wanted to make up for yesterday, but it would have to wait until they were alone.

When Viv got back to Thistleburr, Fern had already cleared the makeshift tables of books and was indoors.

Stacking the planks, Viv stowed them close to the boardwalk. She arranged the trestles over them until Pitts could retrieve them later, while twilight indigo gnawed away the sunset.

When she entered the shop, Fern let out a whoop and Viv started in surprise.

"Eight *fucking* hells!" the rattkin cried. "I can't believe we did it! I don't even know how many we sold!"

Satchel looked up from one of the chairs. Surprisingly, he had his feet propped on the stool, a book across his bony lap. "Eighty-seven books, m'lady."

The rattkin blew out a breath. "Just Fern, Satchel. No 'm'lady' needed."

The homunculus didn't reply to that. Somehow, Viv doubted he'd honor the request.

The remaining wrapped books stood in neat stacks in the back hall, and the shelves throughout the shop were more thinly populated, awaiting the new shipment.

"Maybe you should wrap up *all* the books from now on," said Viv, only half joking.

Fern laughed. "If only it was that easy! We really sold these cheap. It bought me some time and made some room, but if I did that with new stock, I might as well be giving them away. Still. That was *amazing*. And those buns didn't hurt. I hope you thanked Maylee again for me."

Viv bobbed a nod before addressing Satchel. "What've you got there, then?"

The homunculus looked down at the book and back up at her. "M'lady . . . *Fern* insisted I do something that could not be considered labor. This seemed the most obvious option."

"And what do you think?"

He cocked his head to the side, blue eyes flickering. "It's possible I can see the appeal. But perhaps I should sample one of the moist ones."

Viv tried hard not to choke on her laughter.

29

One problem with successfully offloading a heap of books on the visitors and citizens of Murk—one that Fern loudly blamed herself for not seeing in advance—was that the demand for reading material was entirely satisfied. Thistleburr might as well have been a tomb in the wake of the sale.

The shelves had a desolate look about them, too, riddled with gaps, lonely stretches left unfilled.

"How long until that shipment?" asked Viv.

Fern raised her head from her cradling arms. "Who knows? Overland shipping is unpredictable. Maybe a few days?" she said bleakly. "Not that anyone will want to *buy* them. I just occupied the whole gods-damned reading population of Murk with half-priced books. When the *new* ones arrive, they won't need anything to read!" She appended a few choice expletives with precise savagery.

Viv tapped the third of the Beckett mysteries, her current distraction. "They'll finish and need something else. Right?"

The rattkin sighed and grudgingly admitted, "Yes. Theoretically. I suppose." She glanced at Satchel, who'd begun emerging during the day, given the absolute dearth of custom. "Too bad they don't read as fast as him."

The homunculus sat ensconced in one of the chairs with a stack of books at his side. He'd been consuming them at a prodigious rate. Potroast lay at his feet, nipping at the bones of his toes while Satchel gently dipped them away from his questing beak.

"How do you read those so quickly?" Viv waggled her fingers. "Is it some kind of . . . I dunno, magic thing?"

Satchel turned a page with one slender digit. "I look at the page, and then the words are in my mind. That's the accepted way, yes?"

"*All* of the words on the page? All at *once?*" said Fern.

He looked back and forth between them. "You read them one by one?" he asked curiously.

"Yes!" they both cried at the same time.

He appeared to think about that. "That seems quite inefficient, if you don't mind my saying so."

Viv shifted aside the curtains to look out one of the windows. The inactivity in the wake of the sale hadn't done much for her growing impatience. She felt prickly, extremely aware of the passage of hours and days, and increasingly anxious for Rackam's return. Or for *anything* to happen, really. She almost wished another gray-clad stranger would wander into town, just so she'd have something to do.

Only yesterday she'd taken a detour from her morning walk to stand before the bounty board, studying every scrawled offering, daydreaming over bandit camps and ortheg nests and highwaymen. Hells, even a spineback hunt would've been welcome.

Her fingers had ached to hold steel the entire time.

What she wanted at the moment was to return to her room, place her hands on the hilt of the greatsword, and put in some hard work. Really build up a sweat. And to be fair, she did that every day, out back of The Perch.

But she'd also pledged to help Fern with her shop, to try to push it past survival into something more like *living*. Viv had made a commitment, and she liked to think she took her commitments seriously.

She wrestled her thoughts back in that direction. From the limpness of Fern's tail, she could tell she was slumping into her former listlessness.

Viv forced a smile onto her face and turned from the window. "So we'll be waiting a few days, and nobody's coming into the shop. Doesn't matter what we do in here, then, right? What if you just closed, and we took care of some work around the place? That way, when the new books show up, that's not the only thing that's new."

Fern stared at her, chin resting on her arms again, but she didn't say anything for a while. She was thinking about it though, Viv could tell. At last, Fern asked, "Like what?"

"Well, for starters . . ." Viv pointed at the cracked hurricane lamp. "Every time the door slams, I expect that damn thing to shatter all over the floor."

"So you think a new *lamp* is going to solve my problems?" Her voice was a little exasperated, but she was trying for good humor.

"Bothers me every time I see it. But maybe some fresh paint, too. Maybe an actual new rug? This one doesn't stink so bad anymore, but it's still . . ."

"Malodorous," supplied Satchel.

"Can you even smell anything?" asked Fern in surprise.

"My Lady was very particular about such things," he said primly.

Potroast squawked an agreement.

"None of this changes what I sell, though," said Fern. "This isn't a hotel. It's a bookshop! It's not that I don't want it to be *nice*. I do. But it's just hard to believe that any of that will make a real difference. You don't weed the garden when the house is burning down."

Viv tried to figure out how to frame what she wanted to say. She snapped her fingers. "The bakery! If it was, uh . . ."

The rattkin saw where she was headed. "Like my shop is now," she said grimly, motioning for Viv to continue.

"I wasn't going to mention your shop. I was just going to say . . . *dirty*."

Fern snorted. "Nice try."

"Anyway, do you think Maylee would do as well?"

"No, but that's different. That's *food*. If it's repulsive there, you lose your appetite."

"I guess I'm saying that you kind of have to have an appetite for *this*, too."

"Hmmm." Fern didn't seem entirely convinced.

"What's the worst that could happen if we did a little work in here?"

"We could waste all the money I earned in the sale, and it wouldn't make a lick of difference?" replied the rattkin.

Viv blinked. "Okay, I guess that *is* the worst case."

Fern took in the shaggy paint, the cracked lamp, the shabby drapes, and the disreputable carpet. "I don't really even see those things anymore. It's just home. I'm . . . used to them."

"Maybe you're *resigned* to them."

The rattkin sighed. "Okay, so say we *were* to try a few things—"

Satchel perked up. "M'lady, would it be all right if I *were* of assistance *now?*"

"Call me Fern, Satchel."

"Yes, m'lady."

~———

Notwithstanding her furtive trips by the bounty board, Viv really hadn't spent much time within the actual city of Murk. Apart from the distance, there wasn't a lot she needed to do there, and the potential of running into Iridia—even given their temporary peace—usually put it out of her mind.

Now, though, she was eager to find out if the gnome brothers were still selling estate furniture.

With the CLOSED sign posted on the door, she and Fern headed toward the fortress walls. They'd tried to convince Satchel to ride along in his bag, but he'd demurred, saying he preferred to stay back and read.

It occurred to Viv that she'd never really gone anywhere *with* Fern before. Potroast tagged along, trotting by Fern's side and goggling at everything with his pink tongue out.

"Hang on a second," said Viv when they reached Sea-Song. "I think Maylee might like to come. You don't mind, do you?"

"Of course not. If you don't work harder at worshipping that woman, she's going to escape. Then how am I supposed to get free scones? I've got a vested interest."

It took more than a second, but Viv returned with Maylee alongside.

"If the bakery burns down with Helsa runnin' things,

I'm holdin' you responsible," the dwarf groused, but Viv was warmed by the smile underneath it.

The sun reflected off the placid sea in streaks of blinding white, and heat shimmered off the sand. Down on the dry flats of the beach, she could see folk sitting on blankets or under big umbrellas made of sailcloth. Some even braved the waves, swimming and bobbing on the swells like corks.

All three of them were relieved to pass underneath the arch and into the relative cool of the walled city, where the shadows cast pools of refuge.

"First, the most important thing," said Viv solemnly. She hooked a thumb at the chandler's shop—the one where she'd first seen Balthus all those days ago.

Grinning at Fern's quizzical expression, she led them inside, where she purchased a new chimney for the hurricane lamp and asked to have it wrapped to pick up later.

"Well, at least the *important* thing is out of the way," said Fern dryly. "You and that cracked lamp."

Next, they visited the gnome brothers' lot. There was indeed a fresh variety of furniture, ranging in condition from irreparably decrepit to surprisingly sturdy and clean.

Maylee held up an ornate bookend. "Huh. Some kind of seabird?"

"Turn it on its side. Maybe it's a rabbit," said Viv.

Fern snorted a laugh and examined the table it had been sitting on.

The dwarf tilted it sideways and shot Viv a suspicious look, at which Viv chuckled. "Tell you later. But maybe hold on to that. Bookstores need bookends, right?"

"What can I help you ladies with?" asked the bearded

brother, while his clean-shaven sibling fussed over a crate of knickknacks.

"Any carpets?" asked Fern, still running a paw over the table.

"*Far* too many," replied the gnome.

"A *clean* one," said Viv, giving him a meaningful stare.

He looked affronted and motioned Fern over to a stack of rolled rugs and some wider ones draped across the back of a sturdy wooden chair.

Together, they picked through the furnishings, cookware, tools, and oddments. Potroast had to be dissuaded from nibbling the hems of several old dresses piled on an ottoman.

Fern kept coming back to the table.

"What do you have in mind?" asked Viv.

"I'm just thinking about the front of the shop and the new books."

She didn't elaborate further, but Viv saw something in her eyes. Something *almost* like tentative excitement.

They selected a suitable carpet, a couple of vases, two new chairs for the front corner, and the table Fern kept fussing over, as well as a painting that Maylee insisted would add some class when hung behind the counter.

Viv made sure to toss in the gull bookends.

Maylee turned out to be an excellent haggler, and the brothers were both regulars at Sea-Song. Viv could see dismay in the pained wrinkles on their brows as they balanced the baker's good humor against their potential for profit.

Possibly an unfair advantage on Maylee's part.

Viv pitched in some additional cash to have it all delivered, patted her thigh, and declared, "If Highlark saw me hauling any of it back, he'd probably stab me in the other leg."

A few fresh pots of white paint from a cabinetmaker off the
market street, and Viv considered the trip pretty successful.

"Dinner is on me," she said. "About time I ate someplace
besides The Perch."

"I knew there was a reason I came," said Maylee, slipping her
fingers into Viv's hand. She smelled of ginger and sunlit skin.

Viv squeezed them back. Deep down she held the knowledge
of an impending ache, imperfectly disguised. But there was no
getting around that, not really.

Maylee knew it was coming too. By silent agreement, they'd
both pretend it wasn't for a while longer.

～✦～

"And then I said, 'Of course I can't put it away, it's my fucking
tail!'" hollered Fern, banging one paw on the table.

Maylee tried to swallow her beer, but a laugh met it going
the other direction, with predictable results. Viv pounded her
on the back—gently—while finishing off her own mug. After,
it was easy enough to leave her hand there.

At Maylee's insistence, they'd moved on from dinner to a
low-ceilinged tavern tucked into an alley, and they were the
only three patrons. Several drinks in, they more than made up
for the lack of customers with their own volume. At this point,
the tavernkeep dodged in and out to refill their beverages like
they were a nest of angry snakes, and every time he did so,
Maylee only laughed louder.

"So *then*," continued Fern, slurring a little and waving her
glass, "he says, 'I don't care *what* it is, but if you grab my ass
one more time'"—she puffed herself up and deepened her
voice—"'there's going to be *trouble*.'"

Maylee was wheezing for breath now.

Viv leaned back in her chair and regarded the rattkin over the top of her empty mug. "Well. *Were* you grabbing his ass?"

"Of course not," said Fern. "It was not. Worth. Grabbing," she declared, punctuating each word with a stab of her claw. "He had a . . . a whatsit. A . . . a *lantern*. Banging into his butt."

"He was a *Gatewarden*?" Maylee said.

"An *assless* Gatewarden," declared Fern.

And then they were all laughing.

When that wound its way down to relative quiet, Fern looked at the both of them, teary-eyed, and raised her glass again. "To you two. You're . . ." She searched for the word. "Cute. And I'm drunk."

"Cute, huh? You're definitely drunk," said Viv, hoisting her refilled mug.

"Speak for yourself." Maylee clinked her own mug against Fern's glass. "I'm cute as hells."

Viv saw the challenging look on Maylee's face and decided she'd definitely answered too hastily. In fact, the pleasant flush in her cheeks and the bloom in her chest made her want to lean in close, brush her thumb across Maylee's lower lip, and—

She suddenly noticed Fern watching them avidly, with her cheek on one paw, swirling her glass with the other.

Viv cleared her throat, but her words were in earnest. "Can't argue with that."

30

"Gods, it looks pretty grim, doesn't it?" said Fern. She massaged her forehead, still a little the worse for wear after the prior night's adventure.

She, Viv, and Satchel stood together near the center of the shop. The front door was latched, supplies piled in the middle of the floor, the tops of the wall shelves draped with old sailcloth weighted in place with stones. The table, chairs, and carpet they'd purchased were arrayed on the boardwalk out front, along with any other freestanding furniture that could be moved there. The gull bookends sat together on the countertop like a humorous afterthought.

Somehow, their addition made the flaking paint more obvious, and every worn corner of the room looked shabbier than normal.

"At last," said Satchel, his tone gleefully anticipatory. "If I may, m'lady?"

He didn't even wait for permission, cracking open the urn of paint. Viv thought he might actually have chuckled.

"It doesn't seem like I could *stop* you," said Fern.

Satchel and Viv handled most of the initial work. They

used trowels to scrape the walls down and peel away flaking paint, which shed onto the sailcloth and floor like the bark of an aspen. Fern tidied it into piles as it fell. Viv had expected to do a lot of the work herself, given how high much of the exposed wood was, but the homunculus had impeccable balance and certainly wouldn't be injured by a fall. He climbed the shelves with alacrity, even draped in the sailcloth as they were, crouching atop them in impossibly contorted positions no fleshly creature would be able to endure.

Fern filled small pots from the urn and passed them up. Over a series of industrious and companionable hours, they painted the entire front room. Viv could even reach the ceiling, and though it put an awful crick in her neck and abused back muscles that no amount of swordplay ever strained, she managed.

When it was done, Viv removed the stones from the sailcloth and carefully folded it, hauling it to the boardwalk. They threw open the side windows, and Fern swung wide the back door to let the air pass through. Then they gathered and surveyed their handiwork together.

"It's . . . definitely an improvement," admitted Fern.

"Hang on," said Viv, stepping over to the hurricane lantern and removing the cracked chimney. Carefully unwrapping the one she'd purchased, she settled it onto the lamp's base. "*Now* it's better."

"It is indeed," agreed Satchel, the blue flames of his orbits pulsing lazily. "A *very* creditable transformation." He sighed a long, hollow breath of satisfaction, and although Viv never would have guessed a skeleton could look relaxed, he somehow achieved it.

The rattkin rolled her eyes. "It's just some paint." But Viv could tell by the curve of her tail and the way her whiskers twitched that she was pleased.

Over the following hours, Viv muscled the furniture into the shop, and they fussed over rearranging it. Eventually, they repositioned several of the freestanding shelves, or rather, Viv did, by carefully lifting one end and then another, walking them ever so gently into new locations.

They placed Fern's new table at the end of two back-to-back shelves and arranged a small seating nook with the additional chairs near the front windows. The still-empty vases they positioned in the corners. The reconfigured interior allowed more space for the original padded chairs and side table as well, and when they finally unfurled the new carpet, its deep burgundy added surprising warmth to the room.

By then, the paint had dried enough for Viv to bang a nail into the wall behind the counter, where she carefully hung the painting Maylee had chosen.

It did indeed look very nice.

"What was the plan with this table then?" asked Viv, rapping it with her knuckles.

"I guess we'll see," said Fern. She went about the shop, selecting a few different books, studying their covers and nibbling at a paw as she did. Viv and Satchel watched, nonplussed, as she traveled back and forth to the table, arranging the volumes upright or angled, with other books as backing or stacking them just so. Sometimes, she'd take one back and reshelve it, only to replace it with another.

Eventually, she snatched the gull—or rabbit—bookends from the counter and positioned them strategically, sandwiching a series of volumes between them in a few different arrangements until she was satisfied.

Viv didn't know what invisible signal indicated that she was done, but Fern stepped back with a satisfied nod.

And she had to admit, it looked nice.

The rattkin appeared to awaken from a daze.

"Well," breathed Fern, surveying the interior with both brows raised. "Fuck me."

Satchel drew back from her in alarm, and his eyes seemed to widen as the flames within them burned brighter.

Viv leaned down near his skull and whispered, "It's just a figure of speech, not a request."

—~—

"It's a damned good job," said Maylee, scanning the room approvingly. "Looks practically new." She looked over her shoulder at Viv. "And that fresh lamp chimney really ties the place together."

Viv executed a mock bow, and Fern snorted.

Gallina snagged one of the lemon cakes the baker had brought, stuffed it into her face, then settled back into her padded chair. She made vaguely affirmative noises through a mouthful of crumbs.

Fern had gathered beach grass and filled the new vases, and the lantern shushed inside its fine—and undamaged—new chimney as twilight crept down outside. The fresh white paint fairly glowed, and in tandem with the sweetly scented grass, it was amazing how much the removal of the disreputable old rug had improved the smell.

Even the books on the shelves seemed richer. Cleaner. *Tidier*.

"Viv says you've got a new shipment of books comin' in?" continued the dwarf.

Fern sat at the counter, absently nibbling at her own square of cake while Satchel leafed through a chapbook. "Mmm? Yeah, sometime soon. I think I'll just . . . stay closed until they arrive."

"*More* books? Still seems like plenty in here," said Gallina, eyeing the baked goods where they glistened on brown paper.

"Don't think we didn't notice that you showed up for the cake but not the painting," said Viv. Her neck and back still ached, and she sprawled in one of the chairs next to Maylee.

"I'm less than four feet tall. How'm I gonna help?" Gallina started to reach for another cake, then frowned at Viv's amused expression and slumped back into her chair.

"So," said Viv, "did you use your idle hours to read any of those books yet? You know, while we were painting?"

"*No*," replied Gallina, drawing one of her knives and making a big show of trimming her fingernails.

But her face colored slightly, and Viv wondered.

Maylee sank deeper into her chair, propping her feet on the footstool. "It's nice enough in here to nap," she said dreamily. "Feels like a refuge. And my feet hurt like hells."

For a while, there was nothing but the hiss of the lantern and the weary, contented silence that follows in the wake of a day spent laboring with others.

Suddenly, Satchel snapped his book closed and moved swiftly to the side window, pressing his bony palms flat against it. He stared out into the gathering night.

Potroast rasped in his throat, rising onto his front paws.

Viv gripped the arms of her chair. "What is it?" Her mind crowded with thoughts of Balthus and of wights with horned helms and blue eyes, and Varine's symbol burning on their foreheads.

"I thought I saw something, m'lady," replied Satchel, his hollow voice sounding strangely compressed.

She was up from her chair in an instant, throwing the latch on the door. Dashing out onto the boardwalk, she pounded along it to the alley upon which the window gazed.

Nothing there but whispering beach grass, and shadows slowly pooling on the sand.

Potroast skidded to a stop beside her, hooting deep in his chest, his triangular ears flat against his skull, feathers puffed. For once, his ire wasn't directed her way.

Something tickled her senses, the specter of a scent.

Snow. And frozen blood.

Then it was gone, and Viv tried to convince herself she'd imagined it.

When she strode back into the shop, Gallina met her at the door, knife in hand. Viv shook her head. "Nobody there. But . . ." She stared at Satchel, who glanced back at her. "I think you should maybe stay with me tonight. Just in case."

31

I stood upon that windswept promontory, my hair a black flag whipping behind me, as the dark clouds above trailed like tattered banners across the sky. The grasses tumbled in purring waves, moonlight limning their crests.

Far off, the sea seemed still, though it was not. Its heaves and swells were too broad and slow at this remove to truly mark. In my mind's eye, though, I knew their fury, trapped beneath the livid line of the horizon.

And solitary before it, like a pale tree, its autumn leaves storm-tossed, she awaited me.

Her eyes glittered black, finding mine across the seething distance.

The first—

Viv dropped the book onto her chest and sighed. She watched the tiny window high on the side of her room where the lamp quaked its light along the wall. Outside, the wind kicked up—maybe it even seethed—and every breath she inhaled seemed to bring with it the phantom scent of frozen copper.

"This book is not gods-damned helping," she muttered, setting *Stark House* on the floor beside the straw-tick mattress.

She glanced at the satchel resting against the sea chest. "You awake in there?" whispered Viv.

The bag didn't rustle or otherwise respond.

Sighing again, she sat up and doused the lantern, lying back in the darkness. A slash of moonlight raked across the ceiling like a gap of sky visible from the depths of a canyon.

Eventually, the light faded, and so did she.

~

When she dreamed, she dreamed of Varine the Pale.

They faced one another on a familiar dark promontory whose grasses hissed in an insistent wind.

Of course it was familiar. She'd only just read about it.

The necromancer's eyes were as black as words could make them, pits of nothing in white flesh, her hair unfurling in dark ribbons rich as earth watered with blood. Her lips were blue. Lifeless, but full and smiling.

Above her, the moon itself was inscribed with her sigil, a diamond with branches like horns.

Viv's breath dwindled, her chest constricted by what felt like huge, crushing hands. The grass began to shrink away even as other forms rose from the earth. Their eyes glittered with icy blue pinpricks of starlight as they staggered upright, earth falling away in clods and streamers.

"I see you, Viv." Varine's form swelled, as though the grass were her mantle and she was gathering it around herself, magnifying her tenfold.

No, she was *approaching*, gliding fast between the wights that shambled toward their dumbstruck prey.

Viv shook herself and snatched for the saber at her hip, but it was missing. Only then did she notice the heavy weight slung across her back. Her searching fingers found the hilt of the greatsword over one shoulder and gratefully tightened on it. The leather creaked, and a current passed from the steel and into her flesh. She couldn't have let go if she'd wanted to.

She didn't want to.

"You have something that belongs to me," purred Varine, looming impossibly large, empty and enormous, while the world hissed away from her like soot blown from white marble. Until there was nothing, nothing but Varine.

Viv unsheathed the blade and brought it before her, solid and right and *hers*.

"Blackblood." Varine's whisper boomed like thunder, and the necromancer was before and behind and above and, inevitably, below.

And then she was inside her like a blade between the ribs, cold and laughing.

Viv snapped awake in the darkness, clutching at her side and the fading burn of ice there.

Her other arm was flung across the bedframe, fingers tight on the greatsword's hilt.

On Blackblood's hilt.

⁓

Viv sat back on her haunches, her thigh burning and stretching with the motion. She recorked the bottle of bonedust and watched as Satchel boiled out of his resting place and into her room.

When his eyes lit blue, she said, "Couldn't sleep. Do you mind?"

"You'd like some company?" he asked in his hollow, echoing voice.

"I guess so. Glad to see you've dropped the 'm'lady,' anyway."

Satchel stared at the greatsword where it throbbed with lamplight on the bedframe.

"It has a name, doesn't it?" asked Viv. "*She* has a name."

"She does," he replied.

"Blackblood," said Viv.

His gaze sharpened. "Have you been dreaming?"

"So that *is* what she's called," Viv breathed. Then, "Only once," she admitted.

The homunculus sighed, dead leaves on stone. "My Lady will come."

"Not if Rackam finds her first," said Viv. "But if he hasn't done that by now . . . then you may be right."

"Rackam?" asked Satchel.

So Viv told him about Rackam and Lannis and Tuck and the rest of them. It occurred to her that she'd never sat and spoken with Satchel at length, not like this. He was a good listener.

When she was done, she scrutinized him. He'd dropped into a cross-legged sitting position that looked like it would be supremely uncomfortable for someone with muscles and tendons.

"I think," she said slowly, "that you've been lying to us. Just a little."

Satchel didn't respond for a long moment, until he said, "And what makes you say that?"

"A feeling. A *strong* feeling. I do think you have to keep her secrets. I truly believe that."

"I do," whispered Satchel, a ghostly breath.

"But I think you keep more than that. Not to help her. Not to hurt anyone else. But because you're afraid."

"She hears," he said, and there was a note of anguish in his voice.

"Right now?" Viv's pulse spiked in alarm.

He shook his head, and her heartbeat slowed.

"When she finds me," he said, tapping the side of his horned skull. "Every moment, she can retrieve. *Relive.* I can hide nothing from her." His gaze was haunted. "And even *I* can feel pain. She knows how to make it so."

"That's pretty gods-damned terrifying," agreed Viv. She lifted Blackblood from the bedframe and laid it across her lap, trailing her fingers across the steel. "But let me ask you something."

"Ask," he said, and something about the way the flames flickered in his sockets communicated his fierce attention.

"Do you *want* to be free of her?"

He hesitated, no doubt thinking of the moment Varine might witness this admission were he to return to her possession. "I do," he admitted quietly.

"Do you think you're ever going to have a better chance to be free of her than this? If she comes, I'll do my damnedest to kill her, with her own gods-damned sword if I can. Maybe I'm not at my best, but I'm still *good* at this. And coming behind her is the hardest man I know, and more besides. If she's caught between us—" Viv slammed a fist into a palm.

"I am not so sure she can be killed with steel," he said. He tapped Blackblood with one bony digit. "And I am not so sure she can be avoided either."

"Maybe she won't die by steel," said Viv grimly. "But *everything* can be killed."

"And if you fail," he continued, "she will live so, so long. So *very* long. And there will be no release for me."

"Well, then," said Viv. "Maybe it's time to improve those odds. If she can't be killed with steel, then how?"

Satchel stroked his bony chin with two phalanges for several moments, and then the fire in his eyes brightened. "Perhaps there is a way. But it would not be easy."

Viv smiled a predator's smile. A smile nobody else in Murk had ever seen. "Tell me."

32

"Whoof," panted Maylee, flicking sweat from her forehead and flipping her braid over her shoulder. "How'd I let you talk me into this?"

Viv shaded her eyes and gazed out over the sea from their vantage atop the bluff. "The view is worth it," she replied, smiling encouragingly. She didn't mention the powerful need she had to survey the surrounding lands as far as the eye could see, to squint at every shadow and scrubby tree.

No advancing army on the horizon. No bloodless woman with eyes like splashes of ink. She felt some of her itch subside.

To their left, markers poked up from the long grasses of the graveyard like half-submerged boulders in a stream. Fern and Gallina shook out a green wool blanket and laid it across the bare expanse beyond the fence.

"Strange to say, but I've never been up here," said Maylee, scanning north. "Huh, that's quite the cottage, isn't it?" She pointed to the sprawling estate visible from the promontory.

"Fern says that's Zelia Greatstrider's place," said Viv.

"The one that writes all those books with the dirty bits?"

"They're not *that* dirty," protested Viv, although yes, they actually were.

"Didn't say it was bad." The baker grinned at her, a grin with something wicked folded into it. A grin that almost made Viv wish Rackam would take his sweet time.

Maylee set her wicker basket on the blanket. She'd insisted on carrying it herself. "Fern, you should have *her* come by the shop next time you're thinkin' about a sale. Scones and sexy books? Yes, please!"

"Ha! I'd be terrified to ask her. That mansion of hers is forbidding. But as ideas go . . ." Fern trailed off.

Viv unbuckled her saber and leaned it against one of the stone pillars at the corner of the graveyard. She'd seen Maylee eyeing it the whole trip up. She'd felt a frustrating combination of guilt and annoyance at that, and she was still doing her best to wrestle both of those feelings back into their boxes. Nobody would be sneaking up on them at this height, but after her dream and her midnight conference with Satchel, there was no way in all eight hells she was going to troop out of town unarmed. The greatsword—*Blackblood*, she thought—felt best in her hands, but she'd reluctantly left it in favor of subtlety. Or at least as close as she could come to subtle.

This trip had been markedly less taxing than the previous one. Her leg felt stable, only twinging occasionally, and she was finally able to wear her right boot again. She felt almost herself.

"Well, it's good to get some air, anyway," she said.

"You *did* kinda bully all of us into comin'," said Gallina as she removed her boots and dug her toes into the hot sand. "Lookit you. Big, tough, woman of action, organizin' picnics."

"Fern needed to get out," replied Viv.

"Oh, is that what this is? *I* needed to get out?" Fern pretended to be affronted.

"Yeah, you did. Moping around, waiting for that shipment? The shop's closed, the walls are painted. Everything's done that can be done. You needed some air."

Gallina lay back on the blanket, laced her fingers behind her head, and closed her eyes against the sun. "Long way to come for some air, that's all I'm sayin'."

"You know, Rackam really only has one rule," said Viv.

Gallina cracked an eye at her. "Oh yeah?"

"Yeah. Complainers don't eat."

Maylee laughed as she finished unpacking the basket, arraying bottles and crocks and muslin-wrapped bundles on the blanket. Fern shooed Potroast away from them with moderate success.

"Oh, and speaking of not needing to eat." Viv unslung Satchel's bag and flipped it open, unstoppering one of the vials to sprinkle dust over his bones.

As Satchel clambered to his feet, he surveyed the area with interest. He held out a hand before him, wriggling his fingers as though he could feel the breeze. Perhaps he could.

"Marvelous," he said wistfully, looking out over the tumble of blue ocean, at the tiny ships plying the horizon. "So many of my days spent in the dark," he murmured. "So much time wasted."

Viv reflected again that although he had no flesh with which to express his emotions, something about the set of his body and the tone of his voice communicated a great deal. She thought of all those days, made conscious only to labor in some dire service she couldn't even imagine, only to be returned to oblivion when Varine was done with him.

Seeing him in the sun, gleaming under its warmth, blew life into a cooling ember deep in her chest.

"If you don't mind, I'll wander a bit while you share your meal," he said.

Viv thought it was the most relaxed he'd ever sounded.

"Be my guest. It's about time you got out." She thought about their conversation the night before. "We'll try to make it something you can get used to."

A rumbling sound, like stones tumbling over one another, issued from the vicinity of his jaw, and Viv realized that he was chuckling.

"I don't imagine I'll be strolling the streets anytime soon, no matter the outcome," he said. "Some things are foolish to imagine."

Viv couldn't muster a reply that wasn't insulting or false, so she wisely chose silence.

He strolled to the edge of the bluff, gazing after the seabirds that wheeled beyond.

The rest of them sat together on the blanket and worked their way through the bounty that Maylee had assembled. There were long, narrow loaves with flaky crusts. These she sliced lengthwise and spread with a soft goat cheese and pepper preserves, sweet and smoky. Green bottles of summer beer tasted of lemons and wheat fields. Thin ginger cookies snapped pleasingly between the teeth, and there was a crock of sugared cream to dip them in.

Potroast snatched up hunks of bread that Maylee tossed his way, although he stared most longingly at Gallina. Viv never saw her share any of her food with the gryphet, but he followed each of the gnome's bites so avidly, it seemed impossible she wasn't slipping him something on the sly.

Viv caught herself snatching glances at Maylee's knees again, bare and soft as the cream in the crock.

A mild northerly breeze made the air sweet and pleasant, carrying the scent of the thistle flowers and only the faintest hint of salt from below.

When they were replete, Gallina fell asleep almost immediately, and Potroast curled up beside her, his chin resting on her belly where it rose and fell with every gentle breath.

Maylee leaned against Viv's arm, with her own looped through it. Viv liked being clung to. It made her want to cling back, to bury herself in the scent and the warmth of her. She settled for squeezing Maylee's arm in tighter to her side.

Fern had unpinned her cloak and sat with it folded across her lap.

Viv followed her gaze down the slope toward Murk and the tendrils of smoke curling from within its fortress walls. "What're you thinking about?" she asked.

Fern returned from woolgathering, blinking at her in surprise. "That I ate too much," she said with an embarrassed grin.

"Really, though. That was deep thought if I ever saw it, hon," said Maylee.

"Thinking about my father." She ran her fingers along a fold of her cloak. "You know, I never asked him why."

"Why what?" asked Viv.

"Why a bookshop? Why here? Was it what he always wanted? I don't even know."

"Does that matter?" Maylee sat up straighter, but kept her arm curled around Viv's.

Fern shrugged. "It shouldn't, I guess. But I never bothered to ask *myself* that question either. Maybe if I'd asked him, I'd have my own answer? All this work. All your *help*. All this, and . . ."

She raised her paws, and then let them fall back into the tangle of red cloth. "You do something for years and years, and the only reason you continue is because once you stop, you won't really have anything."

She knotted her paws in the cloak. "At least it sometimes seems that way. I'm sorry. What a stupid thing to say, after everything you've done. And all this." She gestured at the remains of their feast. "I sound ungrateful. But I'm *not*. You've probably never felt that way about anything, have you?" She said it jokingly, but Viv thought there was a tiny thread of hope in there, too.

"No, I suppose not," said Viv. "I know what I'm made for. Pretty sure I always did." She might even have believed it.

"I have," said Maylee, and her arm tightened reflexively for a second. "D'you really think you'd feel better if you stopped?"

Fern thought about that seriously. "No, I guess I wouldn't."

"Any idea why?" pressed the dwarf.

"I guess . . . I guess because I'd miss the moment." She made a frustrated noise, casting around for the right words. "That instant when you know that someone sees the same thing you see."

Viv was surprised when Maylee nodded, shifting to meet Fern's gaze squarely. "When they see *you*. When you know that at least right then, you're really not alone. Somebody else feels exactly what you do. Or you hope so, anyway."

"Yes," said Fern, sounding surprised. "Every book is a little mirror, and sometimes you look into it and see someone else looking back." She reached over and dealt Viv's considerable forearm a slap. "I even saw this one a few times."

"Hidden depths," said Maylee with a laugh.

"I feel like you're both acting more surprised about this than you should," said Viv dryly.

"So. *That's* why you do it, hon," said the baker firmly. "And to be honest, it's the same reason I do what I do."

Fern stared back at her thoughtfully.

Viv was still turning the idea over in her mind when a hollow voice rose from beyond the fence, grave and sonorous. "I think that you had best see this, m'lady."

It was the "m'lady" that prickled the hairs on the back of Viv's neck.

"Everybody stay put," she said, her voice flat and low.

She tapped Gallina awake, and the gryphet hooted irritably at her. Then she snatched her saber and located Satchel amidst the grave markers. Gallina trailed barefoot behind her, rubbing her eyes and grumbling under her breath.

The grass of the graveyard switched against the homunculus's ribs as he stared at something Viv couldn't see.

When she drew near, looming over his shoulder, he looked back up at her with his flickering blue gaze.

The earth was blasted black in front of him, as though from a lightning strike or a carefully controlled flame. Shreds of grass curled and twisted into charcoal ribbons around a barren circle the size of a shield.

Etched into the fine black powder was a diamond with branches like horns.

33

They descended the hill in silence as dusk ripened in the west. Viv carried Potroast tucked under one arm, and incredibly, he didn't protest. Viv stolidly refused to glance over her shoulder. There was no way Varine was creeping up behind them, she was sure. The empty horizon was visible for miles.

It was hard to ignore that symbol, though. The mark of some scout? A kind of arcane wayfinding? Gods knew. Satchel said *he* didn't, and she believed him. He rode along silently, tucked into his bag, bouncing against her hip.

She hadn't caught that evil scent again on the way down. That was something, at least.

"I'll tell Iridia about it tomorrow," Viv promised the others. "She's already got the Wardens on watch. It'll be fine."

When they reached the foot of the hill, Gallina split off from the group at The Perch with a salute and a defiantly chipper "G'night!"

Viv walked Fern and Maylee down the path between the dunes to the boardwalk, where shadows gathered underneath the awnings. When they reached the door of Thistleburr, the somber mood broke suddenly as Fern spied a note tucked into the doorjamb, fluttering like a trapped leaf.

"The shipment!" She seized the message and scanned it. "It's here! They'll drop it off tomorrow. Gods, finally!" When she glanced up at them, eyes glittering, it was immediately easier to shrug off the dark cloud that had clung to them.

"I'll be here," said Viv. Reluctant to spoil Fern's excitement, she patted the satchel. "I'll keep him with me another night, though. You know, considering." She tried to make her voice light.

Fern sobered just a little. "I guess . . . that's probably for the best."

Viv and Maylee waited until Fern was inside and they'd heard the click of the latch before they continued onward. Their heights were too different to hold a hand or interlink an arm, but they walked close together, brushing against one another in delicious accidents.

After the commotion around the symbol and that blasted circle of earth, Viv felt grounded in the present now that they were alone. The sound of the surf tumbled in the distance. Maylee's warmth radiated beside her, gentle in the cooling evening air, still smelling faintly of bread and ginger.

She couldn't stop thinking of their conversation on the bluff, before things went sour. Viv felt a growing need, like something expanding in her chest, to ask a question she thought she might regret.

Not to voice it, though? That was cowardice. And she was no coward.

Or maybe that was just when it came to blades and blood, because this was harder than it had any right to be.

Clearing her throat, she finally managed, "What you said before. About . . . about somebody *seeing* you."

Maylee glanced up but said nothing. Neither stopped walking.

"Fern was talking about her work. Her shop. That wasn't all you were talking about, was it?"

The dwarf considered her answer. "No. Not all."

Viv took a big breath. "Do you think we're both seeing the same thing?"

"I'm pretty sure we aren't," replied Maylee. Viv opened her mouth to speak, but the dwarf continued before she could. "It's like bein' up on that hill. One of us is at the top, and the other is down here. We both look out to sea, but we see somethin' different. One of us could climb up, or the other down, and if we did, then maybe things would be different . . . but we haven't. Or can't."

"Maylee—"

Maylee shrugged, moving the basket to her other arm, the one between them. "If we'd met in another few years, who knows? Maybe we'd both be lookin' out from the same hill. Doesn't change that you're still somebody I want to know. Doesn't change what I can do with the days I have. Doesn't make those matter less."

"No, it doesn't change that. But . . ." Viv struggled to find the right words as her face flushed hot. Her throat felt almost painfully thick, every word dragged out forcibly. "If I'm . . . *careless* when I hold on to somebody, I can . . . I can break bones. And I feel real careless right now. Because I don't think you—"

"You don't have to say any more," replied the dwarf quietly. "I know what this is."

"Knowing isn't the same as accepting," said Viv, and then wished she hadn't.

"No. Some things are worth a few cracked ribs though."

They reached the door of Sea-Song, and Maylee laid a hand on Viv's belly, warm through her shirt. "Come here, hon," she said.

Viv got down on a knee and gently ran her fingers along Maylee's braid. The dwarf stroked one cheek with her knuckles, then leaned forward and kissed her on the corner of her mouth.

"I won't break when you're gone. And neither will you. I could wish we would, because then you might stay to keep that from happenin'." She smiled. "But that *would* break you. So instead, I'll see you tomorrow. And we won't talk about this again, because nothin' will change the way things will be, and it's a waste of hours."

Then she unlocked the shop, entered, and closed the door quietly behind her.

"Don't look like *you* slept much," observed Brand as he slid a plate of oatcakes and smoked bacon onto the bar-top before her.

Viv hadn't. She'd dreamed of Varine again, and she hadn't been able to shake the feeling that the necromancer was *actually* seeing her. She'd awakened over and over, until in desperation she'd stretched out with Blackblood lying lengthwise on top of her, both hands folded across the blade.

After that, she'd snatched a few hours before sunlight lanced in through the window, and she'd groggily risen to face the day. Her leg ached as though she'd been running on it all night.

She washed her breakfast down with an enormous mug of hot tea and wished it did more to wake her up. Reluctantly, Viv left Blackblood up in her room and carried Satchel down the hill to the bookshop. The day was going to be hot, and every inch of sand the shadows relinquished swiftly bled out the nighttime damp. At least the heat seemed to do for her head what the tea hadn't.

When she reached Thistleburr, Fern was sitting on the edge of the still-shaded boardwalk, fingers wrapped around her own mug of tea. Potroast stretched out beside her, licking one of his forepaws.

"Anxious?" asked Viv as she approached.

"Mmm. About whether the crates full of books that I spent most of my remaining funds on are actually going to show up at my door? Not at all." She put down her mug. "By which I mean to say, fuck, yes." There was an edge of excitement to her obscenity though.

"Hey, Potroast," said Viv. The gryphet startled and looked at her, his eyes huge. "Yeah, I'm talking to you. Remember, I hauled you down that hill last night?" She crouched in front of him and pulled a scrap of bacon from her pocket, holding it out to him between thumb and forefinger. "Gallina never gave you bacon, did she?"

He eyed her, then very gently extended his feathery neck and nipped it out of her grip.

Fern smiled at them both. "Well. *That's* a good omen, I guess."

Viv eased to a seat beside Fern and the gryphet and gently ran a finger along the silky feathers of his head, down past the point where they transitioned to short fur. His hide twitched and quivered behind her touch, but he didn't protest.

"Huh," she said. "How about that."

They sat in comfortable silence while Viv scratched behind Potroast's pointy ears. She even managed to wring some leg thumps out of him.

"There it comes," breathed Fern, and leapt to her feet.

Clattering along the road from the fortress walls came Pitts, laboring under a bigger load than Viv had ever seen him pull.

When he rumbled to a stop in front of them, she spied three crates in his cart.

"Got somethin' for you to sign," he said, digging papers and a stylus from a pouch on his belt. While Fern attended to the paperwork, Viv began sliding a crate out the end.

"I'll get 'em," called Pitts as Viv hoisted the first off the buckboard.

"I got this one," she said. She grunted as her muscles bunched hard against the weight of it, but she still hauled it to the door without too much difficulty. "Who knew a box of words could be so heavy?"

"Small stones tossed in the river. A thousand tiny prayers. The course is turned," observed Pitts.

Fern furrowed her brow. "Is that from one of the poetry books? I don't remember it."

"Nope," replied Pitts simply.

As Viv returned empty-handed for the next crate, she and Fern shared a glance, and neither could think of a thing to say.

The two orcs hauled the remaining crates while Fern hovered around the edges, whiskers twitching anxiously.

When Pitts had left, Viv unslung Satchel's bag and Fern dusted him awake. Then the three of them stood together in the shop, inspecting the new arrivals while Potroast sniffed around the boxes.

The crates were new, made of raw wood, heavy with the scent of cut pine. The tops were nailed down, but there was a lip around the edge, and Viv found enough of a grip to wrench them back with a squeal of nails.

"I could've found a hammer," observed Fern.

Viv shrugged. "Like you said, there has to be a reason you keep me around."

Inside, packed tightly and precisely, were stacks and stacks of books. The smell of leather and cloth and ink nearly overpowered the piney scent.

Fern bent over and ran her paws along the covers, inhaling deeply. "Gods, that smell." She sighed. "Have you ever smelled anything so good?"

Viv smiled. "I don't think you really had to look that far to figure out why you still have this shop."

The rattkin grinned back. "Maybe you're right. Let's get these unpacked. There's a few in here I ordered just for you."

Viv was more than happy to be distracted from the misty memories of her dream, and of a cruel blue smile.

34

Many of the volumes were surprisingly colorful, with stenciled or foiled illustrations on the covers. And Fern was right, the scent of the fresh volumes was intoxicating, so much so that it made Viv a little dizzy. When she opened one to inspect the fresh print, the spines creaked in a crisp and deeply satisfying way.

"The letters are so *clean*," observed Viv.

"New gnomish printers," said Fern, still grinning ear to ear. "Cheaper to produce *and* they wear better. Which means I can sell them for less, too."

Viv and Satchel unpacked the individual books. Fern made a big production of inspecting each one and created a special pile on the front table according to some unknowable criteria. The rest she shelved carefully, and as every gap was filled, each row of books fattened with fresh additions. It was like seeing a wooden puzzle assemble until the scene painted on it became suddenly clear.

In the middle of it all, the door banged open and Gallina trooped in, startling Potroast from his doze in a slab of sunlight. "So they showed, huh?"

"You're just in time to help," said Viv, straightening with an armload.

"Nah, I'd just get in the way." She ran a hand through her spiky hair. "Besides, I can't reach anything in here. You want me to fall into a crate?"

"You know, your height only comes up when you don't want to do something. So, why exactly *are* you here?"

Gallina flopped into a chair. Viv noticed that she had a folded piece of paper in one hand, which she fiddled with self-consciously. "Uh, well. Just thought when you were done doin' *this* job you might want to do somethin' you're a little more familiar with."

"What are you talking about?" Viv's brow wrinkled.

The gnome held the paper up between two fingers. "Bounty. Pay's not great, but it's pretty close, I guess. I could do it on my own, o' course, but I thought maybe if you were *bored* and not feelin' *too* delicate . . ."

Viv caught Fern's sidelong look and tried not to sound interested when she said, "Bounty, huh? What sort?"

The gnome twirled a hand. "Spineback nest. South a little ways down the coast. Some farmer's losin' sheep to 'em, I guess."

"A loathsome species," said Satchel with sudden vehemence, looking up from the stack of books in his bony arms.

Viv glanced at him in surprise. "You've spent time around spinebacks?"

"More than I care to relate," replied the homunculus darkly. His osseoscription momentarily burned a bright blue.

Still wondering at that, Viv replied to Gallina, "Let me think about it." She passed a book to Fern, who gave her a searching look. "I don't know if I want to be away for *that* long."

TRAVIS BALDREE

What she didn't voice was her worry that if she left Murk for any length of time, Varine or Rackam would show up the instant she was gone. She couldn't decide which was more worrisome.

"Yeah, yeah. I'll pay to cart us down, if you wanna go. Don't wait *too* long, though. I can't just sit around coolin' my heels at The Perch for much longer."

"Mmm. Just going to take care of it yourself, then?" Viv's voice was mild. "How many spinebacks did you say?"

"A manageable number," said Gallina flatly.

Satchel cleared his throat. "If you *do* decide to deal with those creatures, I may be of some assistance."

"No offense," said Gallina, "but I think spinebacks kinda like to crack bones between their teeth?"

"Nevertheless," he said, and the flames in his eyes flashed like a knot popping in a hearth fire.

"You know, Satchel, the longer I know you, the less I think I know *about* you," said Viv. She wondered again what services Varine might have required of him.

As Gallina was getting up to leave, Fern called out, "Oh, that book you wanted should be in here somewhere."

Gallina looked stricken.

"Uh. Yeah. I'll get that later, then," the gnome said in a strangled voice, and hurried out the door.

"Wait, she really *did* read something? What did she ask for?"

Fern finished shelving the volume in her paws and turned back to Viv, her eyes sharp with humor.

She mouthed one word.

"Moist."

When they'd finished shelving everything, Viv carted the empty crates out back to keep for later. When she returned, she found Fern arranging the last of the books she'd set aside on the front table.

With the knuckles of one paw to her chin, she contemplated the entire setup and then reached out and swapped two of them.

"Huh. Looks nice," said Viv. It did. The covers showed well with their fronts out, and Fern had arranged them at artful angles or face up and sometimes rakishly tilted.

There was something modern and immediate about many of the designs. Bold, serifed text in gold or silver, iconography that suggested a dream condensed. Some were covered in marbled cloth with blooms of color like exotic foliage.

Fern studied them with a wistful smile on her lips. "It's funny. I hate to sell them. Did I ever tell you that? If I could keep them all, I would."

"Solid business plan."

The rattkin slapped her on the arm.

"*Desert Heat*," said Viv, grinning. "Greatstrider, huh?" She tapped a volume with a very detailed illustration of an orc and a human on the verge of shedding the rest of their clothing and doing something very acrobatic. A thought occurred to her, and her eyes widened. "Wait, this isn't Gallina's, is it?"

"A good bookseller doesn't kiss and tell."

"So that's absolutely a yes. Anyway, when do you want to reopen?"

"Anxious to go spineback hunting?"

Viv shrugged uncomfortably. "That's not what I meant . . ."

"I know. I'm fucking with you. Actually, I had an idea, and

I wanted to see what you thought about it." Fern sat in one of the padded chairs and motioned for Viv to join her.

As she sank into the seat, she shot the rattkin a perplexed look. "Not sure why you'd need my opinion."

"Well, it's about Maylee. Do you think . . . do you think she might want to sell some of her scones or biscuits here?"

For a moment, Viv's thoughts were knocked sideways as she felt the phantom of Maylee's kiss at the corner of her mouth and an echo of last night's conversation. Her face warmed. Then she shook it off. "Easy enough to ask." She tried a wry grin. "Just cleaned the place, and now you want crumbs all over, huh?"

"That's why I have Potroast. But I think there's something about curling up with a book and something good to eat. And we have the chairs, and, well . . . I like having somebody in here. Having *you* in here day in and day out . . . I like the company."

"And pretty soon, I'm *not* going to be here," said Viv quietly.

Fern shrugged. "Yeah. We've gone to all this trouble, so why not make it a place people want to stay, however we can? However *I* can?"

That shift from "we" to "I" stung more than Viv expected it to. But that was a good thing, wasn't it? When she was gone, she wanted Fern happy and successful, didn't she? That's what a friend would want.

She laced her fingers together between her knees and wondered what it said about her that the thought made her bridle. "I think it's a great idea." And then, crushing that feeling down as hard as she could, she cleared her throat and forged on. "And speaking of Maylee, her idea didn't seem half bad either."

"About trying to get Greatstrider down here? If she showed up on my doorstep, I wouldn't complain, I'll admit. But can you see me bobbing on hers, begging her to parade around my shabby little shop like . . . like some kind of visiting dignitary?" Fern snorted. "I'm not that brave."

"First, the shop isn't shabby." Viv leveled a finger at her. "We painted the shit out of this place. And second, you happen to be sitting across from somebody who makes a habit of charging into things like a damned fool."

"*You're* going to convince her to visit?"

"What if I do?"

Fern considered that. "Well, after I finished kissing you on the mouth, I suppose I'd do my gods-damned best to arrange the finest reopening I could muster."

Viv slapped her thighs and stood. "Just don't kiss me in front of Maylee."

"Mmm, yes. Hard to explain, I imagine."

"Mind the fort, Potroast," said Viv, saluting the gryphet.

He hooted at her sleepily, then settled his feathered head back between his paws.

When Viv passed Sea-Song, she spied Maylee's silhouette through the fogged windows, but she didn't think the dwarf saw her, which was a relief. They needed to speak with one another, but she had a few errands she wanted to get out of the way first. Viv felt like a phantom as she left the bakery behind. She had the surreal sense of setting her affairs in order in case she died. Making sure things carried on when she wouldn't be around to see them.

It unnerved her.

Doing her best to shake off that grim feeling, she hiked into the fortress walls to find Iridia.

There were still more Gatewardens about than normal, but their attention had lapsed from the high alert Iridia had once demanded. And no wonder. Necromantic invasions had been notably thin on the ground.

A few questions asked of one of the women posted at the gate sent her in the right direction.

Before tackling that particular task, though, she addressed something much simpler. Just inside the fortress walls, a busy livery had coaches for let and stalls of well-bred horses. The animals shied at her appearance, and she did her best to keep her distance while she searched for the dispatcher.

She secured transport for the following day, paying in advance. With that done, she threaded her way through the tight warren of streets to the Gatewarden's garrison.

"A symbol?" asked the tapenti when Viv explained why she'd come.

"The same one I told you about, the one on Bal—" She caught herself. "On the dead man's tattoo."

Iridia narrowed her eyes at the slip, but she didn't press.

"Look, you can send someone up to check it out. You can't miss it. I don't know what the hells it means, but it's obviously *hers*. Maybe it's just related to whoever killed him? I'm just passing along the information."

"You know, I can't help but think that if you'd never come to my town, our friend in gray would have gone about his business, and none of this would be my problem."

"Or maybe something worse would've happened," said Viv, her temper kindling. She relaxed her fists with an effort. The idea of hunting down a bunch of spinebacks was suddenly very appealing. "I'm just trying to be a good guest in your town."

Then she took a deep breath and asked the question she'd been trying to figure out how to pose. The one that she *had* to bring up after her late-night conversation with Satchel. "That book. You've still got it? Is it nearby?"

"Near enough," replied Iridia, cocking her head. "Why? It's not your problem anymore. You've transferred it to *me*."

"It, uh, might be important in taking care of Varine if she shows."

"Do you care to elaborate on that?"

"I . . . can't just yet."

"Of course not."

"But is it close?"

The Gatewarden smiled thinly, and then turned away, calling over her shoulder as she strolled back into her office, "Tit for tat, Viv. I'll let you know when you're feeling more forthcoming."

~~~

Viv waited until the bakery closed and Maylee was taking in the sign that hung on the door. The dwarf blinked at her in surprise, cheeks flushed and flour-flecked.

"Hey, you," said Viv, with a small wave that felt ridiculous.

"Hey, hon," replied Maylee. There was nothing reserved in her smile, as open and whole as though Viv hadn't knelt before her on the boardwalk and bruised everything just the night before.

Viv felt the relieved shame of happiness over a problem deferred. "I had a couple of things to ask you."

"C'mon inside then." The baker held the door for her. Viv

brought up Fern's idea and then her own, and it was easy and natural in the yeasty warmth and yellow glow, with the clatter of her assistant cleaning the bowls.

After that, their conversation moved on to other things—stories from the road, the foibles of customers—as Viv helped scrub down the counters and clear the fireboxes. And for a while, the future didn't matter. And that was fine.

35

Viv rode on the back of the coach as it rumbled over the dirt road heading north along low sea-cliffs. She felt like Tamora from *Heart's Blade*, with one hand gripping a bar along the roof and one foot on the backboard. Satchel's bag hung over one shoulder, slapping at her hip. Neither she nor Fern had been comfortable leaving him alone, not after the symbol on the bluff. Besides, he seemed delighted at the mere prospect of hearing Greatstrider's voice.

Her arm stretched and flexed, absorbing every shock of the road, and she found herself grinning at the wind in her curls. She breathed deep the fresh salt air.

Fern poked her head out the coach door. "Are you *sure* you don't want to ride in here? Or on the buckboard?" Potroast's head followed hers out, squawking in agreement.

"I'm fine," she hollered back. "Too small in there, and horses hate me anyway."

The rattkin shot a glance between Viv's hand on the hilt of her sword and the grin on her face. "*Heart's Blade*, huh?" she called.

"What? Um. I don't know what you're talking about."

Fern laughed and disappeared back inside. The coachman spared a look over his shoulder at Viv but didn't slow the horses.

In the distance, on the back of a series of ascending hills, Zelia Greatstrider's estate came into view within a girdle of trees that definitely weren't native to the area. As they drew nearer, Viv spied manicured hedges and a fountain ringed by a groomed drive.

"Fancy," she said to herself, and started to have a few misgivings about the worthiness of the gift she'd brought.

When the coach came to a stop, Viv hopped down and skirted widely around the blinkered horses. The coachman opened the door and folded out a step for Fern and the gryphet to climb down, then reached inside and withdrew a basket covered with muslin and passed it to Viv.

"Just wait here for a bit, all right?" she said, pressing a handful of extra coins into his rough palm.

Fern and Viv both stared along the length of the edifice before them with frank amazement. It was two stories tall, fronted with dozens of arched windows and a set of marble stairs that spread out wider than Maylee's bakery. The roof was armored in blue tiles, the eaves braced with extravagant scrollwork, the doors massive and tangled with a profusion of delicate iron leaves. Water from the fountain behind them pattered into a glassy pond.

Viv whistled. "Pays to write, I guess?"

Fern chuckled. "I don't think *any* writer sells this many books. There's a quote in one of Tensiger's books about elves. 'If you live a thousand years and haven't made yourself wealthy, you're either a fool or a monk.' I don't think Zelia is a monk."

"She's a *thousand* years old?"

Fern shrugged. "No clue. Maybe it's inherited? Anyway, I'm

not going to *ask*." She narrowed her eyes at Viv. "We aren't going to ask. Right?"

"Couldn't imagine it," said Viv, who had, in fact, imagined it.

Potroast was already up the stairs, squatting next to the door, while his stubby tail switched back and forth across the marble.

"Somebody's eager," said Viv, mounting the steps. Without hesitation, she banged one of the enormous iron knockers set on a plate on the doorframe.

They didn't have to wait long for the door to open, but when it did, it wasn't Zelia Greatstrider.

He wasn't as tall as Viv, but he was big and powerfully built. Gone to gray, but not gone to seed, with a neat silver goatee and a handsome jaw. He wore a simple shirt and plain, functional trousers, and didn't look much like Viv's idea of a butler or footman. From the size of his shoulders, the way he held his hand at his hip, and the loose curl of his fingers, she would've bet anything he'd spent more time with a blade belted there than not.

"Can I help you?" he asked, tone mild. From the way his eyes flicked over her and lingered on the saber, Viv wasn't the only one sizing somebody up.

She nodded at him with the most guileless smile she could muster. "Hi. I'm Viv, and this is Fern. She owns Thistleburr down by the sea. The bookseller. We were hoping Miss Greatstrider was in?"

His mouth quirked, and he eyed the basket. "Bread *and* a blade? You know, we don't see a lot of armed visitors around these parts."

"I'll hand it over, if that helps." Viv tapped the pommel of the saber. "Just wary of trouble on the road, and no offense intended."

"Trouble in Murk?" Without waiting for an answer or asking for her weapon, he squatted in front of the gryphet and ruffled the feathers between its ears, not coincidentally baring his neck to her. "Surprising. Iridia must be furious. And who's *this* little soldier?"

Viv decided she liked him.

"I'm afraid his name is Potroast," said Fern with an apologetic shrug. "And of course I'm a great admirer of Miss Greatstrider's work."

The man laughed and straightened, while the gryphet sniffed around his boots and cooed in clear adoration. "I'll let her know you called her 'miss.' It might soften her up a bit. Are you a reader too?" he asked Viv.

She colored some. "I've read one or two."

He marked her blush and *winked* at her before gesturing at the basket. "Smells mighty fine. I'll have to see if she's up for visitors. I'm Berk. I take care of this and that for Lady Zee. Wait here for a moment, would you?"

Leaving the massive door ajar, he strode back into the depths of the mansion without another word. He might as well have told Viv to her face that he'd dismissed her as a threat. It was a strange feeling, and she would've felt insulted if she didn't suspect that he was even more capable than he looked.

When she was sure Berk was out of earshot, Viv looked at Fern and said, "Lady Zee, huh? So, do you think he . . . and she . . . ?" She made a suggestive motion with her hands which could've meant several inappropriate things. "I mean, given what she writes, I have to wonder if—"

"Wonder *what*?" asked Fern archly.

"You know."

"Don't ask *that*, either."

Viv feigned offense. "For somebody who was terrified to do this, you're real brave about handing out rules."

Fern opened her mouth to respond, and then Berk was back, one hand on the door, crinkles at the edges of his eyes. "You're in luck. She's not writing, so she's in a good mood. Follow me." Then he tucked the gryphet under his arm as though he'd done it a thousand times before and motioned them inside.

~

The foyer was massive, featuring an elaborate wooden floor with detailed circular inlays. A grand stair ascended to the second story, and the paneled walls were fairly crammed with paintings in a bewildering array of sizes, all puzzled together with barely any wood between them. Potted trees flanked the staircase—thin, silvery things with graceful, twining branches.

A long corridor extended to the left but had a clear feeling of disuse. Not dusty, but sparely decorated, with closed doors along its length.

Berk led them to the right, into a warmer, shorter, carpeted hall, illuminated by hissing flick-lanterns. Another turn through a narrow passage led into an enormous kitchen, clean and light, with a huge marble counter in the center and a pair of stoves substantial enough to feed a garrison. Fresh herbs hung in fragrant bunches along one wall, and a few saucepans and platters were clustered on one small corner of the counter, part of some interrupted preparation.

From the look of the cookware, Viv got the distinct impression that only a fraction of the estate was used. She wondered how many people actually lived in the Greatstrider household, because the number in her imagination was steadily dwindling.

Another few turns took them to a long office with a solarium at the other end. The walls featured built-in bookshelves from floor to ceiling, absolutely stuffed with books. The ottomans, chairs, and side tables held tottering towers of them as well, and since that hadn't been sufficient storage, they were piled higgledy-piggledy on the floor, too.

It put Thistleburr's stock of books to shame and made Highlark's home library seem miniscule by comparison.

Flick-lanterns on the columns between the shelves provided a steady golden glow. At the far end, a small table squatted in the solarium's light, topped with a metal machine Viv didn't recognize. It was scaled with bronze keys like some misshapen mechanical reptile. A limp tongue of paper unspooled from the top, and piles of regularly sized parchment waited on either side of it. A very old-looking chair crammed with squashy pillows lurked behind the table.

On a long divan behind it, with an open book propped on her bosom, reclined Zelia Greatstrider.

She looked up at their approach, snapped the book closed, and rose to her feet. Like most elves Viv had encountered, she was possessed of a regal beauty. Unlike them, however, she was nearly as tall as Viv herself, and *willowy* was not a word you would use to describe her. Her hair fell silver around her shoulders in unbound waves, and her skin glowed a dusky bronze. She wore comfortable-looking riding trousers and a flowing, open-throated shirt. Her feet were bare, and she occupied all the space she deserved.

"Here they are," said Berk. "Viv and Fern." He seemed to remember his burden. "Ah, and Potroast." He deposited the gryphet on the carpet, whereupon the creature immediately lay across his boots and huffed a huge sigh.

There was a beat of silence during which Zelia Greatstrider regarded them both, tapping her book against her leg.

Viv had considered several opening gambits on the ride up, but they all flew out of her head at once, and all she could manage was, "Uh, this is a lot . . . of books. Have you . . . read them all?"

Fern might have whimpered beside her.

"Never trust a writer who doesn't have too many books to read. Or a reader, for that matter," said Zelia. She approached the desk, shuffling through papers and knickknacks until she produced a quill and inkwell. With some resignation, she said, "So, I assume you've got something you'd like signed?"

Fern nudged Viv in the leg, and she started, remembering the basket hanging over her arm. "Oh! Oh, no. Uh, I—we—had a sort of proposal. Actually, I guess it's a favor? Well, also it would probably be good for—" She realized she was rambling and thrust the basket out instead. "You know what, let me start over. We brought a gift."

Zelia shrugged at Berk, who gently disengaged his feet from Potroast and cleared a space on a side table. Viv set the basket down and flipped back the muslin. "My, uh, good friend Maylee owns the bakery on the beach. She packed up a few things for you."

"Sea-Song?" The first note of real interest entered Zelia's voice.

"Oh, you know it?" Viv asked.

The elf peered with interest into the basket, which was stuffed with scones, lassy buns, and long, gleaming sticky cakes wrapped in paper that smelled strongly of lemon.

Berk laughed, a deep, easy sound. He clapped Viv on the

shoulder. "If I'd known that basket was from Sea-Song, I would've sent you straight in."

Plucking a lassy bun from the assortment, Zelia withdrew to her throne of squashy pillows and gestured to two book-stacked chairs opposite her desk. She broke off a large piece, popped it into her mouth, and chewed with obvious pleasure.

As Viv and Fern cleared their seats, the elf swallowed and said, "All right, you've earned a few minutes. You're the owner, aren't you?" she inquired, tilting the bun toward Fern. "Your father opened that shop, if I recall. An 'R' name, I believe . . . Rowan?"

"Uh, yes, ma'am."

Zelia flashed Berk an amused expression. "I thought you told me they called me 'miss'?"

Berk looked up from where he was rubbing the gryphet's belly and offered a vague shrug.

"And you . . ." Zelia narrowed her eyes thoughtfully at Viv. "You, I don't believe I know. I haven't puzzled out what you're doing in her company yet. Those aren't bookselling arms."

"Oh, I'm just around for a few weeks. A friend of Fern's, I guess. Helping out here and there. Which is what I wanted to talk to—"

"Actually," said Zelia, a sly smile spreading across her lips, "I *do* know you. You're that orc who was dragged into town a few weeks back. Highlark is lucky he made it out alive."

"Um, yeah," said Viv, face flushing hot and honestly feeling a little persecuted. "Yeah, that *was* me, but I felt *real* bad about it. I wasn't in my right mind at the time, because of the fever, and—"

Fern put her face in her paws.

Zelia burst into full-throated laughter and slapped the arm of her chair. Wiping away a tear, she rolled a hand at them. "All right, I'm more intrigued by the moment. If nothing else, I'll work this all into a book. Do go on. Your proposal?"

Viv decided she'd better bull ahead as fast as possible if she was going to get anywhere. "We've done a lot of work on the bookshop and wanted to see if you would come and visit when Fern reopens."

"Visit?" The elf frowned. "You want me to shop there?"

"Oh, no! No, we want people to *meet* you. People who love your books."

Zelia studied Viv. "My dear, why do you imagine I live this far out of the city?"

Viv knew the answer the elf wanted but took a gamble, and said, "Because you inherited a lot of money and a huge estate in the country?"

Fern gasped and slowly turned her head to stare at Viv with huge, disbelieving eyes.

Greatstrider considered her, mouth drawn into a thin line, until it slowly curved back into that sly smile. "You're an interesting person, Viv."

"I think that's the first time anybody has ever said that to me."

"Sometimes, it's even a compliment," said Zelia, and took a satisfied bite of her bun.

"What is happening?" asked Fern helplessly.

Berk patted the rattkin gently on the shoulder, Potroast purring in his other arm. "It means she'll come."

The satchel at Viv's side rustled in anticipation.

36

"What do you think?" asked Fern, holding one of the large sheets up and examining it critically.

She'd just returned from the small printworks in town with a stack of typeset handbills. They read:

THISTLEBURR BOOKSELLERS

est. 1343

New Stock—Grand Reopening

One-Day Sale

With Notable Local Author

ZELIA GREATSTRIDER

In Attendance!

Freyday—Open to Close

BEACH ROW

Viv looked up from the sandwich board she was laboring over, studied it, and nodded. "Seems like it should get the job done, yeah?"

They'd planned the opening to coincide with the arrival of

the weekly passenger frigate, which gave them another day to post the flyers everywhere they could think of.

"Here are yours then," said Fern, dividing the pile of handbills into two stacks.

"Just have to finish this." Viv frowned at her handiwork. "I've redrawn the damn thing three times now, and it's still crooked."

After erasing the previous text with a rag, Viv had done her best to chalk the required words. They still sloped down and to the right, but at least the arrow she'd drawn under them was mostly straight. "Hells. I'm not much of an artist."

Satchel bent over her shoulder to study the result. "Alas, I concur."

Viv sighed and held out the chalk. "Here you go."

The homunculus plucked it from her fingers with a bony hand. "Many thanks. Do you think copperplate or blackletter would be most appropriate?"

"Do both of those make words?"

He looked at her with his burning blue eyes. "I . . . well, yes, obviously?"

"We trust your judgment, Satchel," said Fern.

Viv climbed to her feet, while the homunculus began drafting sure lines in what seemed random locations all across the surface of the slate.

Fern drew Viv's attention by thrusting a mallet and a packet of tacks at her, then followed it up with the handbills. "Here you go. Happy hammering."

Hefting the tool, Viv examined it with professional curiosity and gave it an experimental swing. "Feels good to hold a maul again. Did I tell you I lost mine?"

Fern rolled her eyes. "Don't go braining anybody, please. Not until after they've bought a book, anyway."

"Mmm, yes, I think this will be satisfactory," said Satchel, stroking his jawbone with a skeletal finger.

Viv and Fern stared open-mouthed at the sandwich board.

Wreathed in crisply executed geometric borders, he'd printed the same words Viv had scrawled, but in ornately chalked text.

Books
Reopening
Sale

A gorgeous monochromatic arrow blossomed beneath it.

"What in all eight hells?" breathed Viv.

"Too much?" Satchel looked worried.

"Don't change a thing," said Fern. "It's perfect."

Satchel sighed longingly at the handbills. "I do wish I'd been able to make the Lady Greatstrider's acquaintance. *Sinner's Isle* is a marvelous work."

Fern and Viv exchanged a glance over his head.

Viv laid a hand on his shoulder. It still felt odd to touch the bone of a living thing. "Maybe you can? You know, if you're comfortable with that."

"No," he replied firmly. "I couldn't abide the risk."

"I have a feeling she's open-minded enough to adapt to you, Satchel," said Fern. "She seemed pretty unflappable."

He tapped his skull. "I mean the risk to *her*, if ever the Lady were to find out we had spoken."

Viv grimaced and tightened her grip on the hammer. "Varine has a lot to answer for," she said.

~⌇~

They tacked the handbills throughout the town—on corners, on the side of the livery, and on any surface that would support a nail. Highlark even allowed one outside his tidy office, after examining it with raised brows and a thoughtful expression.

Viv passed Iridia on the street and gave her a careful nod. The tapenti stopped to watch her pass, and as Viv hung one next to the door of a hostelry across from the Gatewardens' garrison, she could feel the woman's eyes on her back.

Iridia made no move to stop her, though.

Maylee affixed one to her door and set another on her countertop.

Viv saved her last handbill for The Perch.

"All right if I hang this outside?" she asked Brand, sliding it across the bar-top.

He looked it over. "I reckon that's just fine. Huh. You got Greatstrider to grace us with her presence, eh?"

"Surprised?"

"Hells, yes. Spied her once only, in all my years in Murk. Keeps to herself, mostly."

Viv shrugged. "I liked her. She's sharp."

"You know, that was my thinking too. Shame she stays away. Now, Berk, seen *him* a time or twenty."

"Have *you* read her books?" asked Viv.

Brand returned his attention to his ever-present copper mug, his tattoos lively as he scrubbed it. He cleared his throat. "Maybe a piece of one."

Viv leaned both arms on the bar-top, lowering her voice. "So . . . Berk and Greatstrider. They're basically alone up in that big house. And her books . . . I mean, she has to get those ideas from somewhere, right?"

"I reckon writers got to have a good imagination," observed Brand, "because they can't all be *that* lucky."

~

On Freyday, Viv set the sandwich board out on the beach, in sight of where the passengers would debark. The air was chill and slow, and the mist curled high up the bluff, like a frozen wave breaking. It blanketed the surf in a silvery hush.

On her return trip, she rapped on the door of Sea-Song, and when Maylee unlatched it, Viv slipped into the warmth and fragrance of baking bread. The quiet of the morning extended to their murmured conversation as she gave Maylee a squeeze and a quick peck on the cheek, slid Fern's payment onto the counter, and then retrieved several baskets of fresh scones and a crock of cream.

The boardwalk creaked under her stride, and the surf thundered its morning song. She heard the neighing of horses and the jingle of harness carrying up and over the dunes from the south.

Thistleburr's bright red door still bore the sign reading CLOSED when she knocked, but Fern opened it to admit her.

The scent of toasted pecans, butter, and burnt sugar mingled with the still-fresh tang of ink and the spice of paper. For the first time Viv could recall, flames crackled in the woodstove, radiating a delicious heat. The gryphet was curled into a feathery crescent before it.

"Let me take one of those," whispered Fern. Then she laughed at herself. "I'm talking like I'm going to scare away the day."

Potroast's head rose, and his stubby tail thumped the floor.

"Didn't forget you, little man," said Viv, and crouched before him to deliver a chunk of scone and another piece of bacon she'd held back from her breakfast. He gobbled them down and bumped his skull against her shin before curling back up.

She blew out a satisfied sigh as she stood. "I don't know why it feels like victory that he lets me feed him."

"Mmm, I can relate. I had the same feeling when you finished reading *Ten Links in the Chain.*" Fern grinned at her. "Here, bring that over." She motioned for the basket.

They piled the scones on a pair of platters next to a pot of hot tea and a cluster of mugs. When Fern was satisfied that they were as ready as they were going to be, she fished the satchel out from behind the counter and dusted the homunculus into animation.

He glanced around the shop, then between the two of them.

"It will be a fine day," he said, his voice thrumming with excitement. "Zelia Greatstrider. Very fine indeed." He opened the slotted box on the counter and poured himself inside, his bones tumbling and slipping over one another until he disappeared within. A hand rose and drew the lid shut, and Viv threw the latch to dissuade any curious customers. The blue flames of his eyes winked in the darkness of the slot, and his voice issued through it in even more of an echo than usual. "Fortune be with you, Fern."

She gently patted the top of the box. "Thanks, Satchel."

Then they waited with the sound of crackling flames and Potroast's wheezing snores, while Fern fussed with the books on the front table and fidgeted with the clasp on her cloak. She'd erected a pile of Zelia Greatstrider's latest work, *Thirst for Vengeance,* with previous volumes arrayed around it.

At last, they heard the sound of boots upon the boardwalk and a sharp rapping on the door.

Fern twitched aside the front curtain to peek and then threw the door wide.

Zelia and Berk waited on the threshold. For some reason, Viv had expected the elf to descend upon them like royalty, but she was dressed in the same riding pants she'd worn when first they'd met, along with sensible boots, a linen shirt with billowing sleeves, and a scarf wrapped around her neck and tossed over one shoulder. Her silver hair was piled high with a long wooden hair pin through it.

"Oh, fuck," murmured Fern, and then she squeaked when she realized what she'd said. "I mean, come in!"

"Thank you, my dear." Zelia's amusement was obvious. She knocked off her boots outside, and when she entered, the shop felt suddenly smaller.

Berk stepped in behind her, this time with a venerable longsword at his belt. He unbuckled it as he entered and passed it to Viv. "Just wary of trouble on the road," he said with a grin.

"Well," said Greatstrider, propping her fists on her hips. "It's a charming shop."

Fern peered down the boardwalk, then flipped the sign on the door to read OPEN, before closing it against the chill.

She opened her mouth to speak, and was utterly paralyzed by the inquiring arch of the elf's brow.

Viv was unarmed, but after sharing a look with Berk, she decided she probably knew how to save the day.

"Scone?" she asked, and offered one to Zelia on a plate.

～

There was much shuffling about, halting reintroductions, and an exceptionally awkward tour of a room that was only a few strides across in any direction, but eventually, Zelia took pity on Fern and seized control of the situation. Commandeering an inkwell and a quill pen—and another scone—she ensconced herself in one of the padded chairs with a pile of books on the table beside her.

She hardly had time for a sip from her mug of tea before the door opened for the first time.

It was Luca, the unfortunate dwarven Gatewarden.

He self-consciously stroked his golden mustaches and stumped into the shop, then stopped short to boggle at Zelia, who regarded him over the rim of her cup with amusement.

"Miss Greatstrider?" he asked. Viv thought if he tugged any harder, he'd yank the braids off his upper lip.

"That's me," she replied.

He cast about, saw the pile of *Thirst for Vengeance*, and seized one, holding it before him in a death grip.

Shuffling closer, he said in a low voice, "I've read all your books. Uh, except *this* one, of course."

"Would you like me to sign it?"

His eyes widened. "You would *do* that?"

She held a hand out to him. "What's your name, then?"

"Uh, Luca, Miss—um, uh, *Lady* Greatstrider."

"Call me Zelia." She took the book, flipped it open, dipped the quill, and signed with a flourish before scrawling a message below her name.

When she handed it back, he read the note while color rose in his cheeks.

Crinkles appeared at the edges of Zelia's eyes. "You have a question, Luca?"

His voice was barely above a whisper as he asked, "Can . . . can I tell you one of my favorite bits?"

"Luca, I think you need a scone. Have a seat and let's chat."

And that was the beginning.

~

Viv and Berk observed from the back hall, leaning against opposing walls, each with a similar expression on their face. A fond and watchful interest.

As Viv studied the customers entering the store, circulating in little eddies throughout the shop, she felt a warmth in her chest that didn't come from the woodstove. Fern's starstruck paralysis evaporated quickly in the slowly building swell of custom. There simply wasn't room for it to survive. Potroast wove between people's legs, alert for any dropped bits of scone. Very few actually made it to the floor.

She was surprised to see Highlark make an appearance, and then highly amused at the youthful awkwardness of his stammered introductions to the great lady.

Zelia's clear laugh and husky voice were a uniting thread as she chatted and signed and shook the hands of those who stopped by to see her.

Viv glanced at Berk. "She's never done this before?"

He shook his head, watching with clear affection. "Never. Still amazed she's here, to be honest." Viv was surer and surer that he was more than a bodyguard or valet. Something about the look in his eyes—sad, but warm. "Must have been the right time."

Fern wasn't there to keep her from asking, but she tried to put it delicately. "So, it's just you two up there in the hills? Together?"

Berk's brows rose. "Oh, there's a groundskeeper, and a few folks come and go. Really just us, though."

"Huh." She let that sit for a minute. "So, you're . . . ?"

"Oh, I make myself useful," he replied. "Mostly."

"Sure." She couldn't help thinking about the lifespans of humans and elves and about the silver in his hair.

The corner of his mouth rose in half a smile, as though he'd heard her thoughts. "Sometimes, it'll never be the right time."

Viv thought about Maylee and what she'd said about seeing people through a tiny window as they passed, and how nothing seemed to happen exactly when it should.

Then she saw Fern's face, bright and laughing as she passed a book into hands that probably needed it.

"And sometimes, we aren't the right people yet," murmured Berk.

While she and he had different individuals in mind, Viv thought they might be thinking exactly the same thing.

～

Fern fell into her chair with an explosive, exhausted breath. Potroast leapt into her lap, still wriggling with reflected energy from the day, and spun around in an effort to find a comfortable angle.

Viv was on the verge of locking the door when a knock came from low on the wood.

She cracked it to find Maylee on the step, peering through the gap as though to reassure herself the shop was still there. "How'd it go?" she asked in a stage whisper.

Fern laughed and gestured at the shop. "Better than it had any right to. And not a single scone survived."

Only crumbs graced the platters on the counter, and while

hardly empty, the shelves did indeed look picked over. Every last copy bearing the name Greatstrider on the cover had been sold, and a great many more besides. When the supply was exhausted, customers had asked Zelia to sign books from *other authors*, which she had acceded to with a very amused smile.

Greatstrider had stayed until the end, when Berk ushered her out the door and into the fog after the last exiting customer, even as he buckled his longsword back onto his waist.

"I'm glad for you, hon," said Maylee, clapping Fern on the shoulder. Potroast extended his neck to sniff at her apron, hoping she'd hidden something in it for him.

After she finished locking the door, Viv threw the latch on Satchel's box, and he appeared in a mesmerizing tumble of bone.

"Sorry you were cooped up all day," she said with an apologetic frown. Maylee sidled up to her and wrapped an arm around her hips.

"It was a pleasure to observe," he said. "Still. I have no memories from the times before . . . this. And yet, I know the heat of a hearth fire, even though I cannot feel it. Today was like that. Knowing the feel of a thing, without being able to experience it."

Maylee's arm tightened, and when Viv looked down, the baker's face had a pained set to it. "Gods-damned isn't fair."

"I think it's time to get you out of here," Viv said to the homunculus. "Tomorrow. Gallina's like to cut herself waiting if she fidgets any harder with those knives. You said you wanted to help with the spinebacks? Let's do it, then. You've been in a box long enough."

"Spinebacks?" Maylee asked.

"Hells, I guess I didn't tell you about that," Viv admitted.

"Just an easy critter hunt south of here that Gallina picked up. Some farmer's sheep are disappearing. Shouldn't be a big thing." She was about to downplay it even further, but thought better of it, instead asking, "You don't want to go, do you? It's been a while, but maybe . . ."

"Nah." Maylee patted Viv's leg, looking up with a tight grin. "Too much to do, and I'd only get in the way."

Viv thought of Berk saying, *Sometimes it'll never be the right time.*

When Satchel was sure that no more words were forthcoming, he said, "I should be glad to go."

"Did you hear that, Fern? You might as well sleep in tomorrow," called Viv.

But Fern was already asleep, her gentle snores echoed by the gryphet in her lap.

37

Viv and Gallina slipped quietly out of The Perch in the crisp hour before dawn, the cool air thick with the scent of wet sand and damp driftwood. It was clear, the previous day's fog settled offshore or hunkered down in the northern hills. The moon was a huge silver coin above, haloed in a phantom of its own light.

Viv tried to let go of the anxiety that had kept her up half the night. She'd shared her plans with Brand, probably to the point of annoyance, in case Rackam returned while she was away. The thought that she'd miss their arrival while she was off gallivanting after some local pests was almost more than she could stand.

Behind that was the concern that kept nipping at her day after day—that they wouldn't show up at all. Neither potential reason for such an outcome was one she wanted to examine.

With the book in Iridia's keeping and Satchel coming along, she'd convinced herself that Fern and Maylee would be in no real danger.

Mostly convinced.

"Can't believe you're bringin' *both*," said Gallina with a snort, keeping her voice hushed.

Viv shrugged, feeling Blackblood shift against her shoulders and tapping the pommel of her saber. "Terrain matters. Better to have options." Satchel's bag jostled against her hip.

Gallina rolled her eyes but didn't argue as they hoofed it down to the main road where it emerged from the long lines of clapboard buildings closer to the beach.

"You're sure they've got a mule?" asked Viv. "I don't want to walk the whole damn way."

"Yeah, yeah, unless they didn't listen. I know. *No horses.*"

There were two mules, in fact. They stood hitched to a short wagon, lipping dispiritedly at the few sprigs of beach grass in reach. A long-legged sea-fey waited on the buckboard while finishing his breakfast, a lantern beside him.

"You know where we're goin'?" Gallina called up to him.

"Yep," he said, licking his fingers and picking up the reins. "Need a hand up?"

"Not likely," replied Gallina. She tossed a small travel bag into the back, leaping nimbly after it, and Viv followed. A few sacks of grain awaited them as seating, piled toward the fore. Viv unbelted her weapons, and they both sat. When Viv reached over to rap the buckboard, the driver flicked the reins, and they got moving.

By unspoken agreement, it was too early for conversation. Viv passed Gallina one of the day-old biscuits she'd tucked into her jacket, and they ate in companionable silence.

For a while, the only sounds were the snort of the mules, the occasional slap of leather, and the rattle and bump of the wagon. Eventually, those were joined by the growl of Gallina's stomach.

"Gnomish metabolism, huh?" asked Viv.

Gallina shoved a hand into her travel bag and withdrew a

hard sausage. Then she remembered the shared biscuits and grudgingly fished out another to offer to Viv. After a pause, Gallina slipped one of the knives from her bandolier and passed it over too.

Viv took them both, but made no move to eat. "You ever done this before?"

"Rode in a cart?" Gallina rolled her eyes.

"Hunted beasts."

The gnome opened her mouth for a fast retort, but then closed it again. Instead, she pared a slice from her sausage and popped it into her mouth. She took her time chewing, and then mumbled, "Sort of."

Viv thought of the way Gallina had grilled her about Maylee back on the bluff.

"What happened?"

Gallina regarded her fiercely. "I can do this job just fine. I—"

"Never said you couldn't." Viv forestalled her with a hand. "You asked what happened to me once, and I told you. Only fair I ask the same. Equals, yeah?"

"Shoulda made you bring a book. Then you coulda read me to sleep instead."

"What did you do before Murk?"

The gnome studied her sausage with great animosity. "Joined up with a couple of mercs I ran into in Cardus. At least, I thought I did. I guess I didn't make a big impression on 'em."

Gallina waited defiantly for a jibe from Viv that never came.

"We were huntin' a bunch of thieves. Kinda half-assed thieves. If you're gonna steal somethin', why a bunch of *scrolls*? Anyway, they were camped in this tangle of woods south of the city, so we head out and set up a camp of our own. The forest is big, and we gotta cover as much ground as we can to find 'em fast. So, we split up, the four of us, and do some scoutin'."

She stopped talking and weighed how much to say. Viv let her.

"So I'm doin' my thing, stayin' out of sight, headin' east beside this old dry river gully. A deep one. And the ground just . . ." She made a whooshing noise and waved her sausage. "Right out from under me, and down I go. Pretty beat up when I hit the bottom. And I can't climb out. It's hard stone and straight up. So instead, I'm followin' this thing and lookin' for a slope. But you know what likes livin' in old dry riverbeds like that?"

"Something that likes to hunt things that can't get away," said Viv.

"Rocktoads. The poisonous ones. A whole bunch of 'em. Course, I did all right, didn't I?" Gallina patted the knives across her chest. "But it was night again before I found my way out."

"And?"

"And by then I figured I should just head back to camp, see what's what. But they were gone, all three of 'em. Camp struck."

"They didn't even wait a day?"

Gallina didn't look at her, but at the hills receding behind the wagon. "I hike my ass back to Cardus, and there they are, countin' out the bounty. They rounded up the thieves while I was runnin' and killin' toads. Didn't really need me, I guess. Probably forgot I was even there."

Viv watched her face. The sausage lay in the gnome's lap, uneaten.

"Fucking bastards," said Viv sincerely.

Gallina sniffed and wiped her nose. "Well, it wasn't all bad. Turns out some people pay a lot for toad tongues."

Viv reached over and squeezed her shoulder.

Then they both sat back and finished their sausages.

When they were done, Viv breathed deep and let the cold air curl down in her lungs and watched the night wick away from the countryside.

She idly ran a thumb along Blackblood's fuller, thought about what was to come, and felt as though she were emerging from the fog of a weeks-long dream.

❧

When they arrived at the farmer's holding, the sun was up, and ribbons of mist were burning off the lowlands in the dawning heat. The farm consisted of a cottage, a jumble of outbuildings and fenced paddocks, a long, thatched barn, and a sizable garden, all encircled by fields filled with hayricks. Bastion oak crowded the slopes up out of the valley.

They heard the bleat of waking sheep, anxious for their morning fodder, and a dog delivered big echoing barks across the breadth of the valley.

The farmer was out on a stool when the mules trundled to a stop in the big looping turnout before the cottage. Even seated, Viv could tell she was tall. Lean and hard, with a tangle of handsome gray hair, she puffed on a pipe in one hand, waving them in with the other.

"So, a Murkie finally decided to take a peek?" she asked around the pipestem.

Viv and Gallina vaulted out of the wagon and stretched.

The farmer looked them up and down, gaze settling on Viv

as she strapped the greatsword and saber back on. "Meg," she said by way of introduction.

"Hey, Meg," said Gallina, flashing the bounty sheet. "Still havin' trouble? My ass hopes we didn't ride down here for nothin'."

The farmer laughed with an edge of bitterness as she got to her feet. "Aye, that I am. Have to keep the flock close, and don't dare take them to the south pastures. Now, they're comin' up around the place after dark. Nothing I can do but bar the door, keep the dog in, and wait it out."

"They're taking sheep at night?" Viv studied the paddocks, the jackleg fences still intact. "Are you fixing the fences when they bust through?"

"They don't come every night, but often enough. And when they do, I'm always a few head shy in the morning. Funny thing, the fences are always fine. They must be leapin' over." She shook her head.

"Blood?"

"Not usually."

Viv frowned. "That doesn't sound like a spineback."

"You've seen 'em?" Gallina asked Meg.

"Once or twice. I think there's a nest near the meadow two hills south. And that sound they make? Like rocks rubbin' together? You don't soon forget that."

"All right," said Viv. "Point us in the right direction, and we'll see what we can do. Can our driver stay here with you?"

Meg nodded. "Tea's on," she called to the sea-fey.

Viv stared south at the hills and stands of bastion oak and, presumably, the meadow beyond. She had seen—and slain—her fair share of spinebacks, and her skepticism was growing by the second.

~⌒~

When they had passed beyond the first line of oak, Viv called a halt and unslung the leather bag.

Setting it on the ground, she fished inside for one of the bottles, popped the cork between her teeth, and dusted Satchel's bones with a few gentle taps of a forefinger.

As she resealed the phial, Satchel assembled himself in a pearlescent rush, flushing with crisp blue light as consciousness bloomed in his eye sockets.

"I don't know why I'm worried about this," said Viv, hiking the bag over her shoulder again and rising to her feet. "What's anything going to do to you?"

"I assure you, there's no cause for concern." His hollow voice held no doubt.

"I guess. Although in my experience, spinebacks like to crack bones between their teeth." She clenched her fist demonstratively. "I feel guilty that you don't have a weapon or something."

Satchel flourished a hand, and the phalanges narrowed to long, wicked points.

Gallina whistled. "Well, I'm convinced."

They trooped together over a set of low hills, with more mountainous terrain humping up to their left, stitched with scattered copses of oak. A rumpled spread of pastureland appeared as they topped a rise. The meadow grass was high and still dewy.

Some grouse startled once, but apart from the far-off surge of breakers, the only sounds were the shushing of their feet through the grass and Gallina's mutters whenever it swatted her in the face.

As Satchel forged ahead beside them, Viv couldn't help watching out the corner of her eye, surprised by his silence and the alertness of his posture, an aggressiveness she'd never observed in him. Her first inkling of potential menace had been those deadly-looking fingers, and that had bloomed into a larger uneasiness.

Although she was increasingly positive it wouldn't matter anyway.

Signs were scarce—no trampled grass or torn earth, no evidence of hunting. Spinebacks were messy eaters and untidy with their leavings. If they were in the area, she didn't think they were nearby, and she had a growing conviction that the pack had moved on entirely.

Still, they'd made the journey. There was no reason not to check the area. She was impatient, but she could be thorough. At least, that was what she told herself.

They combed the meadow and slowly began to track through the shallow valleys between the hills on the other side of it, which were studded with shale and half-buried boulders.

"Well, this is a pain in the ass," muttered Gallina as she shoved away another sheaf of grass at her eyeline. Viv was relieved that she was the one finally complaining.

"We should give it another hour, at least," said Viv, scanning upslope for any sign of a den or burrow.

Satchel scrambled ahead of them, nimbly crawling over boulders and dancing across shale. He was remarkably agile, and little bursts of blue licked along the script on his extremities as he moved.

Suddenly, he stopped and glanced off to his left. Viv froze, following his gaze. A pile of stone sat wreathed in scrubby brush.

The homunculus signaled to them. Viv gestured to Gallina, who straggled behind, wearying of the climb with her shorter stride.

They joined Satchel to survey what he'd found. Fans of tossed dirt flanked an entrance where some animal had excavated a natural cave into a larger space. Splinters of shattered bone speckled the churned earth. Viv would've had to get on her hands and knees to enter, but Gallina or Satchel could probably make their way inside without issue.

That would've been foolish, though.

"They are there," whispered Satchel, an eerie whistle in his echoing voice.

"How can you tell?" asked Gallina.

"Because of what they touch," he replied cryptically.

And then as though in response, a sound like flint dragged down a granite wall echoed from the cave.

"I'll be damned. That *is* a spineback den," said Viv. "Well, we'll just have to flush them out. Nobody's going in there."

She unbelted her saber and stowed it safely behind a boulder with the satchel, then unslung Blackblood, letting its comforting weight drag on her muscles all the way up to the shoulder.

Viv already had a hand to her mouth, sucking in air to shout, before she caught herself. Her companions regarded her expectantly.

"It isn't that complicated," she continued. "I'll make some noise, and they'll come piling out. Then we'll put an end to them. They're not that bright. I'll post up and give them a big target, and then . . ." She raised the point of Blackblood suggestively.

Gallina had a pair of knives in her hands already and glared up at her. "And let you have all the fun? Not gods-damned likely. That big hunk of metal ain't fast. I'll be up top." She gestured at the small outcropping of stone above the tunnel, and without waiting for an answer, she headed off.

Viv almost protested, but then watched as the gnome quietly circled the bushes, until the thatch of her spiky hair appeared above the tunnel. Her blades winked in the sun.

She flicked a glance at Satchel. "This is about as much planning as I ever manage. Are you good?"

"Indeed," he replied. She waited a beat, in case he needed time to do the thing with his fingers again, but he simply stood there.

Well, she hadn't expected to need his help anyway.

And she was impatient to live all the way to the edge of things again.

Sucking in a huge breath, she bellowed at the top of her lungs, "Hey, you gods-damned bastards!"

As a battle-cry, it left something to be desired, but they were just dumb beasts.

Her shout rebounded off the bluffs to the east, and when the echoes died away, there was only silence.

They strained for any sign from the yawning mouth of the burrow.

"You sure they're in there?" hissed Gallina, popping her head up a little higher.

Then the first spineback exploded from the darkness.

Its body was lean and wolflike, ribs like slats, back scaled with rank upon rank of stony spikes. Its eyes were white, gem-like, and its jaw hung low, crammed with teeth like broken fence palings.

Viv brought Blackblood around in a flat arc, catching the thing mid-leap. The stone on its back shattered with a terrific *crack*, and it was flung upslope, folded nearly in half. Its jagged, chuckling roar faded like rocks tumbling down a ravine.

She was dimly aware of a blue glow to her right as Satchel did . . . something. The fragments of bone in the dirt began to shiver, as though the ground were quaking.

There was no time to think about that, though, as two more spinebacks burst into view. Gallina dove toward one, dragging a knife along its ribs, the other plunging for its belly.

Viv grinned wildly, already bringing the greatsword back into play on the backswing, heaving up to take the other spineback in the chest.

She was so committed to the swing that when a blur of motion caught her eye from the left, there was nothing she could do but grit her teeth and fling up an elbow.

She only had time to think, with detached annoyance, *There's another gods-damned exit to the burrow.*

The elbow saved her ribs from the spineback's teeth, cracking its jaw closed, but did little to arrest its momentum. It barreled into her and sent her sprawling.

Though her original swing was fouled, it still caught her first target. The spineback howled and tumbled past, ripping Blackblood from her grip and rolling end over end in a tangle of limbs and teeth.

Then Viv was on her side, breath blown out of her, twisting, bringing both hands up to scrabble for the windpipe of the one on top of her. Its jaws snapped inches from her face, breath rank, spittle spraying her cheeks. She got her fingers around its throat and squeezed, bracing to heave it off her, but the angle was all wrong.

She heard Gallina distantly shouting, and a gathering hum and rattle somewhere above her head. An incandescent flash of blue made her squint, and then the air was filled with the sound of a hundred wasps.

The spineback squealed and shivered as it was struck from every direction at once. Viv was sprayed with something wet and hot, and the creature seized, twitching galvanically, then slumped all at once.

She rolled and tossed it to the side, staring in bewilderment.

It wasn't even alive enough to breathe its last.

Uncountable fragments of bone had punctured it from every conceivable direction.

Viv made it to her knees and stared at Satchel, the blue glow ebbing from the inscriptions along his limbs. His eyes were white hot, already subsiding.

"What the shit?" said Viv.

Gallina staggered up to them both. "Eight hells. You just—" She waved a hand through the air and made a whooshing noise.

Satchel shrugged, and Viv thought he looked embarrassed. "Bones," he said.

"Well, this is a gods-damned surprise," puffed Gallina. "When you said you served your Lady, I gotta say, I thought you meant, like . . . tea."

~

Viv dragged all four of the corpses side by side and examined them. "Something's wrong," she said.

"They stink, that's what's wrong," replied Gallina, making a face.

"No. They're *starving*. Look at them."

Spinebacks weren't beautiful creatures by any stretch of the imagination, but these four were pitiful specimens indeed, their ribs stark, their hides patchy. Gaunt.

"The bones here are many days old," observed Satchel, toying with an osseous shard.

"Then what's eatin' the sheep?" asked Gallina.

"Eating. Or taking," said Viv. "And I don't know. Maybe it's nothing. But it's like they were scared back into their hole. Not much scares a spineback. They're too stupid to be scared. Maybe there's something else out here?"

"The *bounty's* just for spinebacks," observed Gallina. She busied herself gathering trophies from each of the dead beasts as proof of their success.

Viv sighed. "Doesn't sit right with me, leaving the job undone."

"Well, that driver ain't gonna wait around forever," observed Gallina, straightening from her grisly task.

Strapping her saber onto her waist, Viv gathered up Satchel's bag. "Hard to argue with that. I sure as hells don't want to walk all the way home."

~

Satchel poured himself back into the bag before they broke from the last stand of trees near the farmstead.

As she straightened and slung the strap over her shoulder, Viv stopped and sniffed.

A scent on the air.

Winter blood.

The hair on the back of her neck prickled, and gooseflesh rippled down her arms.

"Wait here," she said, and started moving.

"What?" said Gallina. "What the hells are you doin'?"

"Just wait!" she called back.

She followed the odor, and deeper into the wood, in a dark clearing, she found the missing sheep. Or what remained of them.

It was the other things she found that made her blood frost over.

"Is this what I think it is?" she asked quietly, folding back the flap of the satchel.

The homunculus's skull emerged to peer at what she indicated.

"Oh, no," moaned Satchel, his voice filled with dread.

When Meg came to the door of her cottage, Viv surprised her by seizing her hand and hurrying her to a stretch of bare dirt.

"Have you ever seen this before?" she asked, and with the end of a stick she sketched a symbol in the earth.

A diamond with two branches like horns.

The look of surprise on the farmer's face was all she needed.

"How long ago?" Viv demanded.

38

The mules clopped north with agonizing slowness, and the driver couldn't be persuaded to move them any faster. "I don't keep 'em for their speed," he grumbled. "They're doin' what they can."

Viv gritted her teeth, wondering if the threat of the shambling undead might encourage him to hurry them up. Odds were, though, that the driver would head in the opposite direction if he knew what might await them.

She could've jogged faster than the plodding beasts, but even with her leg mostly mended, testing it at such extremes of distance would be foolish.

In the end, she could only fume and drum her hand on the sideboard and glare at the slow passage of the peaceful countryside.

It didn't help that she could still smell the wights in brief whiffs. Or at least, she thought she could. Her mind filled with images of Maylee fending off the undead with her old mace, and Fern's bookshop aflame.

Gallina shot her pensive glances throughout the ride, but

she knew better than to talk about Viv's fears in front of the driver.

The cart rumbled onward as the sun plunged into the sea like hot iron into the quench, and blue night stole down the hills after it.

～

They heard the bells even before Murk came into view—distant, sonorous clangs. Only a rise or two remained between the cart and the outskirts, and Viv could wait no longer. Certainly not with that clamorous ringing giving shape to her worst fears. She vaulted over the side of the wagon with Satchel over her arm, hitting the sand hard.

Gallina started to follow, but Viv seized her halfway down and slung the squawking gnome onto her back like a cloak, so that she straddled Blackblood. Only when Gallina's arms wrapped tight around her throat did Viv let go.

"You're kiddin'," hissed the gnome.

"Hang on."

"What the hells do you think you're doin'?" cried the driver as he reined in his mule team.

"Something stupid," said Viv, and set off at a dead sprint, with Gallina's knees digging into her back with every stride.

～

The city, the clapboard buildings skirting it, and the dunes piled around them all appeared serene. Only the sound of the bells bespoke anything amiss.

Viv pounded over the crest of the last hill, sand spitting behind every footfall, sweat already darkening her shirt.

Gallina's breath was hot against her neck, and the gnome grunted when her body slapped hard against the flat of the greatsword.

Viv had expected flames, screams, an army of the undead—but there was nothing she could see.

After a few weeks of desultory workouts and physical recovery, her lungs burned after a run that she would have easily managed a few months past. She didn't let her pace slacken, though, as she charged down the last stretch of road before it branched off toward The Perch.

"Don't see nothin'," said Gallina.

"You ever hear those bells before, though?" panted Viv.

The gnome's arms tightened a little, and Viv could tell she was shaking her head.

"Must be inside the walls." Distantly, she thought she heard shouts. She spied lantern-glow winking in the window of Thistleburr.

Viv paused in front of the building, heaving huge breaths. Gallina released her grip and landed nimbly behind her. "Like ridin' a horse made out of rocks," she grumbled.

Fern, or Maylee? Viv was paralyzed by a sudden indecision. Thinking about it though, only one option made sense: she had to get into the city, had to find Iridia. "Check on Fern," she said, stabbing a finger at the red door. "Lock up behind you."

"What're *you* doin'? I'm not sittin' with a bunch of books while somethin' *good* is goin' on."

"I'm making sure Maylee is fine. You don't have to *stay*. Just check that Fern is all right and that she's keeping safe."

Without waiting for Gallina to object again, Viv got moving.

~

Sea-Song was locked—which was good—but Viv felt every second creep by as she hammered on the door. She wanted nothing more than to take a few steps back and bash the thing off its hinges, and if she hadn't needed it locked again after she left, she might have done so.

The bells were louder here, and she couldn't imagine Maylee had slept through them. Bakers turned in early, and she was probably tossing and turning upstairs.

In practical terms, it wasn't long before she spied the glow of Maylee's lantern gleaming through the window, but it felt like forever. When she appeared in the doorway, Viv was surprised by the magnitude of her relief.

"You're back," yawned the dwarf. "Can't decide what's louder, you or the bells." She raised her lantern to spill the light across Viv's face.

Viv seized her by the shoulders, leaned in, and kissed her square on the mouth.

"Well, hello to you too, hon," breathed Maylee.

"What do the bells *mean*?" asked Viv, and her grim tone startled any remaining drowsiness from Maylee's expression.

"Fire, maybe? Couldn't see from here. Nothin' we can do anythin' about." She suddenly seemed to register that Viv was wearing two blades. "Hang on—"

Viv glanced over her shoulder, half expecting some shambling skeletal assailant to stumble up the boardwalk.

"I don't think it's a fire. You still have that mace upstairs?"

"Yeah."

"Get it. Stay awake. Lock the door again after I leave. Don't let anybody in."

Maylee narrowed her eyes. "If this is about *her*, then I should come with you. I can still—"

"No. When was the last time you swung that thing? I just want you safe."

"Well, I want the same." Maylee jabbed Viv in the belly with a finger. "Where the hells are you off to anyway?"

"To get a book."

~

Shouts grew more distinct as Viv sprinted toward the fortress entrance. Light bloomed above the walls in a haze of gold, but not from an uncontrolled blaze. Lanterns gleamed on the ramparts, and the bells continued their deafening peals.

At her side, the satchel jerked, and Viv did, too, as skeletal fingers reached from beneath the flap and clutched at her side.

She skidded to a stop and unslung the pack. The homunculus opened the flap himself, his skull and one arm emerging, eyes blazing blue.

"What the hells? The dust—"

"Plenty remained for this," he said. "Quickly! You must let me out."

"I'm heading in *there*, after the book." She stabbed a finger at the walls. "You want somebody to see you and bash you to bits? You haven't met Iridia yet. I don't have time to explain you, and she still doesn't like me a whole lot. I don't think you're going to fare much better."

"She will not harm me. She cannot. Nor can any mortal inside those walls." His voice was coldly certain.

The image of a spineback riddled with shards of bone sprang to mind and quelled her flourishing doubts.

"Your Lady might already be in there," warned Viv.

"If she is, I'd much prefer to meet her on my feet."

She paused, then dropped to a knee, quickly dusting his bones again for good measure. As he clattered into being beside her, she snatched up the satchel once more. "Let's go."

~

The entrance to the city was unguarded, and Viv's fears transmuted to certainty. Satchel kept up with her admirably as she sprinted along the scalloped sand, breath coming harsh but steady.

A short, sharp scream punctuated the shouts and calls.

When she rounded a massive pillar on the near side of the entryway, her footsteps thudding on stone at last, she turned, and a surreal sense of doubling overcame her.

Lanky figures with osseous grins, their eyes pinpricks of blue light, crowded the market street. Gatewardens battled them down the length, and she could have been in the woods again, while Rackam's Ravens hacked at Varine's necromantic minions. There were dozens of wights and only half as many Gatewardens on the long thoroughfare. Who knew how many choked the side streets?

"Shit," she breathed.

"Where is the book?" asked Satchel.

Viv unslung Blackblood and bared her teeth, ready to leap into the fray once more, to batter the wights to dust, to—

"The *book?*" he insisted.

She growled and shook herself. "Iridia has it. The Gatewardens."

"We must retrieve it. First."

She squeezed her eyes shut. "You're right. Can you do that thing with the bones?"

"Not with these creatures," he replied. "They are hers."

"Follow me, then," she said, and dashed forward.

Doors were barred, townsfolk doubtless quailing behind them, although some hung from high windows, pointing and shouting. Iridia's Gatewardens desperately held the revenants at bay in the streets below. She searched the melee for any sight of the tapenti but didn't spot her.

Scanning ahead, she planned her route, and when she drew level with the closest wight, she whipped Blackblood in a diagonal strike that pulverized its ribcage. Its skull went spinning into the distance.

The elven Gatewarden it had been engaged with stared at her in frank astonishment, but she was already gone.

She threaded her way through the mess, finding targets of opportunity and obliterating them like so many rotten tree trunks.

Viv cracked bony legs, hooked her blade through ribs on every backswing, and flung wights into a chaos of gray bone. The blue lights in their eyes winked out as they disintegrated, and she roared in triumph. She didn't bother to look for Satchel. He would follow, or he wouldn't.

She remained dimly aware of her goal. Of the *book*. But present Viv—*real* Viv—was preoccupied with all the savagery she could deal along the way. She was smiling, exultant, and undiminished.

The last few weeks were a wilderness, but she'd found the road again.

Some part of her rebelled, but it was very, very small.

Viv shattered Varine's minions with steel stolen from their master.

She didn't locate Iridia, but she did find Luca the dwarf. Viv towered in the rubble of a dismantled revenant, floured with bonedust, shoulders heaving with huge indrawn breaths.

"Iridia. Where?" she demanded, while Luca quailed in her baleful shadow as though she were a wight herself.

"I . . . I don't know," he stammered, waving his short-sword vaguely in the direction of the Gatewardens' garrison. Then his gaze landed on Satchel, and his eyes widened. "Behind you!" he cried, bringing his weapon up.

"He's with me. Find something else to cut down," she said.

They left him gaping amidst scattered bones, ragged armor, and gray powder.

At last, Viv spied the tapenti at the vanguard of a group of Gatewardens. They fanned out in a half circle before the entrance to their bastion.

Varine's wights crowded close, and more poured from the alleys to join them, swelling their eerily quiet numbers. The only sounds of effort and exclamation came from the Wardens themselves, and Iridia's voice rose above them all, urging her fellows onward. She laid about with her longsword, cleaving bony limbs, the blade trailing plumes of bonedust with every stroke.

Viv dove into the morass with a will, driving Blackblood through unprotected backs, cracking limbs long spent of marrow. For a bare instant she locked gazes with Iridia, and then they both returned their attention to the grim business at hand.

Cutting great sweeping arcs through Varine's minions, Viv fought her way through the press until she shattered the last foe standing between her and the tapenti.

Iridia was streaked from head to toe with pearly dust, her

clattering braids nearly white with it. Her eyes narrowed as she spied Satchel at Viv's side.

"What in the eight hells is *that*?" she hissed.

"No time to explain. Where's the book?"

The Gatewarden seemed set to argue, but quickly changed her mind. "That's what she's here for, isn't it?"

"We need it to put an end to this," replied Viv, because there was too much to say and not enough time to say it in.

"Do I have your word you'll help us push them back?"

Viv almost laughed at the thought of Iridia suddenly *wanting* her blade out and in motion, but there wasn't time for that either.

She only nodded, once.

"Press them back!" Iridia hollered to the wardens beside her, as fresh horrors loped down the street to surge against their defenses. Then, to Viv, she said, "Follow me."

~

The sounds of battle became muffled as Iridia barred the garrison door behind them. The interior was preternaturally quiet in comparison to the street outside.

After a sidelong glance at Satchel, who lingered in their wake, the tapenti wasted no time. She swept past the desks and into what Viv assumed was her office. Small. Tidy. But there was no time to observe details.

At the back wall stood a narrow iron door with a formidable lock. Iridia pulled a ring of keys from her belt, swiftly selected the correct one, and unlocked it. She then laid a hand on the surface, bent her head, and muttered a few brittle words. Glyphs around the border ignited with a brilliant flash and faded, some arcane warding that Viv didn't understand or care to ask about.

As Iridia used both hands to force the door inward, an equally narrow but windowless room was revealed behind, the walls stacked with shelves.

"Stay here," she said, and shouldered past the door, returning quickly with something wrapped in canvas. Again, she placed a palm upon the wrappings and uttered something sharp and purposeful. Once more, arcane traceries glowed.

She flipped the canvas back, revealing Varine's black book of doorways to the underspace.

Satchel uttered a noise somewhere between a sigh and an expression of despair.

Despite the urgency, Viv couldn't help but ask, "What in hells *was* all that?"

"Precautions," said Iridia. "Which were apparently worthless."

"Not entirely," said Satchel, even as Viv seized the book from the tapenti's hands.

All at once, the muffled sounds in the street stopped.

"She can see us much better now," finished the homunculus.

"What is happening out there?" demanded Iridia.

"Can she see what we're about to do?" asked Viv, ignoring the Gatewarden's question.

He shrugged. "I suppose we shall find out."

Viv opened the book, flipped to the middle, and folded the corner of a page into a dogear.

~⁓~

When Iridia and Viv reentered the street, they stepped into a tableau of arrested motion.

The wights stood in ranks beyond the Gatewardens,

immobile, blades and axes and bardiches held at stiff attention. The women and men defending the doorway stood uncertainly, their own weapons up in defensive positions, awaiting attacks that never came.

Then, as one, the heads of the revenants turned to fix their cold blue gazes upon Viv, Varine's symbol burning bright on their foreheads. She stood with the book under one arm and Satchel's bones in the bag slung crossways over her chest.

She'd traded Blackblood for her saber and held it at the ready, but Varine's minions made no move to attack. Instead, their jaws opened in unison, and from them issued a voice that Viv recognized from her dreams.

"Ah, Viv," said Varine, with a sound like sand and syrup. "I've so looked forward to this moment. I've enjoyed acquainting myself with your friends. I think the two of us should meet someplace comfortable. Just you and I, in the flesh."

And all the wights collapsed at once, like monstrous puppets with cut strings.

Viv's stomach hollowed with the sure knowledge of the necromancer's location.

39

Viv stood before Thistleburr's red door, and a hundred dire visions of what she'd find inside crowded her mind. They blackened by the moment.

To her left, Iridia stood with feet planted in a pool of lantern light, a half dozen Gatewardens behind her. Viv had prevailed on her to keep her distance, but she didn't know how long that would last.

Staring at the saber gripped tightly in her right hand, she blew out a breath and deliberately sheathed it.

No sounds issued from within the bookshop. The curtains were drawn. The bells of Murk were silent, and only the roar of the distant sea accompanied the thump of blood in her ears.

Viv tightened her arm against Varine's book, grasped the doorhandle, and pushed it inward.

Unlocked, because of course it was.

She was expected.

"Come in, my dear. And close the door behind you."

She strode in warily, her nerves sizzling with belayed violence, eyes squinting to adjust to the bright lamplight of the interior.

A wreckage of literature greeted her. Jumbles of books in drifts, shelves knocked aside and asunder, loose pages tangled, torn, and bunched in the mess.

To her left, Fern and Gallina hung suspended above the floor, bound in cocoons of bone, as though entrapped by some skeletal spider. Skulls with eyes of blue flame and ragged scraps of armor studded their prison, the cages surely woven from several of Varine's wights.

Tears streaked the fine fur of Fern's cheeks. "Viv," she mouthed helplessly, breathlessly. Beside her, Gallina struggled against the bones that constrained her, her face white with fury.

Alive. Both of them.

A chunk of ice in Viv's chest melted all at once, and her guts went watery with the runoff.

Then her gaze fell upon the other occupant of the room, sitting at her ease in one of the padded chairs. The sheer force of her presence rendered it a throne.

Viv recognized her at once. After all, she'd seen her quite clearly in her dreams.

Varine was beautiful, a sculpture of ivory elegance and icy amusement. Her eyes were just as black as Viv remembered, her hair somehow even blacker, cascading in lightless waves across her shoulders. A furred robe the color of glacial snow radiated a palpable cold. Her bloodless blue lips widened, framing a sliver of perfect teeth.

One of Gallina's daggers was embedded up to the hilt over her right breast, bloodless and disregarded.

"Such a pleasure to meet you at last. The dream so rarely measures up to reality, but my, you are impressive." Her narrow brows rose as she flicked a gaze to the grimoire under Viv's arm. "And so deliciously cooperative."

"What took you so long?" said Viv defiantly, hitching the book up. "I've been emptying this thing for weeks."

The necromancer rose, tucking her robe tighter around her body, as though warding off a chill. "Oh my, Viv. The bluff is cute. We both know the only thing of mine you've been brave enough to take is strapped to your back. Although you *did* confound my pursuit with the wards. I'm surprised at that." Her eyes narrowed, and she glanced at the satchel. "Or perhaps not. My beloved assistant may have something else to answer for."

"What's to stop me cutting you down right now?" asked Viv, although Gallina's inconsequential dagger provided a very compelling answer.

Varine's flat and unamused gaze said the necromancer knew Viv's thoughts as well as she did. The bony cages in the corner tightened with a creak, and Gallina gasped, hollering, "You *bitch!*"

"I'll thank you to hold your tongues," snapped Varine, and her face traversed the distance between beauty and ugliness in an instant. "It's no fault of mine that you've taken what belongs to *me*, and it's my infinite patience that guarantees your continued breath."

Her brow smoothed, and she returned her attention to Viv. "You knew the answer to that before you asked. I understand you a little already, Viv. I will say that I've enjoyed perusing your dreams, as amusingly contradictory as they are."

Viv startled at that, and Varine laughed, a surprisingly pleasant sound. "Oh my, yes, there's a cost to keeping something of mine so close. Did you imagine there wasn't? Blackblood held the door open for me, and I couldn't resist peering inside. It's sad, really, watching you wrestle with your concern for the tiny people you fully intend to discard when you're done here."

Viv's mind raced, wondering how much the necromancer had seen. She could only pray to the Eight it hadn't been too much.

"The struggle must be so exhausting. You've so few days in your short life. Even I can mourn the loss of them. Does that surprise you?"

"I don't know what the fuck you're talking about."

"Don't be obtuse. I'm not here for a *book*, Viv. I'm not here for *him*." She stabbed a finger at the bag over Viv's shoulder.

"Then I hate to break it to you, but this has been a big waste of your time."

Varine laughed again in honest delight. "And yet you've stumbled onto the right answer. I'm here for my *time*. All the days, decades, and *centuries* I invested into priceless treasures you're hauling about like *books* or *luggage*."

"You're the one who named him," growled Viv.

The necromancer's black eyes flared with blue pinpricks, and she seemed to swell, growing in stature and presence. "He is my long ages distilled. His value is what I *put into him*. It's *always* about time. It's the only thing that matters, and I am ravenous for it." Varine's words were as sinuous as the coils of her hair. "I revere the moments you squander on inanities. It's only your poor luck to have plucked what's mine from Balthus's corpse while you wasted your every day."

"If time is what you care about, you sure do spend a lot of it talking," said Viv. "Maybe you let my friends go, I hand your things over, and we put an end to this."

"An end to this," Varine mused aloud, quirking her blue smile. "Yes, well, I've never been fond of endings. I thought that would be self-evident. Your friends will stay where they are."

Viv held up the book and shook it. "I think the only reason you haven't taken this from me yet is because you know I can destroy it. I think that worries you, and I think you want this book more than you want them."

"And I think you want them alive more than you dare to risk my anger," snapped Varine, voice cracking like lake ice in the thaw. The necromancer extended one pale hand. "But you're right, it *is* time to put an end to this. Either test my resolve, or give me what is mine."

"You'll let them live?"

"Let's not pretend you'd trust my word. Any pact between us is a pantomime. My servant, first."

Viv carefully unslung the leather satchel from her shoulder. Her fingers tightened on the strap, and then she extended it toward the necromancer, holding her cold gaze as she did.

"*Don't,*" wheezed Gallina, but Viv ignored her.

Varine plucked it from her grasp, and then twitched it open. She sketched a cursory glance over the contents. "I'll deal with you later, little thrall," she purred, and Viv's skin crawled at the curdled avarice in her voice. The necromancer tossed the satchel carelessly onto the chair behind her and stretched out her arm once more.

Slowly, Viv extended the book toward Varine with both hands.

A book containing a thousand pages like mirrors, reflecting nothing but their owner.

Viv almost pitied her in that moment.

Almost.

Varine impatiently lunged forward and snatched it.

Viv's fingers jerked toward her saber, but she stayed her hand, glancing with concern at Fern and Gallina.

"Ah," murmured Varine, running her fingertips over the cover. The glyphs inscribed into its surface fluttered alight behind her touch. "I've missed you so, my dear one," she said, her words rich with longing, a greeting for a long-lost lover.

With a twist of her wrist, a cascade of bones slithered from beneath the hem of her robe, piling one atop the other into a grotesque lectern, upon which she placed the grimoire.

She flipped back the cover, and then suddenly frowned, her perfect brow wrinkling in dismay. "What . . . ?" She turned to a page in the middle.

Varine gazed in annoyance at the dogeared corner, curled over the black void of the page itself, and reached across to fold it back.

In that instant Satchel's hands burst from the darkness and seized first her wrist and then her forearm . . . and *pulled*.

The necromancer shrieked in surprise as her arm was dragged into the shadows, her black eyes wide with fury. She braced her other hand on the open book and hauled with all her might to withdraw her arm from the night-dark page.

Her gaze snapped to Viv even as the orc unlimbered Black-blood, her fangs bared.

"*You*," snarled the necromancer, muscling herself upright even as Satchel's hands climbed higher along her arm, undeterred. She snapped her free hand toward Viv, fingers contorting and flexing. Blue traceries webbed her palm and wound around her fingers like burning thread. In that blue light, Viv saw her death gathering.

She wound up with the greatsword, putting all her weight

into it and praying she'd complete the swing before Varine could bring her awful magic to bear.

But then a hooting squawk rang out, and suddenly Potroast was sailing through the air, catching Varine's free forearm in his beak and knocking her entirely off balance.

She screamed, a terrible, ragged sound. The gryphet's beak sank deeper into the bloodless flesh of her arm.

Viv brought her swing up short as Satchel seized the moment, and Varine's head and neck disappeared into the page. Her cry bubbled into a muffled wail that echoed into nothingness. The skeletal hands grasped and pulled, grasped and pulled, and the gryphet clung tenaciously to her flailing arm, even as her shoulder plunged into the book.

Viv gaped in astonishment as Varine's body vanished into her grimoire. The physicality of it made no sense, a distortion that hurt Viv's eyes, as though the woman's flesh compressed as she passed through the page.

And the gryphet went with her.

"Potroast!" cried Fern as her companion vanished into the darkness, followed by Varine's hips and then the kicking train of her robe.

Viv flung aside her blade and lunged for the book, plunging her own arm in after.

Her fingers touched fur, but nothing living. The trim of Varine's robe. Viv stretched deeper, dreading the moment when one of the necromancer's hands would curl around her wrist like cold iron.

Fur again, but warm, followed by the silky brush of feathers.

She dug her fingers into the ruff of Potroast's neck and yanked back, dragging him into the light with a sucking noise like a boot from cold mud.

Viv tumbled backward with Potroast on her chest, shattering a chair and falling hard on sticks of wood and scattered books.

Fern cried a wordless sound of relief.

The gryphet scrambled away as Viv leapt to her feet and reached the book in two long strides. She seized and closed it tightly, pressing hard from both sides.

Not a moment too soon, as the book *pulsed*, heavy blows striking the interior of the covers. She grunted, pressing harder and baring her fangs in a grimace. The veins on her forearms stood out as the book fought her with a force that should have been impossible.

Viv dropped to her knees and slammed the book onto the floor, bearing down with both hands as the pounding from within continued . . . and then weakened . . . and then ceased altogether.

The four of them waited in breathless silence for seconds that stretched like minutes, and then all at once the bones that bound her friends collapsed with a clatter and a plume of dust. Gallina and Fern fell to the floor amidst gray clouds and brittle shards. The lectern followed in a fountain of phalanges.

"Faithless fucking *hells!*" cried Fern, pushing herself up to her knees.

"I have to get him out," said Viv breathlessly.

Or maybe he crumbled just like the rest of them, she thought, and felt her stomach twist.

She reopened the book and frantically tore through the pages until she found the dogear. She let the tome lie still, fearing that at any moment Varine's wrathful countenance would surge from the blackness and grab *her* instead. Rising to eclipse that worry was a sick dread that nothing would emerge at all.

Then bony fingers caught the borders of the page, and a horned skull with eyes of blue flame emerged.

"Satchel!" cried Viv, and grasped him by the shoulders to drag him into the open air.

Only his ribcage followed. Viv set him aside as quickly and gently as she could before slamming the book closed and scrambling to her feet.

She snatched Blackblood from the floor, strode to the side table, and placed Varine's awful book atop it.

With two hands on the greatsword's hilt, she drove it through both the book and the table beneath it, with a purring rip of leather and a crunch of splintering wood. A shrieking wail arose from the grimoire, and a cold blast of wind burst from between the covers, twirling the loose pages in the room into a blizzard of print.

Satchel clambered onto the chair, and the rest of his body emerged from the bag, snapping into place. On his own two feet again, he cautiously surveyed the book and the blade piercing its heart.

They all stared at one another as pages drifted to the floor like the ashes of a forest fire.

"Well," he said. "I must admit, I cannot believe that worked."

40

They'd borrowed chairs from The Perch and set them up in a circle, conspicuously mismatching the ones belonging to Thistleburr. Fern thought they'd brought too many. It turned out there weren't enough.

Viv rested against the counter and watched folk fill them one by one, glancing at the battered interior of the shop as they did. It was three days since Varine had wounded the place, and while the bruises were evident in hastily patched shelves, long rents in the rugs, and the mortally injured side table, the shop glowed with the ragged vitality of a survivor. Gaps left by the volumes the necromancer had destroyed stood out like the missing teeth in a pugilist's smile.

She couldn't help but feel an ache of responsibility. A sick throb of guilt. Nothing rooted in logic, of course. Balthus had stashed Varine's book here, not Viv. Satchel had all but assured her the necromancer would've descended on the place regardless.

Still, Viv had braved the pages and stolen something that wasn't hers—and *kept* it—and who knew how events would've played out if she hadn't?

She felt like she'd tracked blood across the floor, all unknow-
ing, and nasty things had come sniffing after her.

In some ways, that made it easier to leave.

In others, it made her wish she'd watched where she stepped
in the first place.

Viv packed those thoughts away as Highlark slipped inside.
He nodded to Viv, a slim volume in hand, and settled himself
neatly into a seat beside Luca the dwarf. There were faces she
didn't recognize, too, but when Pitts sidled through the door,
Viv couldn't suppress a grin. The orc tried to hide himself in
a corner with a book held before him like a wholly inadequate
shield.

"Should've brought more scones," said Maylee, perched on
the stool beside Viv. The pile on the tray before them was prodigious, though, and steam curled from a brass teapot to the
side of it.

Their elbows touched while they watched, and Viv thought
that casual press of warmth was going to lodge in her memory
in a way that other moments wouldn't. She wanted to reach
out with her whole arm and tuck Maylee close, but that felt
too big a gesture.

A parting was imminent, and big gestures felt like lies.

There was an ache almost visible beneath Maylee's deliberate casualness and in the way she never tried to fit anything
further in between her words.

If Viv could've seen herself from the outside, she thought she
might've appeared much the same.

It was an honest sort of pretense, though.

She watched the bookshop brim with conversation and
warmth and community. But while she was surely present with
the rest of them, Viv also felt like a ghostly observer.

Rackam would come soon, assuming he was still breathing. And she had no reason to believe he wasn't.

Any trails they followed would lead them here.

And then, she would go.

Fern emerged from the back hallway with a stack of books in her paws, a bag over her shoulder, and Potroast trotting behind like a proud rooster.

The rattkin blinked at the size of the crowd and then at Viv and Maylee.

Viv smiled back and half shrugged. "It's a good book."

"Um, is everyone here?" asked Fern, raising her voice. "Oh, hells, what a question," she muttered. "Who's going to say no?"

Then the red door opened once more, and three unexpected attendees filed in, one after the other. Viv's brows rose further with each one. Gallina, looking sheepish, followed by Berk and Zelia Greatstrider, somehow resplendent in practical riding attire.

"I'll be damned," said Viv.

"Oh!" exclaimed Fern, as a murmur passed through the assembly. "Miss Greatstrider, this is . . . this is a surprise!"

"Zelia," insisted the elf, smiling benevolently. "Well, you're all here to discuss my book, so I suppose I should be on hand to take the poison with the sugar, shouldn't I?"

Luca's jaw dropped, and Viv thought he might have stopped breathing.

"Of . . . of *course*! I'm so—Well, I'm surprised. In a good way!" Fern stammered. "I think I can speak for everyone when I say that we're all so happy you came."

Luca hurried to offer his seat to her, and Greatstrider accepted with a regal tip of her chin.

Berk unbelted his longsword and edged around the circle, sliding in behind Viv and Maylee.

"Seems I missed all the excitement in town a few days ago."

"Oh, I don't know about that," replied Viv quietly. "Give it a few minutes."

He shot her a quizzical glance, but she only smiled and looked back to the center of the room.

"So, I'm not much of a public speaker," apologized Fern. "You'll have to forgive me. I sell words. I don't *say* them." A good-natured chuckle from the group gave the rattkin some courage. "Anyway, I hope to make this a regular event. You've all read *Thirst for Vengeance*, and I hope you enjoyed it as much as I did. We're here to talk about it together, and I, uh—" She looked at the stack of books in her paws as though unsure how they'd gotten there.

Highlark rose and gently took them from her, and Fern patted at the pockets of her cloak while shooting him a grateful expression. She found a folded piece of paper in one, which she opened and held in trembling paws. "I've made a list of topics to discuss—if we want to—although we can talk about whatever you like. But, before we get to that, there's something I'd like to say. Someone I'd like to *introduce*."

"Here we go," whispered Viv, catching Berk's gaze. "Just leave the sword where it is, yeah?"

Fern set the bag carefully on the floor. She opened the flap and took a step away.

Several indrawn breaths overlapped as the horned homunculus boiled up from within the satchel, his bones clacking into place with rhythmic musicality, until his eyes ignited in twirls of cobalt flame.

With Varine's departure, no further bonedust was required, as though her presence had been a sickness it kept at bay.

Viv could feel Berk tense beside her and then relax as he noted her inaction.

"This," said Fern, "is Satchel. And he'll be staying with me for a while."

There was absolute silence, during which the homunculus rubbed his phalanges together anxiously before him.

His gaze came to rest on Zelia, and he executed a hesitant bow. "Lady Greatstrider. It's my profound pleasure to meet you. I must say, I've found your works most enjoyable. My days are entirely my own for the foreseeable future, and I do look forward to devoting some to whatever you write next."

Viv hadn't known the elf could look astonished. It was kind of impressive.

There was a long beat of silence during which nobody seemed to know what to do.

Then—

"Hey, Satchel. So, Fern, when do we eat?" asked Gallina.

And after that, things were fine.

But for Viv, it was also like the end of a story.

Except the story was somebody else's.

41

Pembroke kicked dust over the ashes of their morning fire and watched the last curl of smoke rise above the dawn mist. He felt his years from his shoulders to his heels, creaking like an unrosined bowstring.

Marret busied herself with the horses, and when he saw her in profile he smiled at the hale ruddiness of her cheeks. He wished he were younger.

His knees popped like dry branches as he crouched to gather his bedroll. In all of a few moments they'd packed away their camp.

They'd chosen a lovely little hill, surrounded on three sides with birch and looking out over a silver thread of river that neither of them could name.

"I suppose this is our last morning before we get back," said Marret.

"The blood and mud is done," agreed Pembroke. "But it's altogether more final for me, I think. I'm headed for the peaceful pasture of retirement. You? Why, you've only just jumped the fence, with a world to grab by the throat."

She tried to glance at him in surprise, but he knew she understood that this was his last ride. Marret gave up the pretense and frowned, almost bitterly. "It feels gods-damned wrong. We were . . . we were good together. Weren't we?"

Pembroke laughed. "I've never felt safer with another blade at my back, nor any other eye while I slept. We mend the holes in each other's britches, as my old da used to say."

"Then why does this have to be the end of it?" The plaintive note in her voice almost made him reconsider. Almost.

It took him a while to reply. Patching the last cracks in his resolve.

"Because I'm headed down the hill, and you're headed up it. I'm just glad we chanced to meet on the way."

Viv snapped the book closed and rubbed her eyes with two fingers.

An errant grain of sand had blown into her face, surely. There was wind enough.

Seated atop one of the beach-facing dunes, she looked out over the tumbling waves, every curl ripening to red before churning into its fellows. Gulls hacked and cried above, scolding her intrusion.

She slid a finger over the foiled lettering on the book's cover. *Crossed Purposes* by Kest Brindleby. Fern's last suggested book. More than any of the others, it felt personal in a way she hadn't anticipated.

Viv supposed that was what Fern had meant up on the bluff. About books and mirrors and that perfect moment of feeling *seen.*

Which was fine. Wonderful even, Viv could admit. But

also terrible, because didn't it make things harder than they should be?

Wasn't it so much more comfortable to duck out the door without somebody pointing out your departure? She couldn't help but see Maylee's face, feel her thick braid between her fingertips.

She wished Rackam would come, and it could all be done.

Then from behind her came the clink of harness, the groan of axles, the tromp of boots, and the armored creak of folk who traded in blood.

Viv turned and saw Rackam's Ravens trooping down the road to Murk, and until that moment, she hadn't known you could feel dread and relief at the same time.

—~—

"There she is," said Viv, sliding Varine's book across the table. The slit in the cover was surgically clean, a testament to Blackblood's preternatural sharpness. It was strange to think, but to Viv, the book *felt* dead. The unnerving vitality it once possessed had fled. All that remained was leather, paper, and the faint whiff of blood on a frozen lake.

Rackam sat across from her in The Perch, and near a dozen of his Ravens stood crowded around the table. He drew it toward him, furrowing his brows at the symbols on the cover. Then he opened the book.

The pages were still black, but they were no longer depthless, and each was split crosswise.

"Not much of a trophy, is it?" said Rackam, sighing. "Weeks of false trails and backtracking, snow and mud, scores of blue-eyed corpses—and this is how we catch up to her."

Sinna tossed her red hair back and skeptically examined

it. "Nobody is going to pay us for this. How do we know she's even dead?"

"Oh, she's dead, all right," replied the old dwarf. "Or whatever passes for dead for her kind. Malefico saw her thralls drop like sacks of flour all at once, and we haven't seen one since."

Malefico nodded but didn't say anything.

"Still not clear on how you stuffed her in a book, though," rumbled Rackam.

Viv had briefly considered mentioning Satchel, but introducing an animated horned skeleton to a group of folks who'd been bashing them to bits for a few months straight seemed like a surpassingly bad idea.

"It was complicated. And lucky."

He held her gaze with his flinty blue eyes, but eventually he slapped the cover of the book and handed it off to Sinna to take care of.

"Well. Nothing in all eight hells that can be done about it anyhow. They'll pay us, or they won't."

But, knowing Rackam, Viv thought they would. He was a persuasive man.

The conversation shifted on to another sort of business altogether.

"So, who's this now?" he asked, gesturing toward the gnome seated beside Viv.

Viv waited a moment for Gallina to introduce herself, but when the knife-studded gnome only sat with mouth slightly parted and eyes wide, she took pity and intervened.

Smiling, she slapped Gallina on the back. "This is the girl that saved my ass in a street fight."

Viv didn't have much to pack, but she supposed Brand would appreciate having the mattress heaved back onto its frame. Just as she let it fall with a thud and a protesting creak, a knock rang out at her door.

It was Maylee.

Without asking, she entered and closed the door behind her, and simply stood with her hands at her sides.

The walls of the room seemed to float away in the silence, and Viv couldn't stand to let it extend any further. She opened her mouth to speak.

"Hush," said the dwarf. "I know you wouldn't leave without sayin' anythin'."

Viv wanted to believe that was true about herself.

"I just couldn't do this out there, in the world." She gestured vaguely behind her and met Viv's gaze for the first time since she'd entered. Her eyes glimmered at the corners. She sniffed and then roughly ran her forearm under her nose. "You're too gods-damned tall," she complained in a thick voice.

Viv sank down onto her knees, so they were nearly face to face.

"That's better," Maylee whispered, and put a hand to Viv's cheek. Viv could smell yeast and sugar and warm skin. "I know what I told you at the beginnin'. About knowin' you for a while. And I even believed it. Guess I still do. But here's the part where I pay for it. And maybe you too, but I won't ask about what it costs you. I'm not sure I want to know."

The lump in Viv's throat was too big to fit words around. Instead, she mirrored Maylee's gesture and laid her huge hand along the side of the dwarf's cheek.

"I'll probably never see you again," continued Maylee, and one tear overspilled, tracking through the fine flour on her cheek. She leaned into Viv's touch and added fiercely, almost angrily, "But I don't regret it."

She pushed forward, and her lips pressed against Viv's, warm and lush and longing. And all too brief.

Then she pulled away and left the room, closing the door quietly behind her.

Viv never managed to say a word, but their time was over.

One had gone up, and the other down, and the crossing would not be repeated.

～⌒～

When Viv walked into Thistleburr for the last time, Satchel was shelving some repaired volumes while Fern curled up in one of the surviving padded chairs, perusing a catalog. Potroast looked over from taking experimental nips at Satchel's ankle-bones to hoot at her.

Fern put the catalog aside and started to rise, then saw the pack on Viv's back. Her expression made a few detours on the way to a smile. "So, you're going, then?"

"Soon," said Viv. After Maylee, she'd figured this would be easier, and it was, but not by as much as she'd hoped. "I wanted to give this back to you before I did, though." She held out Fern's copy of *Crossed Purposes*.

Fern snorted. "I knew there was a reason I lent you that. Kept you from slipping off on the sly."

"I wouldn't do that," protested Viv.

"Hm. I know you warrior types," she replied, with a pained smile. "Tear the damned place up and leave. Just look at this mess!" She waved dramatically at the shop, which still clearly bore the marks of Varine's trespass. "Anyway, that book is yours to keep. What did you think of it?" She asked it offhand-edly, but Viv didn't think it was an offhanded question.

She studied the cover and understood that to give a thought-less answer was to break something she didn't want broken. "Well," she said slowly. "At first, I decided it was maybe a little on the nose. Sad. Pembroke is so sure he's done. They'll never see each other again, and maybe that's just because they're both too stubborn to see things another way. That's how the author leaves it. Still. The more I think about it . . . it seems like it ought to be obvious, but people in books are wrong all the time. Hells, the *authors* are wrong. So maybe that's what the story says in the words that got put down, but if you could read past the end? The words that *didn't* get written? Maybe it ends up being something else altogether."

"The story past the story," murmured Fern.

Viv shot her a startled glance. "Yeah."

Fern nodded. "You've been a good friend to me, Viv. And I'm going to miss you." She held out her paw to shake. Viv did. "Property damage notwithstanding."

Viv laughed and sniffed. "You, too. I *did* get the better end of the deal."

Satchel approached and sketched a neat bow. "You have my undying thanks, m'lady," he said, and something about his voice kept Viv from correcting him. "I never dared dream of my liberty."

"Are you planning to stay here, then?" asked Viv.

The homunculus tilted his head. "Fern has agreed to have me on for a while, and I believe I will enjoy the quiet. For the days yet to come? I cannot say. There are so many to account for."

A hoot from Viv's feet made her look down. Potroast nuzzled her boot, his soft feathers flaring against the leather.

"Now you get affectionate, huh? I guess I'll even miss you, you little monster." She fished the final chunk of bacon she'd saved from her pocket and showed it to him.

He stared up at her with his huge golden eyes, and then delicately took it from her hand. The gryphet held it in his beak for a moment, then gently placed it on the floor, as if to say, "I'll save this for later." Then he very deliberately licked one of her outstretched fingers.

"Huh," said Viv, because her voice was too choked for more. Somehow, this on top of everything else was too much to endure.

She stood and offered more words of increasing inadequacy until there was nothing to do but go.

As she opened the door to leave, she took one last look back at the three of them.

"See you in the story past the story," said Fern.

And then the red door closed behind her.

EPILOGUE

Many Stories Later

Tandri opened the door to Legends & Lattes, and a spring breeze just this side of a winter chill followed her in. She unwrapped the scarf from around her neck and swung a canvas bag from her shoulder, setting it on the counter.

Viv looked up from where she was wiping down the gnomish coffee maker.

"Thimble already gone?" asked the succubus.

"You just missed him," replied Viv. The rattkin baker had scurried home only moments before. "Still a few of these left, though." She nudged a plateful of Thimblets with the back of a hand.

"I'm just back from the post, and the orders are out, but this was waiting for you there. I saved them a trip." She searched her bag and withdrew a brown envelope with a red wax seal. "I don't recall any business we've done in Murk?"

Viv put down the rag with a prickle of surprise.

Taking the envelope, she studied the Territorial post marks

that charted its path to Thune. The wax on the back bore the impression of a page and quill.

She cracked the seal and withdrew a folded letter.

Viv,

It's been many years, and I don't know how to sum them up, so I'm not even going to attempt it. I thought of you often and hoped you were out there alive. I confess, sometimes I doubted it, because the life you chose is a hard one. Imagine my delight when I heard you were well, and more than that, your life took turns I never could have imagined. I received the news of your shop, and your success, from Zelia Greatstrider, of all people. Coffee? I'm afraid it hasn't arrived on this sleepy end of the Territory, but I'm intrigued.

I'd love to say that my life has been perfect, that I've seized every moment, that after you left there were no struggles or doubts, but that wouldn't be true. It has been satisfactory, though. There have been many good days.

But hearing word of your ambitions made me think of the book I gave you. Crossed Purposes. It made me think of the story past the story. I think you found yours. And knowing that, it makes me imagine that I can find mine, too. And that I need to seek it out.

I love what I do. I know that. Once, you showed me how much. But I want to smell different air, to see different faces, to forge new connections. I cannot tell you how much you've inspired me.

Satchel is gone now. And I'm relieved that he chose to do more than stay here with me, but I'd be lying if I said I wasn't lonely in his absence.

I will be traveling to Thune in Maias. A sabbatical, you might say. I do hope to see you when I arrive. I can picture you in my mind, with your sword and your impatience, and so look forward to holding a new image alongside it.

Have you been reading since you left Murk? I hope so. I find myself wondering if a seed was planted in you when you were stranded here so long ago, and maybe it took a long time to blossom. If I helped water it in any way, then that would make me very happy.

Yours,

Fern

P.S.—Maylee is well. I think you helped her understand who she needed to find, and then, at last, she did. I thought you might like to know.

"Fern," murmured Viv.

"That must have been quite the letter," observed Tandri with a curious smile. "Your face went a few places, anyway."

Viv laid it down on the counter and gazed around Legends & Lattes. At the shop and the home she'd built. In her mind, she could see Thistleburr and the red door and the hurricane lamp and the warm press of books on all sides. She glanced at the stack of chapbooks and novels tucked under the counter.

"I never told you about Murk, did I," said Viv.

"No, you didn't." Tandri joined her on the other side of the counter and squeezed her shoulder. "But by your expression, it's a good story."

"We'll probably need a drink or two. It's not a short one." She could already imagine Tandri's amused expression when she recounted her fumbling summer romance with Maylee.

"Start talking, I'll fix us both a hot cup."

"Yeah . . ." Viv trailed off as a series of gears meshed in her mind. Something interlocking after twenty years. "Hey, that place next door is still for sale, isn't it?"

"Jeremiah's place? I think so. Why?"

Viv did some sums in her head, thinking about the savings they'd amassed over the past few years and about old connections and little windows. "Just thinking. An old friend is coming to town. Could be she decides to stay, and if so . . ." She glanced at Tandri. "What do you think about maybe . . . a bookstore next door? I wonder if Cal is up for another renovation . . . ?"

"A bookstore?" Tandri blinked. "Is this to do with that letter?"

Viv thought of the words Berk had said to her all those years ago. *Sometimes we aren't the right people yet.*

But now, maybe she was.

"Yeah, a bookstore." Viv stared at Tandri, and without thinking about it, tucked a lock of hair behind her wife's ear. "You know, books are what brought me to you."

"Mmm. Not coffee?"

"Long before that."

"I guess I'm thankful then."

Viv thought about that for a moment.

"Actually, it was probably getting stabbed in the leg that did it."

And as Tandri laughed, waiting for the full story, Viv was grateful for all the wrong times that had led to this right one.

ACKNOWLEDGEMENTS

Well, none of this went as expected.

I'm writing these acknowledgements, and it hasn't even been a year since *Legends & Lattes* was released. I'm still trying to wrap my head around that.

When Tor UK acquired the rights to *Legends & Lattes* to republish it, part of the deal was that I'd write a second book. Fortunately, I knew exactly what that book would be. I already had it in mind, crystal-clear, and *surely* I'd be able to write it in six months. After all, it only took a month for the first book. Easy-peasy, right?

Ha.

Friends, that's not the book you're holding.

My second book was going to be cozy fantasy mystery set in the city of Thune – Fantasy *Murder She Wrote*. It centered around the magical college of Ackers, involving a five-hundred-year-old elf and instructor of Thaumic Forensics. After being passed over for the deanship of Ackers for someone infinitely less qualified, she angrily retired from her professorship to become a romance novelist. A not particularly successful one. Thus, when contacted years later to investigate the death of the dean who took her job, she returned to Thune and Ackers – with her affable himbo in tow – to investigate the mysterious death, if only to shake the hand of whoever did it. Along the way we'd learn about the way that magic functions in the Territory, more about the Madrigal and Lack and Thune's underworld, and we'd follow the formation of her fledgling detective agency in the rooms above a university bookshop.

Gosh, I knew exactly how it was going to go. I had a tenthousand-word outline. I was unstoppable.

I got about twenty thousand words in and loathed it. Everything felt mechanical, making sure person A got to place B, and information C was discovered. It felt like a big list of chores. There were glimmers of things there that I really liked, but deep down, the book just didn't have any heart.

I confessed this to my editors Georgia & Lindsey in absolute terror, but they were kind and supportive as I lurched to another, alternate book.

And then another.

And then another.

And that's the one you're holding.

It wasn't all wasted – it sounds gross, but I harvested a lot of organs from those three failed books, and they're here, pumping away in *Bookshops & Bonedust*. Several characters emerged from the wreckage to populate Murk.

Everyone tells you the second book is the hardest, and they're right. The real challenge for me was untangling what I was feeling while I was writing. Was this horrible nausea I was experiencing because the story was bad, or was it because I was now writing for expectations, and didn't want to let anyone down? I couldn't tell. It took me three attempts to untangle it, and correctly identify those emotions.

So here we are, with a prequel I never intended to write. And I'm happy with it. It says things I want to say, and if I'm lucky, it interlocks with *Legends & Lattes* in a way that makes both stories better, while still allowing them to stand on their own.

I hope it gave you a nice afternoon or three, and that it left you warmer than when you started.

I'd like to thank my family – my wife Katie, and my kids, Gavin & Emma. I love you all.

Aven Shore-Kind made sure this book got written, tireless in her support, enthusiasm, and insight. I am eternally grateful.

Forthright reprised her role in editing this once before it was even submitted to Tor, to make sure I stayed true to the characters and bedrock of the last book, and because she cares about every word.

To my agent, Stevie Finegan – I am so grateful for you. You're the best.

Seanan McGuire – you really gave this swing an enormous push, and I will never forget it.

Carson Lowmiller yet again knocked it out of the park with the lovely US cover art that has defined this series so perfectly. I am thankful every day for your artistry.

To everyone who has made or sent me fanart – I treasure every piece of it.

To the many influencers on TikTok, Bookstagram, Booktube, and all the other social media communities that have been such great advocates for *Legends & Lattes*, I appreciate everything you do.

At Tor UK, my huge thanks to Georgia Summers, Bella Pagan, Holly Domney, Grace Barber, Rebecca Needes, Kieryn Tyler, Lloyd Jones, Becky Lushey, Jamie Forrest, Ellie Bailey,

Emma Oulton, Carol-Anne Royer, Elle Jones, Ellen Morgan, Alexandra Hamlet, Andy Joannou, Will Upcott, Holly Sheldrake, Sian Chilvers, Jamie-Lee Nardone, Nick Griffiths, Stuart Dwyer, Kadie McGinley, Richard Green, Rory O'Brien, Becca Tye, Leanne Williams, Joanna Dawkins, Lucy Grainger, Jon Mitchell, Anna Shora, Mairead Loftus, Elena Battista, Toby Selwyn, and Hannah Geranio. I so appreciate you.

At Tor US, my unending appreciation to Lindsey Hall, Aislyn Fredsall, Rachel Taylor, Gertrude King, Eileen Lawrence, Sarah Reidy, Khadija Lokhandwala, Angie Rao, Peter Lutjen, Bernard Scott, Lauren Hougen, Sam Dauer, Jacqueline Huber-Rodriguez, Michelle Foytek, Rebecca Naimon, Erin Robinson, Alex Cameron, Lizzy Hosty, Will Hinton, Claire Eddy, Lucille Rettino, and Devi Pillai. You are all spectacular.

Special thanks to my sensitivity reader, Sophia Babai.

Last, but not least, I want to thank Kel, Mireille Tessier, Jory Phillips, Kalyani Poluri, Sam Baskin, Linnea Lindstrom, Mark Lindberg, and Bao Pham for all your help and care.

ABOUT THE AUTHOR

TRAVIS BALDREE is a full-time audiobook narrator who has lent his voice to hundreds of stories. Before that, he spent decades designing and building video games like *Torchlight*, *Rebel Galaxy*, and *Fate*. Apparently, he now also writes books. He lives in the Pacific Northwest with his very patient family and their small, nervous dog.